I0456606

DON'T LET GO

THE SWITCHBOARD DUET
BOOK TWO

HEATHER LONG

Don't Let Go/Heather Long – 1st ed.

ISBN: 978-1-956264-89-0

I said what I said.

They shenan-again.

FOREWORD

Dear Reader,

I can't thank you enough for taking a chance on Talk to Me and now picking up Don't Let Go. If you, have perchance, not read Talk to Me, I would suggest grabbing that one first. Yes, this is a duet, and this book picks back up, right in the middle of the action so you really need to read, Talk to Me first.

As I mentioned in the first book this duet was nowhere on my writing schedule one day, it was just there, whispering in my ear. I could hear the characters coming to life.

Not only were they "talking" to me, they wouldn't *shut up*. I had to start writing as soon as possible so I could also work on other things. What the muse wants, sometimes, you have to let the muse get. This book *demanded* to be written. I was grateful that Don't Let Go waited a bit patiently for me, but between traveling, and other deadlines, they went a little mute. I guess they needed more attention than I was giving.

It's fine, Patch and I had a word, and I told them

what she tells everyone else: *Talk to Me*. What I have loved about this series from the beginning, is they walked in fully-formed, bad habits, histories, attitudes, and more just right there. They didn't spend a lot of time on their backstories. They were who they were and that was who we were getting.

I expected I would get more of their story out of them in some ways and in others, I am dead certain I know everything I need to know about them. I hope you enjoy them as well as I did.

For a quick previously, in Talk to Me, we were introduced to Patch aka Fallon, a hacker and operator who was recruited to work for a super shady agency when she was young and idealistic. When she discovered what they were up to, she made a choice to cut all ties, but she also took a huge swath of their files and disappeared to build herself a new life—one in secret.

For the next five years, Patch existed in a carefully curated bubble, never leaving her home and only interacting online. As an operator, Patch worked with other contractors, her clients. The three main clients are Michael Remington, a British assassin, John McQuade, a rough and tumble former military man turned mercenary, and Justus Locke, a suave, international thief.

The three are as different as can be, but when Patch suddenly stops taking calls all three go to find her. It takes all three of them, because they know very little about *her* life or *her* past. Rescuing her is only the first step, because she's been taken by her former employers and tortured for information she refuses to give up.

It will take all three of them to keep her alive, especially when she arranges a meet with a possible source and everything goes to hell before they can get out.

Of course, that brings us to Don't Let Go.

For a little housekeeping. The Switchboard Duet is a dark romantic suspense why choose. This means all the romantic heroes are matches for the heroine and she will not have to choose. It's also worth noting that romance was not the key focus of the first book, but it does play a very strong secondary beat in this one. It's a harrowing journey of discovery for all four, from trusting each other to earning her trust and a chance at a possible future together. You know, if they survive...

TWs: Mentions of SA. Kidnapping. Intimidation. Torture. Interrogation. Car accidents. Threats of violence. Scenes of combat. Violence. Be kind to yourself, this is a dark romantic suspense duet.

Thanks for checking out Don't Let Go, I can't wait to hear who your favorite is.

Happy reading.

xoxo

Heather

P.S. Human voices only. All the work involved in this and all my novels from the stories themselves to the covers, to editing, to the audio are human-produced materials and voices only.

PROLOGUE

LOCKE

Everything about the plan went great—until it didn't. One moment Remington guided Patch through the quad of the outdoor mall, cold air nipping at them. The next he suddenly veered course and started running.

I barely had time to acknowledge the abrupt shift when a brick wall barreled into me and slammed me to the walkway. Three things registered at once: the pop of gunfire, the plumes of shattered clay exploding where the bullets struck, and screams.

Lots and lots of screams.

I twisted and managed to stay behind the oversized concrete planter as McQuade moved upward, braced on one knee. He raised his gun, and waited a beat until there was another shot. The crack of it was almost too quiet but it might have been muffled by the screaming.

McQuade barely reacted as little plumes of debris went up from the planter and the ground right in front of him. The bullets were close, but he raised

1

his gun slightly higher, eyes narrowed and then squeezed the trigger.

No silencer could muffle the explosion of sound as he fired three shots. The last one silenced the gunfire coming from above. I caught movement in my periphery, and flicked my wrist, releasing the catch on the knife holster on my forearm. The slim handle landed in my palm.

I threw the blade even as I sat. At this range, accuracy was relatively easy. Anticipating the guy's speed was not. Still, the cold steel struck true, lodging right in the guy's throat. He went down with a spray of bullets upward, gurgling as he clawed at the blade.

"Nice," McQuade commented before he fired twice more. Two more targets went down.

"Can you see them?"

"No," McQuade answered. "You hit?"

"No."

"Good, then get ready to move."

"Getting my knife first." I didn't wait for his agreement or not. I had a gun, despite being familiar with firearms, I was far more comfortable with my knives. They gave me more non-lethal methods, but since these assholes were targeting Patch, I was fine with the painful ones.

"Comms are out." The constant buzz of static betrayed a weakness in the plan. One I really didn't want to think about.

People were still running, the screams had left the main quad where we were and retreated. Sporadic gunfire erupted and I moved swiftly to yank out the knife. The blade might be staunching the wound, but the guy was definitely dead.

Wiping the blood off on the guy's jacket, I ripped open the pockets and emptied them. He mostly had more weapons, but I found a plain white security card and a phone. I also lifted the guy's ear piece. The pop and crackle of speech over it carried.

Guess their comms *weren't* out.

Assholes.

"Oh," McQuade exhaled. "I like that plan."

I tossed it to him. He tucked it over his free ear, then did a sweep. Squealing tires ripped through the parking lots around us. The piercing shrill of sirens approached.

"We need to go," McQuade said. "British fucker isn't answering."

He wasn't...

Son of a bitch.

"I'm right behind you."

He took me at my word and headed in the direction we'd last seen Remington and Patch. Movement flickered and I'd no sooner caught sight of it than McQuade fired. He stalked across the open shopping center, a man on a mission.

The gray skies and cold weather did nothing to deter him. When we were almost to the clock tower, he froze for a minute, head cocked.

When he motioned to the earpiece, I nodded. Not that he glanced in my direction. The shift in his posture was my only warning. Something was up.

From minute one, this plan nagged at me. Not because it was a bad plan—it wasn't a great one, but I'd definitely done more with less. No, what I didn't like was putting Patch out there. She would be exposed.

Remington went with her. Of the three of us, I think I might have preferred McQuade, only because he was a mad dog and would likely gut someone as look at them. That was definitely the kind of energy I wanted protecting her.

Where McQuade blew hot, Remington was cold and precise. He might not look like he'd burn the world down, but I really didn't like the chances for anyone going up against him directly. He had been the one to notice the assassins before we did. Right, so maybe not my first choice, but definitely a good one.

"They're pulling out, but I want to get eyes on them or one of them to question..." McQuade scowled.

"Do we risk it?" Cause I saw the benefits. "Or do we extract and find Patch?"

My choice was pretty easy, but I was far more about stealth than open warfare. Fighting our way through the streets? That was McQuade's bread and butter.

"Split the difference," McQuade said as he flattened his back to the clocktower. "Go east." He pointed to a breezeway between the shops. "They came in on a containment pattern. They are gonna have to withdraw the same way."

And there were cars that way.

I had the keys for the car we'd used to get here. No guarantee that wasn't compromised—why we hadn't left anything in it.

4

Never thought my car boosting skills would get this much work. I jogged ahead, not rushing out but playing decoy. It took almost reaching the end of the breezeway where it opened to the parking lot to work.

The man in all black combat gear just stepped out of the shadows and swung. Apparently, we weren't the only ones looking to take prisoners. I blocked, then swung, rotating his arm as I flipped the blade's angle and brought it down and stabbed him through the back of his shoulder.

The jacket was designed to be bullet resistant and to pad from the impact. Digging the knife right through the seams planted it right into the fleshy part of the muscle.

Then McQuade was there and he jerked the gun from the guy's hand before coldcocking him with his pistol.

It was almost anticlimactic how fast he went down. "Get a car," McQuade ordered. "Big one."

Since that was already my plan, I scanned the lot before I sprinted toward one of the larger Land Rovers. It was the upgraded luxury type.

Good.

It took me a minute to pull out the scanner and plant it against the door. Two buttons and it was skimming signals, testing them. There were only so many—the locks clicked and it was open.

No electronic key, but since I had the frequency, I waited until all the lights went green then pressed the start button. All the gadgets were fun, but I kind of missed digging a knife in and popping the ignition or just twisting some wires in the engine.

The past had a lot more fun.

I backed out then drove straight toward Mc-Quade. Right up onto the sidewalk, I cut the wheels and spun so the rear faced him and I could push the button to release the tailgate.

He loaded our passenger in with a distinctive thump, then slammed the door shut before he climbed into the back seat. Good, I didn't fancy our guest deciding to attack us if he woke up. I didn't wait for him to close his door before I was already speeding for the exit. So many vehicles were trying to leave, I didn't want to get caught in a choke.

I also didn't miss the black-garbed men moving between the cars in the lot.

They were looking.

For us? For Patch?

I touched the comms at my ear again. Still static, then shot a look at McQuade.

He shook his head once. "They don't have her. Fucking Brit got her out."

That was good. I turned onto the green, jumping the curb and driving over the dried mud and dead grass to hit the street on the far side. Apparently, I started a trend, because more cars did the same.

How the hell had they known we were there? Had she been set up? Dammit.

Ten minutes and several blocks later, the comms were still static, but we had no tail.

"Call him." It was my turn to give the orders. McQuade already had his phone out. It took three attempts before Remington answered.

"Where are you?" McQuade demanded.

"Patch was hit..."

He said something else, but I barely registered it. She was hit? Where? How bad?

"Meet us there. Stay off the open air." Then Remington was gone, the call cut off.

"He's taking her to our secondary rallying point," McQuade told me.

That was almost an hour away. Was she okay for a drive that far?

Goddammit.

"Go faster," McQuade snapped, but I was already accelerating.

"We need to make sure our passenger doesn't have any trackers."

"We will. Just *drive.*"

CHAPTER
ONE
PATCH

TWO WEEKS LATER

"*C*asualty reports are still incoming..."

The half-light cast by the dim lamp in the bathroom kept the murky darkness at bay. The world seemed fuzzy around the edges.

"*Unexpected complications. Collateral damage within acceptable limits.*"

The world seemed coated in grime and my eyes watered.

"*...don't you dare! Patch! Talk to me dammit!*"

The last voice penetrated the haze and I shook my head a little. Were the voices real or was—

A movement shifted the bed. A movement made by *someone else*. I jerked a little and turned, my gaze locking on a pair of dark eyes. Little bubbles of hysteria fizzed up through me like I was a carbonated can given too hard a shake.

The dark eyes were steady, unblinking and while I was sitting up, he remained where he was—

laying down. Some distant portion of my brain still capable of rational analysis said his posture reflected a lack of threat.

Lack of threat...

That information accompanied one other pertinent nugget. Probably the important one...

"McQuade..."

Recognition bled through me and I sagged like someone had cut my strings. Fear dissolved into the sick effervescence rioting in my system.

"It's just me," he said in that rough way of his. The words had to bounce over that gravelly tone, but in some ways that was so much better than the soothing notes.

I really didn't want to be soothed.

Not while my heart jackrabbited and my stomach did flip-flops and my memory...

My fucking memory needed to be defragged so I could get rid of all the broken bits of data cluttering things up and put the rest back together again. I lifted a hand to touch my face.

Despite half-expecting bruises, all I found was a pillow impression on my cheek and some drool.

Very attractive.

"I'm going to sit up, Sugar Bear."

Sugar Bear—

"You know," I said. "I never told you that you could call me that—" Then I hesitated. I hadn't told him that was okay, right?

The murkiness discoloring everything was like trying to stare through sooty pinholes to what happened over the last few weeks. One minute, I was in my home working, doing my job. The next I was in a clinic, with three men I'd only ever spoken to on the phone hovering over me.

It wasn't just days that were gone, it was *weeks*. Whole chunks of time I couldn't account for but that couldn't have been fun based on my injuries. Even more, based on how Remy, McQuade, and Locke behaved around me.

Something terrible had happened and I couldn't access it. I hated the not knowing almost more than I hated the visceral physical reactions I kept having.

"Just because you didn't tell me I could, doesn't mean I won't do it," McQuade said, a smile curving his well-formed mouth. The stubble on his face was also kind of charming, and emphasized his more rebellious side.

As interesting and handsome as he was, hadn't I gone to bed on my own the night before?

"You were having a nightmare," McQuade said, the ease with which he spoke so damn familiar.

More familiar than the flirtations on the phone. This had substance and texture. It made me want to lean on him

"I know you said you wanted to sleep on your own. I heard you last night. And I heard your nightmares. When you're having nightmares, I'm going to show up. You sleep better when I'm here." He delivered the information with all the confidence of being straight facts.

Hard to dispute facts. Even if I didn't quite remember the nightmares. I remembered... The shadows slipped away before I could get a grip on them.

It wasn't like I could argue that point. He seemed to be speaking from experience and, frankly, I had slept. So I just kind of nodded, but I couldn't go back to sleep now. He seemed to understand, because he motioned towards the bathroom. Despite the gesture, it wasn't until he kept that long stare fixed on me that I finally forced myself to get out of the bed.

A split-second's hesitation marked me pushing back the blankets. What did I go to bed in? It took a moment to register that I did have on a t-shirt and panties. It covered everything important. Relieved by that much, I headed for the bathroom.

McQuade said nothing until I flipped on the light in the bathroom and began to close the door.

"Patch," he said in a very low voice. It was the kind of cadence I couldn't ignore. No one could. He only used it when he wanted you to pay attention to him, because it was serious. He needed you to listen and believe him.

Over the past few years I'd only ever heard him use that tone a few times. Then it was only to those people he'd rescued and he still needed to get out. Hearing him use that tone with me offered both comfort and the most disquieting unease that I'd ever experienced.

Licking my very dry lips, I steeled my shoulders and lifted my chin. As much as I wanted to escape everything his voice implied, I refused.

I wasn't a child. I wouldn't run away from what went bump in the night, even if I didn't know what that bump was or who caused it. The man sitting on the bed we'd ended up sharing was no stranger.

I'd known him for years, even if we'd never met in person until...

Well, I couldn't actually remember meeting him the first time at the moment, so I'd just go with recently.

McQuade continued to stare at me until our gazes locked. He raised his eyebrows, was I paying attention to him?

I nodded in response to the silent question. "I'm listening," I added while trying to infuse those two words with every bit of confidence I could. It still came out weak, but whatever.

"It's going to be fine." Five words delivered in a manner that said there were no other options. Everything would work out. It was going to be *fine*.

Because he said so dammit.

"That's what you know?" I asked and maybe I was daring him a little to prove it to me. "I mean, is that really what you know?"

Grinning, he flipped back the blankets revealing the rest of his very well-muscled, trim, and fit form, that was damn fine if you didn't mind all the scars. I definitely didn't mind them. Every single one was—

He cleared his throat and I jerked my head up to meet his incredibly amused gaze.

"That's exactly what I know," he said. "And you can look at me anytime you want, Sugar Bear."

My face flamed. Choosing tactical retreat, I shut the door then turned to lean with my back against it, eyes closed while desperately trying to ignore the masculine laughter wrapping around me from the other room.

At least he wasn't completely repulsed by my involuntary gawking at him. Not that he had a damn thing to worry about, he was so ruggedly built and...

Shit, what am I doing? I rubbed a hand over my face before staring at myself in the mirror.

What the fuck am I doing?

I'd had quite a few injuries when I woke up in that clinic, head pounding, vaguely nauseated, and really out of it. The last thing I'd expected was the three of them hovering over me, varying degrees of relief on their faces.

~

"Fallon?"

Blurring. Heat. Light. Cold.

The world seemed to drop and nausea swept through me. Then the world darkened again.

"You're safe." *The softness of that voice, the absence of the clipped tones to his British accent washed over me.* "The others are on their way."

Darkness.

Light.

Splintering.

"Gentlemen, yelling will not wake her up faster. I would caution you against increasing her stress until we've gotten a coherent answer from her." *The almost lyrical voice scolded in such a firm tone. It was kind of magical. Not that I'd heard any yelling.*

The darkness swallowed me again.

"Hey, Fallon." *Locke? Locke was here.* "I know you don't necessarily like us using that name, but I think it's *pretty. Patch is a badass, but Fallon—she's something special too."* A chair wheel squeaked against the floor. *"Fuck, sorry. We're splitting up time with you. You're never left alone. I promise. No one is going to get to you here. You're safe."*

The stress on that last word stirred something inside of me. *Safe.* Safety, like time, was relative. An illusion. An all too brief respite.

Even if I kind of wanted to believe him.

A hand flexed over mine, the gentlest stroke of fingers slotting with mine, until they were interlocked. It was like he reached into the darkened pool and dragged me toward the surface.

"It's okay, Sugar Bear. You take as long as you need. The fact you can sleep with all this beeping is impressive."

McQuade.

"Doctor said you needed time. No stressing that sexy fucking brain of yours. So, pick one thing and just focus on that." Silence lingered, but not absence. I wasn't alone in the dark.

They were all here.

McQuade.

Locke.

Remy.

I squeezed the hand holding mine.

"Hello, luv. There you are. That's it. Hold on to me."

Blink.

Brightness.

Darkness.

Cold.

Hot.

Blink.

15

Blurs moving around.

The world swayed.

Darkness again.

Another blur.

The light sharpened gradually, forming a frame around a set of red-rimmed blue eyes that stared back at me. I blinked slowly, adding more clarity to the image. It was so real...

"Hi," Locke whispered. A smile softened the corners of his mouth. His usually perfect hair was mussed, his face unshaven, and his clothes wrinkled. Something was wrong for him to be in such an unkempt state. "You still with me?"

Was he here? For real? Or was this some kind of dream? Why was he here? Maybe I was imagining it. Focus was so damn hard at the moment. Arm trembling, I tried to lift my hand. It was like it was totally disconnected from me.

He ducked his head, meeting my touch. The roughness of his whiskers scraped at my skin. Locke was real.

He was real and I was touching him.

Why—how had he found me? Were the others real too?

His smile deepened and he covered my hand on his cheek, keeping it pressed to his face. "It's really me. We're really here. Been waiting for you to open those gorgeous eyes."

Movement behind him. The others? But even as I raised my eyes to focus, they were already closing. Dammit.

Blink.

"There you are." Remy had replaced Locke. Maybe I was hallucinating. These two didn't even know each

other. But the shadows under his eyes and the paleness to his face suggested more than worry. "The doctor is actually here this time."

Irritation ruffled beneath those words.

"Mr. Remington." Oh, the doctor was the lyrical voice. "I've told you that just telling her off is not going to work."

"Yet, she is looking at me and she can hear me," he retorted, before glancing back at me. His cooler demeanor softened. "Can't you, luv?"

I squeezed his hand. Even as I searched for the words to say, a woman entered my line of sight. Her darker skin and eyes seemed so warm in contrast to the violent white of the room. Was it really that white? I couldn't really see much past either Remy or—

I had no idea what the doctor's name was. The room seemed to swim again, then there were two fingers moving back and forth right in front of me. Oh, that helped. Easier to focus on what was closer.

"Can you follow this motion?" Her tone had turned brisk, direct. "Excellent. That's good tracking. I need to test your pupil response."

The only warning she gave me before she pierced my brain with a too bright pin light. It flooded my eyes, fading everything around me. Eventually, it left a corona effect around Remy, then Locke, and McQuade as they crowded in behind him.

They were all there.

Exhaustion had marked them, but it was worry that stamped their features. I'd seen them in a lot of situations.

This one was new.

They were here and terrified.

17

For the first time since I woke up, fear pierced me.

❦

Maybe I imagined it? But that didn't seem likely. No, they'd been incredibly relieved. I'd also been shot. With trembling fingers, I traced the thin pink line right along my hairline. I could feel it, but it wasn't visible unless I pulled my hair back tight.

A furrow where the skin had split open after a bullet creased me. They'd used these little butterfly bandages on it and skin glue after it kept reopening for a couple of days after. The blinding headache had been insane.

The pain had been off the charts. The pain and my completely obliterated memory.

The physician said it would come back. Eventually. He assured me that it was a trauma reaction, probably not anything to do with my brain. Or maybe just my brain protecting me. Great. I didn't like maybes and shoulds.

I liked concrete facts. For example, between my physical condition and everything the guys hadn't said, I'd definitely experienced the trauma to have this kind of reaction.

Specific type of trauma?

I could guess. My last memories before waking up in the clinic had been being in my house in Estes Park, and working in my safe room.

Someone had to have taken me. Taken me. Tortured me.

But where? And who?

Had I told them anything? Was it already too late?

The guys didn't think so, or so they insisted the spare once or twice I'd actually managed to get Locke or Remy to answer a question regarding it.

Dammit.

I wanted to push. The first few days, I let them call the shots, but the headache was better. More manageable.

I needed answers.

Remy insisted I needed to let them worry about things right now while I took it easy. My brain needed the time to heal. He reminded me what the doctor had said about trying to force it could make it worse.

What he'd actually said was forcing it could exacerbate the trauma and hurt me more than help. The minute he said those words, the guys dug in, McQuade, in particular. We wouldn't be pushing. End of story.

Hating every part of this, I shoved away from the door. I used the facilities, then washed my hands before staring at myself in the mirror again. There were new scars in addition to the thin one along my hair line. A couple on my chin, and another on my throat.

Scars I didn't recognize, from injuries I couldn't really remember.

Stripping off the t-shirt and panties, I braced to study the scars on my chest and the ones along my arms.

Cigarette burns were hard to think of as anything else. They were stained pink, the skin waxy, and the circles kind of oblong. It made me think whoever had inflicted them had moved the cigarette in circles to extinguish it on my flesh.

There was evidence of more burns over my breasts and abdomen down to my thighs. These looked more electrical than cigarette. The lines thin, almost ribboning over each other.

A crop? A whip? Hot wire?

No matter how much I studied them, the marks only gave me more questions, not answers. The thud in my head increased, as though the pound of my heart echoed in my brain.

After twisting the shower on, I didn't wait for it to heat up all the way and just ducked under the water. The chill in the water braced me, the spray washing away the fog and the cobwebs. Gradually, it heated before I could get too cold. McQuade might still be in my room, but if he heard the shower come on, he wouldn't bother me.

So far the guys had all been good about respecting my privacy unless I called for help. Something I'd ceased the moment I could stand and walk on my own. My feet still hurt, the wounds there mostly healed, but it made my arches tight and I didn't think the ball of my right foot would ever not be bruised.

It had been my nightmares that pulled him into the room. Had I cried out? Screamed? What were they about? But no matter how hard I tried, the dreams were no more substantial than wisps on the air.

Showering relaxed some of the tension out of me, even as it washed away the cobwebs. By the time I finished and toweled off, I was ready for coffee. What I wanted was coffee and my computer.

The guys weren't exactly forthcoming with the latter. That needed to change. Dressed in my t-shirt and panties once more, I opened the door to the bedroom. It was empty. McQuade had also pulled up the bedcovers and made it.

It was kind of sweet. It only took me a few minutes to pull out a pair of leggings, some thick socks, and a sweater I could pull on over the t-shirt. I didn't bother with a bra.

Some of the wounds on my back had left the skin there very sensitive and I hadn't had time to figure out a solution for it. Later, I promised myself.

Later, I would get all of this sorted out. I would also get all the answers I wanted and needed. First, I needed to persuade my erstwhile guardians that I could handle the tough stuff. That meant I needed my computer back and some straight answers.

They could give them to me or I would figure it out on my own. Healing meant I was more mobile and independent. My computer had to be in this house somewhere.

Second, figure out where *here* was so I could plan accordingly. Squaring my shoulders, I took another deep breath. The guys needed to understand that no matter what, I wasn't letting this go.

I couldn't.

TWO

REMINGTON

" S he's getting restless," McQuade warned when he emerged from her room.

The first time he'd gone in there had been following a nightmare that woke all three of us. Everyone *except* Patch. It hadn't woken her at all. If anything, she'd been trapped in that nightmare until McQuade settled next to her, then put a single hand on her shoulder.

Even in the low light cast from the hall into her room, there was no mistaking the frown easing on her face. More telling had been how the muted, almost smothered cries had ceased. She didn't *scream* not long or loud. It was somehow worse, those near inaudible cries of pain. Censoring her own suffering, even in sleep.

It was a load of tosh, but she didn't ask me.

McQuade eyed the coffee where it brewed. Locke and Patch both seemed to enjoy the espresso machine more, but espresso was not what she reached for all day. I preferred to give her options. I nodded to him. "Help yourself."

The restlessness had been apparent over the past couple of days. She'd reduced the amount of sleep she needed. The lingering signs of the concussion had faded and taken her light sensitivity with it. She hadn't *asked* for her computer the day prior, but she had been looking around for it.

Or presumably, that was what she was seeking.

"You're thinking awfully hard over there," McQuade commented. "Going to share with the class?"

I spared him a look. "Locke is the one who likes to discuss his feelings."

His cough and splutter following his inhaling of the coffee amused me more than the comment. It also, almost, masked the sound of her bedroom door opening again. I cut a glance toward her reflection on the glass of one of the wall photos. It was blurred, indistinct—yet her. The long blonde hair that fell well past her shoulders and more than half of that length was a darker color. It was as though once she'd colored it years previously, she'd never changed it again.

Instead, she let the hair grow out. The blonde length a declaration for how long she'd been in hiding. A testament to her self-imposed exile, I supposed. Then again, she hadn't gone below the grid for so long because it was a vacation. She'd genuinely constructed a prison of sorts out of her bolthole.

There she stayed, until she'd been dragged out of it. I couldn't imagine her not kicking and screaming. So no, she'd given them a fight and they'd repaid her in blood and tears. Anger pulsed sluggishly through my blood the more I considered everything that had been done to her.

Including the latest—her memory loss. It wasn't permanent, or so the doctor had sworn. But he also said he wasn't sure if it was a true trauma response physically *or* emotionally. It could be both. So he strongly advised us to let her remember on her own. Thankfully, she hadn't forgotten who *we* were, even if she'd been stunned by our presence.

She remembered nothing of her incarceration or so she said... I believed her. She had no reason to lie to us. We'd been very up front about what we wouldn't discuss. No one pretended we didn't know, but the doctor thought for her sake, mentally *and* emotionally, it would be better if she retrieved her memories when *she* was ready.

Information was power. I would listen for now, but I refused to let anyone have that kind of power over her.

"Are you all right?" The softness in the question grounded me almost as much as the concern filling her gray eyes.

Frowning, I glanced from her eyes to where her hand rested lightly against my chest. I'd missed her passage from the doorway to where I stood. Compromised. I was very much compromised for this woman. It could prove problematic, because none of us could afford to lose focus in a combat situation.

"I'm fine," I assured her. Then because I wasn't certain what had given my mood away, I added, "Why do you ask?"

"You looked—fierce," she answered in a slow, almost sleepy voice. Not too drowsy though, she was waking up, yet still ready to do battle. We wouldn't be able to delay her much longer. Whether she was ready or not, I had total faith that she would absolutely find out the information on her own.

"It's early and McQuade isn't the best company first thing."

"Fuck you too, mate." The cheerfulness belied the bite, but the snap was still there.

"Don't call me mate," I reminded him, then covered Patch's hand on my chest. Closing my fingers around hers, I eased the contact that threatened to brand me through my clothes. "I made coffee. I was just considering breakfast. How are you feeling this morning?"

Initially, all but the blandest of foods had left her nauseated. She had vomited once or twice at the clinic. All consistent with a concussion. We'd kept the foods mild and eased her back into it. The night before, however, she'd eaten the grilled fish easily. I took that as a good sign.

"I'm hungry," she admitted, her faint smile not quite erasing her puzzled expression. Though she didn't say anything until I pulled out a chair for her at the table. Then I went about getting her coffee prepared. "Remy—"

"I'm gonna grab a shower," McQuade said and I cut a glance to where he leaned over the table and pressed a kiss to the top of Patch's head. "Be good for Remy."

"You have—"

"I'm aware." He didn't even let me finish the reminder. Yes, he had a supply run to do today. Supplies and information, we were spreading out where we retrieved them from. At the moment, no wireless or analog signals were leaving this location. Our phones were off when we were here and they were in shielded bags.

The only electronic devices were on a local network *only* that had no external access. It let us watch the security system. The need to keep this location as far under the radar as we could meant isolating that contact. I still wasn't sure how they tracked us when we'd been so damn careful.

Until we figured it out, I didn't think there was enough of a level of paranoid to keep her safe.

"You're aware?" Patch prompted, focusing on McQuade. I didn't like the interception of her attention. She'd been watching me before, yet the loss allowed me to study her a little more covertly. There was an awareness to her that had been lacking since she woke from the shooting.

A vitality in the faint flush to her cheeks and the determined lift of her chin. I didn't know *her* micro expressions as well as I might. Her tone of voice was far easier to read and to understand. She had so many different ways to speak.

Teasing.

Affectionate.

Exasperated.

Cooly professional.

Sharp, dangerous, and solving problems only half-aware of the fact someone was on the line with her.

Afraid.

Hurt.

There were easily more, I could catalog them all if I took the time. I understood the nonverbal cues in her voice. Not in her face. It didn't help that when I tried to study her to learn more, or at least begin to identify what a faint frown on her forehead meant versus the tightening around her eyes, I stopped looking at her expression.

Instead, I found myself studying the contours of her face. How defined her cheekbones were. The fact her collarbones jutted told me all I needed to know about her lack of nutrition while they held and tortured her. She seemed wound too tight, her skin pulled taut, and all of it stretching like a mask to keep the damaged parts cobbled together.

The woman with so much strength, she prevailed on pure determination alone. That quality merely added to her overall appeal.

"I'm aware of what I have to do today," McQuade was saying in answer to her earlier prompt. She wouldn't be brushed off. "If we wanted to tell you directly, we would." Not an unfair point.

"Maybe Remy was about to, before you cut him off." The tart response pulled a real smile to my lips and I started the grinder as McQuade opened his mouth. His glare toward me just made me smile wider.

Once I had the perfect puck, I pulled her shots before retrieving the milk. "Go take your shower," I said. "I'll fill her in on what she needs to know."

McQuade snorted, but it was Patch's turn to give me a flat look even if the corners of her lips tilted. She was more amused than she wanted to let on. "You need me, press the button."

The panic button. She had it with her always now and it buzzed to all of us. The device was more for our comfort than hers. Locke pointed that out the night he set it up, not that it slowed his hand even once.

"I will," she said. "But I doubt I'll need it. Remy is here."

I appreciated both her vote of confidence *and* McQuade's grumble in response. The mercenary didn't linger after that, vanishing back toward the room he'd claimed for himself. Steaming her milk didn't take much longer and I was getting better at creating the foam she enjoyed. When I carried the coffee over, I met her assessing gaze.

"I'll make you a deal," I offered.

"For what?" Head tilted, she accepted the coffee and grinned at it. "Also, thank you for this."

"You're very welcome, the deal is, you answer a question and I'll answer a question."

"Quid pro quo." She summed it up beautifully. "That seems almost too easy."

"Does it?" It was an open-ended question. So while she pondered that, I continued, "Breakfast?"

"Yes please, and I think I would like some eggs with the toast this morning."

She sipped her coffee. The flick of her gaze away as she drank didn't fool me. I'd laid out the bait neatly. If she missed it at all, then she was definitely not ready for the conversation. She waited until I was getting the eggs out.

"What are you keeping from me?" The broadness of the question was almost too wide in scope.

"I'm sure we're keeping a great many things," I told her. "I'm afraid you need to be more specific and I can't answer for the two of them on everything. Do you want your eggs fried or scrambled?"

Most of the time, she seemed to prefer the scramble. Or so I thought. I'd been getting to know her habits before. Despite her injuries, most remained consistent. Her food preferences shifted some. I suspected that had more to do with the aftereffects of the concussion than an actual personality-level change.

"Hmm, scrambled. The fluffier the better. Might be lighter to eat." The explanation answered a couple of questions for me, so I saved those. "What caused my head injury? The most recent one."

When it came to whittling her focus down, she took it to a razor's edge. An excellent sign. Critical thinking skills and application could be compromised and we had scant few resources for testing them.

"I believe it was a ricochet, but I don't have the evidence to validate it fully. We were on our way to a meeting. We walked into a sniper's ambush. Multiple shots were fired and exchanged. One of them creased your head."

She traced the line of her injury with her fingertips. I studied it every single time I saw it. Four centimeters in length, curved at the ends. Slightly flatter on the anterior versus the posterior. The bullet creased her along the curvature of her skull.

The line was still pink, the skin around it

flushed. Too recently healed to hide against her hair. It stood out, the stain of color against her pale golden hair. Once I had the eggs going, I dropped the toast to cook.

I gave her another minute to process the direct answer. She'd been shot. Ricochet or direct, the only thing that mattered was she survived. That said, it was still a harsh reality to realize that someone really had tried to kill her. The holes in her memory aside, she didn't seem shocked by the news.

Good sign? Bad?

Undetermined.

"How is your headache today?" It had been rather ongoing, easing off but then returning for several days. Partially eye strain, or so I suspected. "And do you know where your glasses are?" The last question slipped out even though I had already asked one. Choice in eyewear hadn't made it to the list of our earlier discussions.

"It's not bad," she answered slowly, as though she had to do an assessment first. "Actually, I don't really have one this morning."

"Are you sure?" Because the lack of certainty echoed under the last few words.

"Pretty sure," she murmured, then lifted her shoulders. "I think I had one when I woke up, but more of a nagging one. It went away with my shower. So—that's good."

I was in no rush to agree or not. Not without more information. Patch continued to be something of an enigma, and while it intrigued me on so many levels, it also frustrated, because I needed to know all her tells. I needed to know she wasn't holding anything back that might indicate something more was wrong.

"Yeah, I don't. That's kind of weird." Her laugh was far more bemused than entertained. Not that I could blame her. So much she didn't remember yet. Some parts, I would never be eager for her to reclaim. "Anyway... no, I barely know where I am, Remy. Besides, I only need them when my eyes are tired."

I nodded. "We need to find yours then or get you a new set made. I should have realized." She hadn't had them when we pulled her out, but she hadn't even had clothes. Then we were too focused on getting her out and safe. While she hadn't complained before, now I had to wonder how much eyestrain she'd been subjecting herself too.

The toast popped up as I turned the heat off under the eggs. It was into that silence that she asked, "Why don't you want to tell me what happened?"

This close to her, I couldn't miss the vaguest note of hurt in her voice nor the way her gaze latched on to mine. Protecting her shouldn't involve leaving her vulnerable. This question, however, closed off the easier avenues to avoid it.

"Because we aren't sure if the reason you don't remember is due to physical or mental trauma." It was the truth. I carried the plates over and set hers in front of her before I grabbed the silverware and the butter dish. "The missing days are fairly specific..."

"And you know what happened?" She asked as if it were almost an involuntary reaction.

"Yes." I nodded once before pulling out my chair and twisting to focus on her and not the food. Leaning forward, I held out a hand. Would she take it?

She didn't hesitate and that helped to ease a jagged weight off my soul. A weight that had fallen in and begun to crush me from the moment I'd realized she'd been shot.

"I know you want to know," I said, closing my hand around hers. "I know you want to dig and to look. We aren't answering you because we don't know if telling you will do more harm than good."

She searched my face and whatever she was looking for, she must have found because she gave a slow nod. "Something happened to me. I need to know what it was."

"Can you give yourself a few more days to heal?" She was doing so much better now, and I wanted that improvement to continue. The last thing she needed was to suffer a setback. Particularly more than an hour away from the closest medical intervention.

"If I say no, will you answer me?"

I saw things so much better from a distance. I lacked the kind of distance I needed to be as cool and rational as she deserved. She was so much more than a job.

So. Much. More.

"Yes."

THREE

PATCH

"So I told you about my job before?" Each word came out a little slower than the previous. More out of disbelief that I would confess those facts to *anyone* much less these three.

"Be hard for us to know the details, Sugar Bear, if you hadn't told us." McQuade gave me a wry look.

"Unless you worked for them and this was a ruse of some kind to pull information from me." Even giving voice to the idea didn't really sell the concept to me. Escaping the concern in their eyes, I looked down at my arms.

I'd been in sweatshirts or sweaters since waking at this cozy little cabin in the far reaches of Michigan. It was Michigan. That sounded right. With the fire burning merrily, hot coffee in my cup and all three of them surrounding me like a sexy wall of testosterone, I'd been far too warm in the sweater so I stripped it off.

There were circular scars all over my arms. Scars that hadn't been there before. I traced one of them with a fingernail that wasn't particularly attractive. I'd had longer nails before. Not super long or anything fancy, but long enough that I could shape them.

It wasn't like I'd been able to go get a manicure in years. So I made do with giving them to myself. I'd gotten pretty good at it. Most of my nails were either ragged down to the base or lower.

One had been ripped right down into the quick and there was a cut that circled the finger. My fingers ached and there was definite stiffness around the joints. The headache pulsing behind my eye seemed to increase in its tempo.

Lifting the hand in question, I rubbed at my forehead just above my eye. The area was still tender so I had to be careful. The bruise there had faded to a sickly greenish-yellow, and the lump had begun to decrease in size.

"You don't believe us," Locke said, disappointment salting the neutrality of his voice. Or maybe I was imagining it.

"It's not that I don't believe you," I said, testing every word. "I'm just trying to figure out why I would..."

"Why you would tell us secrets you haven't told anyone else." As unexpected as having one of them finish my thoughts was, it was more than a bit discomforting to hear it detailed in that distinctly sexy as fuck British accent.

Remy folded his arms as he leaned back against the counter. It was the first defensive posture I'd seen him—or any of them take—since I woke up here. His steady gaze held me captive as I tried to figure out what thoughts were rolling through his head.

"That's part of it," I admitted, despite the absolute truth in the statement. The last thing I wanted to do was insult them. They didn't deserve that. "The other part is—I'm used to talking to you on the phone not..."

"In person where we can enjoy a little old-fashioned face-to-face interaction?" Was McQuade taunting me? The hint of sarcasm underlining the last few words of his question seemed a warning.

"Before two weeks ago," I said, picking my words carefully. "We'd only ever spoken on the phone. You didn't know me. You could have walked past me on the street and not noticed me."

"luv," Remy sounded disappointed. "I would definitely have noticed you."

I sighed, then rubbed a hand over my face. We were going in circles.

"Now, if you meant we might not have recognized you as Patch, the glorious goddess on the phone who has saved my life more than once..."

"And mine," Locke and McQuade said in one voice.

With a wry wave of one hand, Remy gestured to them. "We know you, Fallon. We're aware you don't remember our first meeting or everything that happened. We also know how difficult this is..."

"Or maybe we don't," Locke added on with a shrug. "I can't say I'd be happy to be missing any moments in my day, much less my weeks and months."

"The point, Sugar Bear," McQuade half-growled with a roll of his eyes at the others and the corners of my mouth twitched despite the sobriety of the moment. "We know you're learning to trust us again. You trusted us enough to tell us before. Or maybe you accepted that we were the best of a bad situation. That's possible. Either way, it worked because you read us into your recruitment and then your subsequent realization that maybe you weren't working for the people you thought you were."

The sinking feeling of that reality threatened to drown me. I worried at the nail on my thumb. It was already beaten and broken down to a bare nub. It wasn't like I could make it worse.

"I hate this," I said, closing my eyes even as my heart started to race. Every single time I tried to dredge those memories up, pain drove a spike through my brain.

"We know," Locke said and he was suddenly a lot closer. When I opened my eyes, he was crouched in front of me and he had one hand on my knee. "We really do. Now, all of this other stuff aside. You don't remember what happened between the last calls you had with us and then waking up here two weeks ago."

It wasn't a question.

I resisted the urge to shake my head in answer. At the moment, it would probably leave me nauseated and I'd had enough of that.

When Locke didn't withdraw, I focused on him. He seemed to be waiting on me to acknowledge the statement. Fair enough. "No, I don't remember."

"Okay," he said, giving me a small smile. "That wasn't so hard, was it?"

"It sucks." I wasn't sure whether it was my words or my tone that made McQuade chuckle. At my glance, he just shrugged and folded his arms. Like Remy before him, he seemed to be adopting a more defensive posture.

To be honest, that was weirder coming from Crazy McQuade than it was from Remy. The latter had always been more guarded and infinitely patient. The former? Well, I doubted if McQuade had ever met a risk he wasn't ready to take.

"Agreed," Locke said, recapturing my attention. "So since we can't just decrypt your memories at the moment or load up what is missing, let's tackle what we can do."

"What can we do?" Remy asked, a sudden sharpness in his tone. "We want her to rest and continue to heal."

"No kidding," Locke said, giving Remy a dirty look over his shoulder. "Pretty sure we're all on the same page, Lord Obvious."

Lord Obvious?

I had to bite the inside of my lip. Talk about giving a promotion to a captain. A little bubble of laughter escaped before I could contain it. "Yes, what can we do?"

That snared all three of them once more. Three weighty gazes pressed in on me. The air seemed too warm and the room too small. These guys all possessed such large personalities.

One corner of his mouth ticking higher, McQuade made no effort to suppress his smile. The light squeeze to my knee from Locke pulled my gaze back to him.

"Tell us what you need from us to prove you can trust us." Locke raised his brows, the offer as much a dare as it was a request. "While we can make it work without the trust, I think we'll all feel better about it if you know you believe what we say."

Remy blew out a harsh exhale. "Bloody thief has a point."

"Thank you," Locke commented with a smirk, but he didn't take his gaze off of me. "Talk to us?"

Another burst of laughter tinged with hysteria escaped. I pressed a finger against my lips in an effort to stifle the inappropriate humor. It really was very warm, and I couldn't seem to lock my gaze down on any one of them.

"I don't even know where to start." That admission cost.

"Go operational," McQuade suggested. "You had to vet us when we became clients. I know it was more than a deep background. In theory, you saw something worth investing in with each of us."

"Huh." He had a point. I tapped a finger against my lips. It was as much a reminder to give the idea a chance as it was to think it through. "I did... Yes, I was probably a little more thorough with the deep background than I used to be. But I needed to make sure that not only were you who you said you were, but that you had no ties to my former employers."

"So, we all passed?" Remy confirmed, his cool eyes rock steady on me. "No hiccups?"

I opened my mouth to respond then closed it as I considered the question. Finally, I nodded. "Everything I can recall says you passed my first vetting, then the second where I watched you for a few days."

"Watching us?" Locke asked, both brows up as he leaned slightly away from me and studied me. "Were you playing the spy, Fallon?"

I didn't quite flinch when he used my name. It had been so long since I'd been around anyone who even knew what my name was, much less used it to speak to me.

It was odd.

"Yes," I said, not bothering to sugar coat it. "You're all very dangerous people. I'd have been a fool to be the one who would open doors and clean up behind you without knowing more about you."

"Smart," McQuade said, approval radiating through that word. "Though it begs the question, how did you manage to 'spy' on us before we finalized the contracts?"

With a wince, I lifted my shoulders. "I sent you a deconstructed worm over the course of three emails that only activated when I sent the last one asking for a few days."

The simple fact was, I wouldn't take on every single person who tried to hire me. In fact, I answered only about five percent of the requests in those first weeks. Of that five percent, it was less than point zero zero four that earned a place on my roster.

"You infected our computers," Locke said, the half-twist of his smile betraying his amusement despite the attempt at a stern tone.

Licking my lips, I nodded. "All of your devices.

Pretty much anything that shared data. Most people link their email on multiple devices, so it gave me a good snapshot."

It let me access their equipment remotely. I could turn on their cams, scan the area around them. Location services could be turned on if they were off and it let me track them locally.

"You know where we live," Remy said abruptly, the surprise on his face turning troubled. "You know a great deal more than you've ever admitted."

"Guilty," I said. "So maybe you three should decide if you can trust me too."

"I don't need to decide," McQuade said flatly. "You've saved my life, Sugar Bear. I'm here for the long haul."

"Same," Locke said. "Though now it makes me think I'm going to need to be more clever about birthday presents."

Unlike the others, Remy wasn't as quick with his assurances. His eyes narrowed as he studied me.

"I'm sure that's discomforting," I told him by way of an apology. "I needed to know. That doesn't mean you aren't going to be happy that I know your secrets. It's making me crazy that I don't know how they found me."

He nodded slowly but still said nothing. My stomach bottomed out. If the deep dives turned their trust, then I had no one to blame but myself.

"For what it's worth, I disabled the worms after we decided to finalize the contracts. Everything else I sent you, I told you about." They each had devices I could access remotely, and I'd always told them to make it a secondary one. It protected their privacy and it was easier to ditch and destroy in the event they were compromised.

Scratching his jaw, Remy looked more thoughtful than annoyed. I could almost read the unasked questions in his eyes. He wanted to talk to me. He did not want to talk to me in front of them.

I nodded to him and some of the stone seemed to ease out of his expression. "I'd apologize," I said slowly. "But to be perfectly honest..."

"You had a job to do and protecting yourself is the first step." Locke gave my leg another gentle squeeze. The contact had been a little uncomfortable at first. The feeling proved fleeting the longer he rested his hand in place. "Never going to complain about that, Fallon. You should never apologize for it, either."

"What he said," McQuade grunted. "But he wants to know if you saw him naked already because it might cost him some points overall."

"Fuck off," Locke said, cutting him a look. "You best hope she hasn't seen me naked. You're already running behind in the points department."

McQuade snorted, but Remy just rolled his eyes even as I tried to keep from laughing

"The point," I pressed on, lips twitching. We needed to get back on topic. "Yes, I did research you and investigated you to make sure you were who you said you were. Some of your career choices were colorful. I needed to know you weren't... horrible people." I winced. "Do you have some questionable career choices? Maybe."

It was my turn to shrug.

"My hands aren't exactly clean. But I wanted to

know..." How did I phrase this that didn't sound condescending or shitty?

"That we were honorable," Remy said, the lilt to his words softening the implication that I'd questioned the fact at all. "That you could trust us."

"Yes."

"So," McQuade said, pouncing on that fact. "If you could trust us then, don't you think you can trust us now?"

Lips parted, I studied him for the longest moment, then looked to Remy, and finally down to Locke. While I detected no signs of malice or dishonesty, it was still uncomfortable.

"In theory," I began slowly. "Yes, I should be able to trust you now."

"Except?" Locke prompted.

I licked my lips again. The answer was right there on the tip of my tongue, but it was a terrible confession. My heartbeat seemed almost too loud, too fierce. If I admitted it to them, I was also admitting it to myself.

Closing my eyes, I blocked *them* out. I concentrated on regulating my breathing and bringing the sudden gallop of my pulse under control. Locke flexed his hand on my knee again. I covered his hand with mine more on impulse than anything else.

He was offering comfort and I wanted to accept it. Forcing my eyes open, I said, "I'm scared. If I'm wrong... it's not just me, I'm risking."

Understanding crystalized in Remy's eyes even as McQuade frowned, but it was Locke who blew out a slow whistle. "If one of us proves untrustworthy, you're worried about what he'll do to the other two?"

"Yes." As much as I hated to admit that, I hated thinking it more. "I want to trust you. I think... on some levels I do. But so much of this is confusing. It's all messy and strange. Like I said before, I still don't know how they found me. Or how you guys found me wherever I was and you've been very circumspect about the details."

"You're right," Locke said. "Then this is what we do. SITREP, gentlemen. Let's brief her on how we discovered she was missing, when we met, and how we found her. I would prefer, however," he continued, gazing up at me, "to avoid the specifics of where you were and how you were when we found you until you're ready to process it."

A careful recitation of the details without exposing the memories that had apparently been excised thanks to a bullet glancing off my skull.

It was a compromise, but a good one.

"Yes, please."

Locke shifted his grip to take my hand as he stood and then he tugged me out of the chair. "We're going to do this somewhere more comfortable. Who wants to go first?"

"Me," McQuade and Remy said in the same breath.

"Well, as long as we're clear on that." Locke's droll tone pulled another laugh from me and he grinned.

FOUR
MCQUADE

I t was late when Patch went to bed. The briefing had been far more circumspect than she cared for, but we didn't skimp on *our* details. The only ones we edited were her condition when we found her.

Seeing her injuries, the filth of what clothing she had left as well as the blood and dirt embedded in her skin played on repeat my mind. The absolute darkness in her eyes haunted me. The memory of her wounds was seared into my brain, a permanent reminder of what she'd been through.

We'd catalogued every single injury, not only to treat them, but also so I could keep a running tally of what I would be doing to the people who took her. The fact the facility in Louisiana was still there was a sore point for me.

Though Remington had suggested the site might have been scrubbed since we penetrated their defenses. Not good enough. I wanted certainty, not speculation. I wanted blood, not escape.

The near inaudible, strangled sound came from

her room. Rising, I abandoned the chair I'd claimed after she'd bid us all good night. Locke and Remington both stared at me when I said I'd take first watch. Neither of them cared for me going into her room to sleep.

I didn't much care what they liked or didn't. I checked the exterior cameras on the handheld monitor on the way around the chair to head to her room. If Patch needed me, I was not letting her suffer. Not when I could help.

Everything showed clear, so I turned the sound down. The motion sensors would send an alarm if they picked up anything. We'd scrubbed our route back after the cluster fuck at the mall. Switching roads and vehicles until we were certain we'd eliminated even the suggestion of a tail.

Still, someone had tracked us to that meeting. The logical conclusion was her ally had sold us out —sold *her* out. No one wanted to broach that subject yet. While I didn't think she was as infinitely fragile and likely to shatter as Locke and Remy did, I also didn't want to inflict more harm than good.

The door opened silently. I'd oiled the hinges because I didn't want to disturb her if at all possible. The fact another strangled sound came from the vicinity of the bed tugged at me to hurry my ass up.

She needed extraction.

Closing the door behind me, I circled the bed to the far side. She preferred to sleep closer to the windows than the door. I got it, though I wished we had a room with no windows on it at all. I didn't like the exposure. We'd covered the windows, however, and the blackout curtains were always closed.

Remy had also trapped the site lines to make sure anyone trying to set up would get a nasty surprise. The Brit was annoying, but he knew his shit. Any fuckup that came after her that way was going to lose more than a hand.

"Stop..." Her voice sliced through the darkness. Blood, sweat, and tears coated that single word. It made me fist my temper in both hands. She didn't need my rage right now.

Phone and gun on the nightstand within easy reach, I slipped my shoes off and eased onto the bed. The sheets were twisted all around her. One bare leg was out and the other hidden. Her shirt had rolled up, leaving her panties visible, but I dragged my attention upward and firmly on *her* and not her ass.

Even if she had a very nice, very rounded, sweet ass that would be a generous handful. Mind out of the gutter, I snapped internally. Even if my mind wanted to be further into the bed rather than the gutter, I resisted the urge to slap myself.

"No..." The choked noise underscoring the word strangled my libido silent.

Gliding a hand to her shoulder, I settled it there. No words, just my hand. A shudder went through her whole body before she stilled. It was almost preternatural how the thrashing ceased so abruptly.

Sometimes, all I had to do was rest a hand on her. The weight would be enough to push the dreams away. Despite her lack of motion, she wasn't rousing and her breath still came at a rapid rate.

The short, harsh gasps punctuated the air, warning that the nightmare still held her captive. Squeezing her shoulder gently, I shifted my weight on the bed. Sometimes, if I laid down with her and just kept my hand there, it was enough.

Then she flailed.

Sometimes it wasn't. She struck out with one hand. The glancing blow barely registered. As strong as she was, she didn't hit hard at all. It was more the abrupt surprise in the action.

"Shh," I soothed as I loosened the sheet so she wasn't trapped anymore. Keeping my hand on her shoulder proved a little tougher when she struggled, but then I curled her over against my chest and wrapped my arms around her.

I had to be careful, the last thing I wanted to do was hurt her. Keeping my arms loose, I was ready for her to pull away. It had happened a couple of times when she woke and found me here.

Other times?

She rubbed her cheek against my shirt, it was almost like she was burrowing into me. I didn't mind in the slightest. Flattening a hand against her back, I spread my fingers out.

With slow circular motions, I tried to ease the knots from her muscles. Another little wet gasp escaped her as I settled her more firmly against me. Bit by bit, though, she began to settle.

"There we go," I murmured, keeping my voice soft and easy. "Go back to sleep. No bad dreams for you."

The nightmares had been bad before. Since the shooting, they'd seemed to have grown worse. I had to wonder if this was how her mind was trying to process her trauma. Or was it something else?

Was she just retraumatizing herself each night? Was that why the memories weren't coming back? Or was this just how she dealt with the PTSD? Fuck, I had far more questions than answers.

Her breathing evened out, the rapid gasps fading to longer, deeper breaths. The fact she went almost boneless against me pulled a real smile to my lips. There was something utterly captivating about this woman.

I hated that she'd been scarred by what she'd been through. More than physical scars, too. The wounds they'd inflicted on her had gone deep. Her fisted hand against my shirt relaxed slowly as her leg hitched against my thigh.

Bit by bit, she sank deeper into sleep and I angled my head back against the pillow to stare up at the ceiling. If I turned my head, I could see the camera views on my phone. They were still clear, so I settled for mapping out the information we had so far.

Section Five.

Even the thought of them being involved turned my stomach. Admitting my father had been a part of the effort to set it all up had only been a partial admission. The rest... if they needed to know —if *she* needed to know—I'd tear open that wound and empty it out for her.

Until then, I could only hope that they were merely tangentially related. They definitely involved themselves in multiple operations, domestic *and* foreign. But would they take someone and torture them?

The automatic yes my brain supplied offered no comfort. How had my father put it? *"There is no honor in war, son. Make no mistake, we are waging war."*

Except, we should never be waging a war against our own people. Section Five didn't distinguish between enemies foreign and domestic. It just counted all of them as enemies. Treated our citizens like they would foreigners and made no distinguishing calls.

Ugly business.

The shift in her breathing warned me she was waking before she flexed her fingers against my shirt.

"Good morning," I murmured, keeping my voice low. "Go back to sleep. I'll keep the nightmares away."

Her huff defied me and I let myself smile. She couldn't see it in the dark. It was a good time to just enjoy her reactions. Her absolute impatience with us coddling her amused me, but I found her way of arguing with herself utterly endearing.

Even if I didn't care for the content of the arguments. Could she trust us or not? The fact she *wanted* to trust us helped. Now, if she could just *let* herself trust us. When she pushed herself upward, I forced my arms to loosen further and to stay still.

I was not the trap. I didn't want her to ever associate me with that. Thankfully, she didn't pull away or try to retreat, she just eased up and stared down at me.

My eyes had mostly adjusted to the dark. I couldn't make out her features, but I could see her silhouette. I could almost imagine the byplay of emotion flitting through her eyes like storm clouds.

The idea of being a storm chaser had never appealed to me so much.

"This keeps happening," she said, the sleep absent from her voice though the huskiness was present.

"It's fine," I said. "It's why I always take first watch. If you're going to have nightmares, I'm going to be here to chase them off."

Another huff escaped her, though I couldn't quite tell if it was more laughter or scoff. It could be both. Or neither. The fact I wasn't sure kind of annoyed me. I wanted to know everything about her.

"I'm not really sure we should be cuddling," she said, speaking carefully like she didn't want to offend me.

"No?" I wasn't playing dumb. But I did want to know what she was thinking.

"No," she said, as though turning that single syllable over and testing the taste of it. "I'm... I'm not comfortable with this. We're still strangers."

"Well, I understand you being uncomfortable, but not the why. We're *not* strangers, Sugar Bear. Pretty sure we went over that earlier today."

A sigh escaped her and I let my fingers trail down her arm. It was just a light petting motion. The first sign of resistance and I would stop. But I could practically feel the stress draining out of her.

Yeah, her mind was still trying to reconcile what it could remember—the past, the present, and the gap in between. As much as I wanted to put her at ease, a part of me did not have a problem with her memory loss. If it meant she got to forget the pain and the torture, I was fine with her not having to deal with it.

Except, she was still dealing with it. Not knowing ate away at her. Not remembering also didn't protect her from encountering those assholes again. If she couldn't recognize them, how did she avoid them?

"You do realize this is weird, right?" The question dared me to disagree with her and my smile grew.

"Not all that weird. I've been comforting you out of those bad dreams since they started." From the first night I'd heard her crying. No fucking way was I staying on the other side of the door and letting her suffer.

It wasn't going to happen. Not while there was breath in my body to stop it.

"That's the weird part," she admitted. Then to my surprise, she settled back against my chest. Her ear pressed right over my heart. "You guys have this history with me I can't access, and it's shifted our relationships, clearly. But I don't know all the details."

"That's the part that bothers you." It wasn't a question. "Let's see if I can ease this for you. You have all the control here. If you really want me to let you go. I will."

I paused right there. She was awake and the

dreams had let her go. So, it was safe for me to release her. Rather than accept the offer, she relaxed more against me. I went back to my light petting of her back, rubbing gentle circles there.

"Thank you," she said in a voice so low it was nearly a whisper.

"You're welcome," I told her and then kissed the top of her head. Some of her hair snagged against my stubble, so I smoothed it away. I should probably shave in the morning. It was getting to near whiskers again.

"John..."

I went still at the use of my given name. "Yes?"

She didn't respond for the longest time and I half-thought she'd gone back to sleep. Finally, she sighed. "Never mind."

"Hmm, talk to me Sugar Bear."

Her half-snort wasn't quite a laugh, but I'd take it. "That's my line."

"But I said it this time. So talk to me. Tell me what's going on in that beautiful head of yours?"

"I don't even know the answer to that." She shifted against me, but she didn't pull away. I lifted my hands so she could make herself more comfortable and she settled against my side.

One thigh hitched against mine, but safely away from the not-so-subtle boner I'd been sporting since she started wiggling. She moved her cheek to my shoulder and spread one of her hands out over my chest right above my heart.

"Right, let's try this." I settled my arms around her again and just rested my hand on her hip. If I started rubbing her back now, I'd be playing with her ass too. Not the best idea at the moment.

Later, I promised myself.

We were going to have a later.

"What were you thinking when you called me John?"

More silence, but I waited her out. Her breath feathered against my throat, teasing the skin and electrifying me with each exhale. I stroked my thumb up and down in a short, isolated motion that didn't venture near her ass.

Course, now that I'd thought about her ass, I couldn't stop imagining gripping her ass as I sank her down on my cock. That made the boner about ten times more uncomfortable.

Right, I needed to start thinking about bullets, gunpowder loads, and distance between targets. Not that it was distracting me at all from the weight of her resting against me.

"That maybe you could tell me a story." It was such an unexpected request, I blinked and waited. Waited long enough that she let out a little cough. "I know it's ridiculous but each time I close my eyes, I feel like he's right there waiting to burn me again."

He.

Anger was acid in my blood.

"The problem is, I don't know who he is. I can't even describe him. It's like this deep, dark living shadow. All I know is it terrifies me and I don't want to be scared."

Of course she didn't.

"Okay, what story would you like to hear?" Mission accepted.

"Um... you mentioned something once about target shooting?" She didn't sound quite so certain about it. "It's when you headed into Libya for that quiet extraction. I said it was probably going to be like shooting fish in a barrel. You said to remind me sometime to tell you how not easy that is..."

I turned the request over in my head and then chuckled. It took me a minute to even remember what she referred to, but then I had it.

"Ahh," I said. "Right. Fish in a barrel. It was during some specialized training when I was in the army. We were being tested for combat technique and thinking outside the box. It doesn't really matter what they had us doing, but the live fire range covered about five acres. You had to make entry at one point, locate the hostages, mark them for pickup and eliminate all the enemies along the way."

"Sounds tough," she murmured, she was drawing little circles with her finger against my chest.

"Eh," I said with a half-shrug. "I loved live fire exercises. It gets the blood pumping. The thing was, our trainer had a real whacked sense of humor." A chuckle worked its way free. I hadn't thought about Sergeant Billy in a long time. What a dick. "He always set traps so if you had a misfire or hit the wrong target, you paid for it in the moment and not just points docked."

"What happened?" Her voice was far more alert. Maybe I should have picked a different story.

"Well, I took out one of the enemies but the bullet passed through him and right into one of the hostages. Winged the guy, so at least I didn't kill him. Then a barrel of fish water soaked me from above."

"Fish water?"

"Yep," I said. "It sounds about as rancid as it was. It *reeked*. It also cost me points in stealth because there was no way to not smell me coming."

"Oh my god..." She pulled her hand from my chest and pressed it to her lips.

"Yep. Got to spend the next four hours stinking of three-day old fish and briny water. By the time the day was done, I couldn't smell it anymore, but my team didn't want to be anywhere near me."

Her shoulders were shaking.

"So yes, shooting fish in a barrel is very easy until the barrel gets you back."

Her giggles surfaced then and I grinned. She was going to wake herself up, but it was better than the nightmares.

"Enjoying my misery?" I asked and she snorted, but couldn't quite contain her giggles.

"Yes," she admitted. "Should I apologize?'

"Nah. Want to hear another?"

"Yes, please."

The dark of the night wrapped around us and I glanced at the camera angles on my phone. Still all clear...

"Well, it all started when I had to steal an airboat..."

FIVE

PATCH

After a third night in a row of dark dreams where the shadows writhed around me, inflicting pain via a thousand cuts, I abandoned trying to sleep the first time I jerked awake. I half-expected to see McQuade right there. To my surprise, he was absent.

Frowning, I glanced from the empty space next to the bed to the window. The black out curtains made it impossible to tell the time of day. I was not supposed to open them either. No lines of sight into the house.

Shoving the blankets back, I climbed out of the bed. Everything was stiff and sore. My neck cracked as I stretched and then my right shoulder popped. The relief spreading in the wake of the stretching and crackling was enormous. With a twist, I added popping my lower back to the list before I headed into the bathroom.

Trying to smother the yawns assaulting me, I emptied my bladder before washing my hands and my face. The cold water chased away the cobwebs and the exhaustion left in the face of more nebulous nightmares.

The dark, abstract nature of the dreams themselves unsettled me at the best of times. Not that any of my recent days qualified for that. The guys were still holding their own counsel on the specifics of what happened to me.

Though, to be fair, I could probably guess. If the burn marks on my arms weren't a giveaway, some of the other scars I'd found would be. Maybe my brain was right to not focus on that information.

Would recall help us solve the current challenges?

Hands braced on the cool counter, I studied myself in the mirror. I had no answer for whether it would help or not. None.

Frankly, I failed to see how more information would be a detriment unless they were worried I couldn't handle it. The longer I stood here, the more mental circles I seemed to get caught in.

Whether I remembered or not, *this* right here, this dithering and worrying about it, wasn't doing anyone any good. Least of all me. With that in mind, I braided my hair to pull it all back from my face before I got dressed.

The lack of McQuade in the bedroom made me think I'd find him sitting in a chair in the living room. Or maybe holding up the wall just outside of my door. To my utter shock, not only was he *not* present, none of the guys were.

That was... weird. The door to the little half-bath was open, and the light was off. The kitchen was mostly dark except for a couple of night lights. The windows were all covered, but the clock on the wall said it was after four.

Clearly, it had to mean four in the morning. Unless, I slept some ungodly amount of time and it was well into the next day. That wasn't possible, right? They would have woken me up if I'd slept that long.

I was halfway to the kitchen when the first inklings of panic struck.

Wait.

I hadn't been able to take a breath in days without running into one of them. No matter the time of day, I had one or more of them right here. Whether they were talking to me or not, I wasn't alone.

Locke would be at the table in the kitchen, making notes about something. Remy would be in the kitchen, preparing food or reviewing the security cameras. At least, I thought it was the cameras. Maybe he was reviewing other video footage. As unsettling a thought as that was, he was still usually here.

As for McQuade, I woke to him in my bed more often than not. The other night, he'd held me for hours and told me so many funny stories. They had chased away the shadows so effectively, I'd half-hoped it meant they were gone for good.

Never thought of myself as a dreamer before and maybe I shouldn't be now. Either way, the fact I was out here and they *weren't* put me on edge.

Crossing to the kitchen, I opened the cabinet where I could literally pull out a television screen mounted on a stretch arm.

As soon as I activated it, six different areas popped up. The security cameras were all external as far as I knew. It gave me a good sweep of the property. Had I known what the land here entailed? Had I helped to set up the cameras?

The guys generally used their phones. I did not have a phone that would let me tell what was what. Still, there was a keyboard inside the cabinet, so I pulled it out and flicked it on. Then using the arrow keys, I paged through the numerous angles.

We had far more than six. The landscape wasn't familiar. Snow was still on the ground. The various images showed an outbuilding several meters away. There were no vehicles parked outside. The drive leading away from the house was smooth, unbroken snow.

I frowned. How were they coming and going if not by car? Or maybe it was a new snow? Each answer I found seemed to give me two more questions. As annoying as the wondering was, discovering such basic gaps in my intel was a slap in the face.

Not only did I not know how they were coming and going, I didn't know how they set up this location. What the next steps were going to be. I didn't even watch my own back. Some irritatingly contrary part of myself whispered, *"You must trust them more than you realize."*

Bitch.

I stared at the pair of coffeemakers. The espresso machine was my preference. It was also noisy though and more likely to alert my roommates to the fact I was awake.

Not that they would mind. It might throw them as hard as it had me. Deciding to just go for regular coffee for now, I set the pot up to brew. Then I filled the kettle and flicked it on.

Remy didn't drink much coffee. Of course he didn't, he preferred hot tea. Hadn't he asked me for an actual decent place to get a cuppa when he'd been in Turkey? The memory presented itself in detail. The job. The target. The five days of patient waiting.

Then the exodus from the country with me smoothing the way. That had an element of fun. It was also the first time I could recall he'd been quite that tired. Unwilling to linger longer than necessary, he was loath to stop and secure a place to crash for twenty-four hours.

Rubbing my thumb against my lower lip, I turned that part of the memory over. Arguably the job was done, I hadn't needed to stay on the line. His weariness worried me. It led to me breaking into a few local systems, particularly a transit bus that could get him to the border.

The buses all had cameras. After securing him a ticket, I sent him on board. The bus wasn't even half full. He managed to take up the back seat comfortably. With me watching his back and his comm turned all the way up if I needed to wake him, he'd slept.

He'd slept because he *trusted* me.

Kind of like how I was resting and recovering, without being read in on every part of the current operation. I trusted them and I couldn't even put my finger on exactly *why*. Obviously they were looking after me, but offering friendship in place of torture could soften a target up.

"Except, you know these men," that bitchy little voice observed in the back of my head. *"They are exactly who they say they are and for two of them, this is not the type of job they would take. As for McQuade? He doesn't get off on the sadistic shit."*

They weren't the trap. My uncertainty had nothing to do with lack of faith in them. The smell of the coffee brewing filled my nostrils with its heady scent. I got down a mug and poured myself a cup as soon as it was ready.

Both hands wrapped around the hot mug, I savored the first swallow. It was almost scalding. Almost. It blazed a trail through me, lighting the torches of awareness in my system. I pictured it like it was actually happening, the animation of it amusing.

"Enough," I ordered myself. A full computer sat waiting in the corner of the kitchen. It totally looked like my set up. It had from the first moment I saw it. But I'd been sleeping so much and I didn't spend time out here without them.

That meant they didn't entertain me sliding in to take a seat and booting it up to find out. I scanned the room around me one more time before carrying my precious coffee over with me.

I flicked on the power switch. I'd booted it all the way down, or someone had. I preferred to leave my equipment offline fully when I slept. It helped prevent infections from worms and other malware when I wasn't sitting in the chair.

It also meant I could be damn certain of each task I had it running. Sure, it took more time and some of it was tedious but tedious kept me safe.

Well, until recently.

Fine, tedious kept me alive.

As soon as the password challenge displayed, I set the coffee down and then typed in the code I most typically used on my equipment.

Muscle memory was a good thing.

The screen unlocked to a basic window.

Oh, so familiar. I appreciated the elegance and launched the operating system. Then I began working my way backwards in time by the dates on files. It wasn't hard to see that all the files dated to the window of time that was currently a blank for me.

Made sense. This was a new setup. I tried to picture my workspace at home. The locked room, the comfortable chair, the multiple monitors, and the security of doing what I loved. Was that all still there?

Presumably, whoever took me had to have taken me *there*. I never left the house. I hadn't left in years, not since I'd carved out that space for myself and settled in. The disquiet sliding through me at the idea of strangers in my space left an ache behind.

"Okay," I murmured. "Time to talk to me." While that was directed mostly at myself, I picked up the coffee cup and took a long drink as I began to scan the file system, reacquainting myself.

Encrypting and hiding everything was second nature. It was also training. No wipe could ever be trusted to be one hundred percent full proof. Scatter the files so they need to be stitched back together and only if you had the right keystrokes and software.

I had always liked puzzles.

After firing off decryption to open one of the last files I'd saved, I'd sipped my coffee. I was done with it all too soon. Shoving back, I stood and turned only to find myself breast to chest with Remy.

A shriek of surprise locked in my throat as I dropped the now empty mug. Shock and adrenaline left me shaking as I stared up at him. I hadn't even heard him *move* much less walk right up behind me.

Belatedly the lack of sound following the mug's fall had me glancing down to see the cup in Remy's hand. He'd caught it. The light cast by the screen left his beautiful face harsh relief.

"Didn't mean to scare you, luv." It wasn't quite an apology, but it worked. "Also don't think you're meant to be working on screens yet."

The adrenaline slammed headlong into my irritation and left me hopped up and vibrating. "I'm tired of not knowing. You said if I asked you to go ahead and tell me anyway, you would."

"Yes." No denial.

"This isn't any different."

"Beg to differ," he murmured, then shifted to

wave me past him. The fact he hit three buttons on the keyboard and the screen went dark had me narrowing my eyes at him. "You doing it yourself is putting eye strain on you, it's dark, that's a lot of blue light, and you're still recovering from a concussion."

Rolling my eyes, I headed toward the pot and flicked his kettle on. It boiled swiftly so it wouldn't take long. I pulled the mug he tended to favor from the drying rack and flipped open the container of tea bags on the counter as he slid my mug to me.

"Thank you," he said, taking the tea bag from me. Though, he also caught my fingers before I could turn away. Hand locked on mine, he tugged me right to him and then wrapped an arm around me as I impacted against his chest with my hands.

"What are you doing?" The warning in my voice should be enough, but he kept one arm locked around my waist and his free hand wrapped my braid up in his grip.

One corner of his mouth curved upward as he brought his face down to mine. He moved so slowly, it telegraphed his every motion. The teasing warmth of his breath on my lips had my heart racing for a whole new reason.

"This," he said finally when I made no move to stop him. His lips brushed mine, barely there, a whisper of a kiss that seemed to magnetize until his mouth slotted firmly over mine, drowning me in the sudden, and surprising, sensuality.

My heart slammed against my chest as he tugged my braid once, angling my head better. Then his tongue swept over my lips, demanding entrance. We weren't just in the kitchen anymore, but the back of a car. The hot, albeit swift, kiss he gave me imprinted on my soul.

Jerking back, I blinked up at Remy. "For luck?"

Had I imagined him saying that?

His smile deepened and then he kissed me again. His tongue dueled with mine and I forgot all about the fact he hadn't answered the question.

CHAPTER
SIX
LOCKE

The alert hit my phone within seconds of me opening my eyes. I had no idea if it was the alert that woke me, or something else. I rolled off the bed, already dressed. I had final watch for the night. It was the most challenging, because it was in the slower, darker hours when I most often wanted to sleep

But I'd trained myself to be a light sleeper a long time prior. I always woke at two, dressed, did a sweep of the house and confirmed that McQuade or Remy—whomever had the first shift—was knocking off to get sleep. Then I returned to my room and put my feet up. I could doze just as easily as sleep.

My internal clock was more reliable than any watch. It knew exactly how long I was allowed to sleep before I did a sweep. It had been less than thirty minutes since the previous sweep. The fact the alert hit my phone confirmed why I was awake.

One glance at the screens told me why.

Fuck.

Straight out of my room, I crossed the hall and opened McQuade's. "We've got company," I told the man who sat up as soon as I pushed the door inward. He was up and I pivoted to alert Remy on my way to scooping up Patch.

Remington's door was already open.

Convenient.

Go bag in hand, I headed for the kitchen, following the scent of coffee. The assassin was definitely in the kitchen, wrapped around a dynamite package with dark tipped blonde hair and a sassy mouth.

Not that I could see said sassy mouth because the British assassin was currently devouring it, while gripping her braid in one hand. Filing all of it away for later, I cleared my throat.

They didn't spring apart so much as Patch gave a jerk and twisted in Remy's arms. While he just gave me a look of mild irritation. Swollen, pink lips that were extremely kissable parted as she stared at me. In the half-light of the kitchen, her pupils were the size of saucers and she was absolutely delicious.

Right. Filing that away too.

"We've got company. Patch, grab your go bag. You're with me." The passion on Remy's face vanished as he released her and pivoted to study the screen showing us the SUVs coming up the long drive.

Five of them.

If we could see five, then the chances were highly likely there were far more out there.

"Go," Remy said, turning to Patch and giving

her a gentle push toward him. "Trust Locke. He knows where we're meeting. Stay with him."

"I—"

"Don't argue, woman," McQuade snapped as he strode through the room, armed for bear. "You can tell us off later. Right now, you need to trust us the way we trust you. Go."

The hitch in her step lasted for three seconds. If she resisted too much, I was going to have to throw her over my shoulder and go. *Not* ideal.

"Be safe," she said, sounding more Patch than she had in days as she swept her gaze from Remy to McQuade and back. "Don't get dead." Then she looked at me. "I want my machine." She pointed to her computer. "Just the tower, we can replace everything else."

"Got it."

She was already striding for her room and I pulled the plug on the equipment and yanked the cords from the hard drive. Remy slid a case toward me that he'd grabbed from the closet and I set the tower inside it, then locked it closed. It wouldn't protect it from everything, like bullets, but it gave us a better chance of not damaging the equipment on the go.

Not even sixty seconds later and she was back, coat and boots on. She had a bag over her shoulder and she met my gaze as she tugged on a dark hat over her blonde hair. Smart girl. We didn't need any light playing off of her.

"I'm going to move fast, stay with me. If you start to lag at all..."

"I'll say something. Do you need me to carry anything else?"

I shook my head. The plan was pure extraction for us. We were leaving and not looking back. Mc-Quade and Remy would find us *after* they dealt with the wet team coming to scrub us.

"Let's go."

McQuade and Remy were readying the welcome party for our uninvited guests as Patch followed me out into the snow. The cold air was biting, but it slapped what little sleep out of me that remained.

We needed to double-time it across the open field to the trees, then continue southeast at a jog. Keeping Patch in my periphery, I set the pace. I had a longer stride than she did, but we were going to create a disturbance in the snow one way or another so I didn't bother with trying to keep it clear.

The wind might do us some favors. Her breath came in swift pants by the time we reached the woods. We'd just cleared the first tree when I caught the sound of a motor. They were moving fast.

We had to go faster.

I shot her a look, her face had been flushed pink under the half-moon shining above. But what little light it had provided us was gone in the trees.

"Can you grip my belt?" I asked.

"Yes." She slid fingers around one of my belt loops. Close enough.

"Try to follow my steps. I know the route by heart and I'll avoid the thicker roots."

We couldn't afford a flashlight out here. Patch

soldiered on, staying with me and not complaining. The distant sound of gunfire made her jerk once. If I had a hand free, I'd take her hand but all I could do was glance over my shoulder.

"They were ready for them," I said. "Keep moving."

Three miles had never seemed to take so long before, but we exited the woods less than thirty yards from the oversized storage barn where we'd moved the mobile unit. We'd done some of the harder work *prior* to the trip south.

After that went sideways, McQuade relocated it so we had it ready for a fast exodus. Her breath still came in swift pants but she wasn't slowing down. At the door to the barn, she went around me and hauled it open.

At my gimlet glare, she said, "You have your hands full. I can open a door."

Yes she could, but it also put her in the line of fire if someone was in there. Since no other alarms had been tripped, we were safe. Didn't mean I had to like it.

She let out a gasp when she saw the massive 18-wheeler parked inside. The tires were reinforced and bullet resistant. It had full armor plating, though hidden under a few coats of paint. The back was fully outfitted and even had a generator.

"Close that and come on," I told her as I headed for the cab. I got the passenger door opened. Climbing up, I stored the case with her tower and my go bag, then reached for hers.

Her breath fogged the air as she passed it to me. Then she shot a look to the other, larger doors.

"Trust me," I said, holding a hand to her. "Up you come."

She caught my hand and though she was climbing, I hauled her up and gave her a boost into the passenger seat. She let out a little laugh, that was more stress than humor. "These things are huge."

"That's the idea." I winked and once she was in, I closed the door and dropped to the ground before circling the building. I double checked we weren't plugged in or tangled up with anything.

Last time I'd been out here, we'd gone over everything one more time. All three of us had keys. So it didn't matter who had extraction, we could get her out of here. In the driver's seat, I got the engine started. Diesel engines weren't the quietest, and something this large was bound to be noisy.

Could be worse. I went over the console, and the controls. Reminded myself where everything was then shut off the auto lights that had come on as soon as I started the vehicle.

"Buckle up," I told Patch. "And be ready to climb right up into the back here behind me." With a thumb I gestured to the bed area at the back of the cab.

"Okay..." The half-dazed note made me focus on her closely.

"Minimizing you as a target, Fallon." The use of her real name gave her a little start and she shot me a look. Good girl. Stay alert. "Right now, you're fine there. We have two shotguns behind the seats and locked in. Just pop the notch next to them and pull it out if you need it."

I also had a handgun and my knives. I was

never going to be the biggest fan of guns. They were effective, however, and McQuade loaded these with enough buckshot to challenge an elephant. They wouldn't necessarily kill someone, but they would definitely take them down and leave them in a lot of pain.

There was also a 12-gauge with specialized frag shells. Those could take out an IED or blow the hinges off a door. Removing limbs wouldn't be a problem.

"Shotguns behind us. Use the notch to get them out, point and shoot."

"More or less." I wasn't going to go over it any further. She knew how to shoot a gun. That was enough. If it came down to her having to fire one of those guns, we were going to be in a world of hurt.

I checked my watch then hit the remote on the sun visor. The double doors on the far side began to roll open swiftly and silently. They'd been oiled to hell and gone to prevent the sound from carrying. Putting the truck into gear, I accelerated out slowly.

One glance at my side mirror told me the running lights were still off. So we pulled out onto this narrow little road that barely qualified for the designation. The gravel under the snow crunched as the tires left deeper grooves. Again, we were gonna leave a footprint.

Ideally, it would be a very long while before anyone saw it. The slow pace might have aggravated me if I hadn't spent a lifetime cultivating patience. Every job was different. Faster was not always better. In fact, faster could sometimes just get you caught and nothing else.

Behind us the huge doors to the barn would have closed once we'd cleared them. I didn't look back or turn us around to check. Everything important was already on the hauler except for the two men who would be meeting us down the road.

If they made it...

I kept that part to myself too. The seriousness of the situation was absolutely present. We agreed to only split up if the arriving force was too much for two people to take easily.

Five SUVs?

That was easily twenty guys, probably more. It was always the ones we couldn't see. I resisted the urge to keep scanning the skies as we crawled along the tree canopied road deeper into the frozen night.

The first turn was to the left and I eased us around it and then we were on a slightly *larger* road. This one had two lanes instead of only one. It wasn't as heavy with the snow. Sand and salt mixture provided grit for the tires. It also let me accelerate.

Patch sat silently next to me. Almost too silent and too still despite the agitation vibrating the air around her. She was worried, and who could blame her. The plan had been solid because we'd mapped the route to follow to get away and to avoid the most natural routes that approached the cabin.

The barn wasn't even located on the same property as the cabin. So it wouldn't necessarily get flagged right away. Fifteen grueling minutes later, I flicked on the headlights and the running lights. Patch let out a little gasp of surprise. I kind of wanted to tease her, but I would save that for later.

At the state highway, we turned fully south and increased our speed. There were more vehicles on the road. Trucks like ours. A handful of cars. It would get thicker soon. In fifty more miles, we'd reach the interstate and a main transit artery for the state.

For now, we looked clear. I checked the side mirrors and then glanced at Patch. "We're good."

"Are you sure?" she asked in the shakiest voice I'd ever heard from her.

"Yep," I said, injecting a little more confidence than I probably should at this point. But it was seventy-thirty in our favor. Okay sixty-five, thirty-five, but close enough. "They'll handle the cleanup and we'll see them by the end of the day."

She blew out a long breath. I could almost feel her trying to get her breathing under control. It was okay for her to be scared, but she didn't need or want platitudes right now.

"I've learned a very important thing this morning," she said finally.

"What's that?"

"I have serious control issues."

The deadpan delivery of the unexpected line made me laugh. She glared at me as I chuckled, but not for long. Soon her laughter joined mine.

Was it a little hysterical? Probably, but we could both use a break.

SEVEN

PATCH

They'd mentioned a mobile unit, but I had no idea the size or the scope of it. The flight through the woods in the dark hours of the morning reminded me of how tenuous our whole situation was. More, it left me terrified for Remy and McQuade.

Locke just radiated confidence, from collecting the gear, and carrying my computer tower, to the hike through the darkness. If he worried about a single step, he didn't betray it.

It was my first real hike out of our safe house since I'd woken up there. Not that there was much to see under the heavy canopy of darkness beneath the trees. The scents of snow, crisp pine, and a hint of something muskier—maybe Locke wore a particular aftershave? I wasn't sure—filled my nostrils with every breath.

The crunch of our feet in the snow seemed almost too loud in the silence. That was the other thing about the rush through the dark woods, it was eerie how quiet it was. Something I used to love about the world during a snowfall or after a fresh snow proved unsettling as hell when I knew we were running.

More when I caught the sound of engines in the distance. That low rumbling noise sent my pulse jumping far more than it should have. It took both forever and no time at all to arrive at the barn hidden beyond the trees.

Locke helped me climb up inside and then he was in the driver's seat and we were rolling out.

"You okay?" Locke asked after we were on the interstate. The whole time we'd driven that narrow little road through the woods then onto the state highway and past the sleepy little towns had left me on edge. I'd been torn between alternately holding my breath and trying to regulate it.

"I'm fine." The answer was practically automatic. Was it a lie? Probably not, but it had been a while since anything was truly "fine." "I'm surviving," I told him. "Maybe a little jumpy."

The fact my pulse still raced betrayed how upset I truly was.

"I hate that we left them." More because I had no way to check on them. I had Locke's phone. Maybe we could check the cameras via the surveillance they had in place. But what would I do if something was wrong? I couldn't warn them. I couldn't work to back them up.

I was practically useless.

Wasn't that a bitter pill to swallow?

"It was the plan," Locke said, his tone soothing. "We've been refining it over the past few weeks."

"Did I have a say in this plan before?" As circumspect as they'd been, it was clear I'd been with them longer than the couple of weeks I could recall currently.

"Yes," Locke answered, swiftly. Too swiftly. Then he released a grunt as he favored me with a sheepish smile. "And no."

"Well," I retorted. "Thanks for clearing that up for me."

He snorted. "You gave us specs before. Specs to help make sure we had the right equipment on board and some solutions for possible technical issues we might run into once we were on the move."

That sounded like me. "Okay," I exhaled the word. "I—have a thousand questions and I don't know whether asking any of them is a good idea or not."

"No such thing as a bad question," he informed me in the most sing-song of tones. The throwback to him asking if we should play twenty questions once during a planning session for one of his jobs rushed in to fill in some of the gaps.

"I think we proved that sentiment is a little flawed."

A huff of laughter escaped him. "A *little* flawed?"

"Okay," I conceded. "Maybe a lot flawed. But you were the one who decided to see how many inane questions you could throw in at random intervals."

"Absolutely true," he agreed. "I was also trying to figure out what you liked. Hard to get presents for people if you don't know what they enjoy or not."

Of all the things he could have said as a response, that one surprised me. I shot a look at him.

"Yep," he commented with a kind of ease I envied. "That look isn't insulting at all."

"I'm *not* trying to insult you," I said, trying to not roll my eyes. "Trust me, if I'd wanted to, I do know how to deliver an insult."

His swift grin helped to ease away one of the rocks that crashed down on me at his earlier observation. "You know, I vaguely recall you putting me in my place once or twice."

Once or twice?

I *snorted* and his laughter smoothed away more of the jagged points of stress. "Don't play with me," I muttered.

"Sorry," he said in a cheerful tone that indicated he was *anything* but sorry. "I like playing with you."

He flashed another easy grin at me and I had to shake my head.

"Really?" I went for dry. Utterly dry and skeptical, but his grin was undiminished.

"Yes, really. I've always enjoyed playing with you, Patch. You're great at witty responses and one liners."

"Good to know I've got some skills." The wry observation earned a snort from him this time.

"Don't play the pity party anthem," he retaliated. "You have all the skills. You know how to hack into systems old and new. You are creative in finding solutions that would never have occurred to me and you're rather honorable."

Heat warmed my face and I was glad for the fact it was still dark enough to hide it. Keeping my gaze turned out the window, I couldn't help checking the side mirror a few dozen times.

"Hey, don't retreat on me now. I need you to keep me awake."

"What?" I twisted to look at him. The charming asshole wore another smile.

"Made you look."

"You're twelve." It came out a huff.

"No," he said. "At twelve, I lacked the imagination I have now. I also couldn't maintain a boner for hours with no relief. Not to mention I had zero appreciation for how fucking sexy a smart woman's brain is."

Fresh heat flooded my face. "Stop it."

"Stop what?" It was like playing a dangerous game of verbal dodgeball and he kept spiking the damn ball.

"Stop flirting," I said, rubbing a hand over my face. I was probably bright red.

"No can do, Fallon."

The jolt of my real name chased away some of the embarrassment. It probably shouldn't be so weird to hear. Even more when it seemed to imply an intimacy we shouldn't be sharing.

Then again...

"You get that Remy isn't the only one interested, right?" The sudden subject change threatened to give me whiplash.

"We're talking about that now?" The words came out way more defensive than I meant for them too.

"No," he said slowly, elongating that one syllable. "We don't have to, *however*, I think we should."

My stomach sank. At least the reality of it acted like a splash of cold water on my earlier awkwardness. "Maybe we shouldn't."

"Running away?" It wasn't a taunt. Everything in his tone said it wasn't a taunt. But there was no escaping the fact he was calling me on my bullshit.

"Maybe," I admitted, stealing a look at him before I studied the road ahead. "I'm scared for them. I still don't remember the past few weeks or however long it's been. I'm still trying to wrap my head around the fact that I keep waking up to McQuade in my bed and the fact that Remy kissed me this morning."

"I get that," he said easily enough. "I also get that avoiding a discussion isn't going to make this any easier for any of us, especially not now."

"Now that what? We're on the run? Again?"

"We were on the run before." He had a point. "There's a time for playing coy. This isn't that."

I sighed. "I know." As much as I would rather avoid the more uncomfortable topics, especially with us on the road and no idea of how the guys were doing... "I'm not a coward."

"Fallon... Patch... Hey," he added the same stress of care to each name. "The very *last* thing I would ever label you as would be coward. The word doesn't even belong in the same hemisphere you occupy."

"Except—"

"No. No excuses or caveats. None. You are brave as hell. Braver, I think than anyone could have realized. I mean, I certainly had no idea just how much of a badass you are." He shook his head. "You're not a coward. You are, however, in a difficult position."

I sighed. "You saw Remy kissing me."

"Yep." No judgment lived in his voice. "Saw you kissing him back too."

More heat swept through me. That kiss had been... soul stealing. I hadn't even really had time to process it or the fact I'd forgotten about where we were or even what we were doing there when Locke appeared to interrupt us.

Probably a damn good thing he had.

I licked my lips. "I did."

I caught a flash of his smile from the corner of my eye.

"Thought I would deny it?" Was I really challenging him?

"Maybe," he said, shrugging. He handled the big rig like he drove them every single day. In my experience, that wasn't the case. He preferred fast cars, expensive suits, and even more expensive and rare items including art, wine, and jewels.

"That seems like a bad idea right now." I folded my arms, fighting against the chill that seemed to expand from my core. "I am trusting all three of you. Probably a bad idea to make you not trust each other or me."

"Agreed." At least he wasn't sugar-coating it. "While I probably should keep this part to myself, I find it a bad idea to also isolate *all* information from you."

I stole another look at him.

"That wasn't your first kiss with Remy."

The flashes of his lips on mine. The words... *for luck*... hanging in the air. Was that Remy or...

"And in the interests of full transparency on the subject. When we kiss again, it won't be our first one either."

The word *again* seemed to clarify the answer before he said it wouldn't be our first. "We've kissed before."

"We did. You said it was for luck," he told me. "I definitely felt lucky."

The sentiment collided with the other memory and I lifted one hand to touch my lips. Had I said it to Locke *and* Remy? Or had I said it to Locke and then Remy said it to me? "I wish I remembered..."

"You and me both," he said, then he was holding a hand out to me and I had to unlock my arms so I could accept it. When I glided my hand over his palm, he gripped my fingers tight. There was strength in his hold and he gave me a gentle squeeze. "Maybe you get back and maybe you don't. Not going to stop me from treasuring that memory or making sure you know my hat is definitely in this ring."

Emotion clogged my throat.

"Point of fact," he continued, stroking his thumb over the back of my hand. "I've been planning how to seduce you for years, Patch. When you were just a voice on the line. The voice that saved my life over and over. More than once, you saved my sanity."

"Justus..." Even saying his first name felt too intimate, and the world around us seemed to shrink until it was just the two of us in this cab.

"I know what I'm saying," he continued. "I've been saving presents for you for years. I have a whole collection to give you."

I stopped pretending he didn't have every ounce of my attention. Instead, I just gawked at him.

"Diamonds. Emeralds. Gold. Platinum. Ancient. New. Paintings. Sculpture..."

He let out a little laugh that from anyone else might have sounded self-conscious. But Locke... Justus was the most coolly confident man I'd ever met. He walked into the craziest scenarios with only his wits and his skills and sauntered out the far side with the prize.

"So I'm kind of like the kid in school who wrote you notes about homework and asked for your help cause I wasn't sure how to ask you for what I wanted."

There was a brutally familiar feeling. "You're not shy."

"No," he said, giving my hand another squeeze. "I am not. But when you don't know what the lady likes and what the lady will respond to? You do a lot of fishing and finessing."

I licked my lips. "I don't—"

"You don't have to say anything," he continued, then kissed my hand before he let me go. "You don't. But I am telling you right now, Remy isn't the only one interested. You have to know McQuade is too."

"I had gotten that impression." Hard to miss when he came in to soothe me out of nightmares regularly. "Have I kissed him?"

"Not sure," he said. "Wouldn't surprise me. Mc-Quade's pretty fucking direct."

So was Remy... except, he definitely knew how to play a long game. McQuade was the guy who tore down the front door. You would always know when he was there.

Locke? He was stealth and care. You may not realize he was there until he got past all the barriers, but that was part of his charm.

Remy? No one ever saw him coming.

"I have no idea how to respond to any of this." Admitting it aloud eased more of the tension knotting my spine. I definitely didn't want to pretend right now. Not when Locke was being so direct. "I want to know," I continued before he could brush it off or tell me it was okay. "I want to figure it out. But there is so much going on."

"Agreed," he said. "So we keep it open and upfront. The next time I kiss you, I'll give you a heads up."

It was my turn to laugh. "What if I decide to kiss you?"

"Well, darling," he drawled. "You can kiss me whenever you want. Let me be absolutely clear... my answer? It's always going to be yes."

The flirt was unmistakable as was the fresh tidal wave of heat that swept over me. "Justus..."

"Fallon?"

"You're dangerous."

"Not to you," he promised. Fuck, I wished I remembered that first kiss.

Especially now that I was thinking about a second one. For a minute, okay maybe a couple of minutes, I forgot about the horror behind us. I didn't forget the others or the danger they were in, but that little reprieve let me catch my breath.

"Dammit."

"What?"

I blew out another breath. "I hate to say this...I really need to pee."

CHAPTER
EIGHT
REMY

N ot tracking Patch and Locke all the way
to the mobile unit required discipline.
We had multiple SUVs incoming.

"Twenty to twenty-five," McQuade said, his
tone dry. "Starting to think someone out there has a
hard-on for our woman."

Our woman.

The term implied a great deal of possession.
With her sweet taste still lingering on my lips, it
wasn't a conversation I wanted to have. Particularly with her rapid exodus alongside our resident
thief.

So, I snorted. "Twenty-five? Not really offering
much of a threat." I could take that many on my
own. "I'm going up. You good down here?"

"Hell no," McQuade said with a smirk as he
checked over his weapons, verifying his magazine
loads and sliding more into his pockets. "I haven't
been good in years."

Another alarm went off. "Hmm, looks like we
have more company on the way," I murmured,

checking my phone on the way to the roof. Grabbing the drawstring, I pulled the ladder down.

"Ground assault." McQuade checked the weapons he'd lined up on the counter in the kitchen. "Not on the trail?"

At the top of the ladder, I glanced at the screen. As much as McQuade had laid out and prepared for the best avenues of attack for our location, it was still nice to see it confirmed. "Not on the trail. They're coming up from the south. Pincer move."

"Bastards lack any kind of creativity." McQuade's derisive snort needed no other explanation. "Keep them focused on us."

I held up the remote. "Don't get dead."

"You too, mate." His toothy grin was all viciousness with just a scant bit of amusement.

I rolled my eyes and headed up to the roof. I had a lovely perch that allowed me a full 360 view and access to multiple targets. I tucked the ear bud into place. Noise cancellation would let me hear McQuade and shield my ears from the decibels of the rifle firing.

"The party has arrived," McQuade damn near drawled. "Table for five, corner right. Looks like a bunch of irritating bastards."

On my stomach, weapon set, I checked the sight and scratched off two stealthing toward the front of the cabin. Their all white garb let them blend in where the rest of the crew were in black. Interesting.

"Optical illusions. Two tried to jump the line. Two eliminated. Take care of your first guests. I'm on the next wave."

McQuade drew their attention nearly as much as he took down his targets. But it was my job to flush them out of hiding, particularly those who went to ground when the first of their camouflaged people didn't get past me. I was scanning for the three I'd spotted earlier, when I caught one of the SUVs roaming backwards.

"Hmm, someone's walking the check," McQuade practically tsked.

"I see them." Lifting the remote, I set off the first wave of charges. They exploded upwards in sequence, the pattern seeming to increase in speed as it approached the attackers trying to flank us.

Lowering the remote, I sighted the secondary explosive device we'd planted. Like obedient sheep, the freelance guns scattered, following the path I'd left open. In three, two... I squeezed the trigger in between the heartbeats and hit the mark.

This explosion went upward in a plume of displaced snow, and smoke. The snow muffled some of the sound and helped with the shrapnel, but the concussive force they rushed into blew them backwards and took all seven men out.

"Nice," McQuade complimented before he shutdown another grouping who lined themselves up.

"Thank you," I said, evenly, scanning the field for my next shot. The hotheads and the reckless ones were always the first into a fray. Currently, they were all down and removed from the field.

That left us with the cagier, more experienced members of their assault team. The ones who understood the value of patience. A glimmer of light in the distance pulled my attention from what was directly in front of me. I shifted, every so slightly, using the scope to check the farther ranges.

Another flash.

I zeroed in on the location, just a quarter of mile to the southwest. A blue scarf wrapped to a sapling, fluttered faintly in the near nonexistent breeze.

Tracking back from the scarf, I located the faint movement. The sniper had hunkered down. Probably aware that the milky sunlight fighting to penetrate the cloudy gloom of dawn had given him away.

Or at least worried that it had.

Touching my tongue to my teeth, I fired three shots in rapid succession. The first went wide—on purpose.

The second also went wide, but ahead of him instead of behind.

Be cocky, I said internally. The third shot went four inches above that flash of motion.

Keeping watch via the scope, I nodded as the weapon suddenly dangled like a poisonous fruit in the trees.

Gunfire strafed the roof, the bullets chewing up the sealed wood and sending the chips of it flying. The shards peppered me, slicing cuts along my cheek. They might have done more except I wore gloves and a heavy, dark coat that helped me to blend in.

The gunfire came from two separate locations. Smart. An experienced pair, working in tandem to cover each other while keeping me pinned. It was an excellent maneuver. I spared about ten seconds of admiration for them as they got to where I needed them.

Squeezing the button on the remote, I dropped my head for cover as I set off another daisy chain of explosions. Unfortunately for the tandem pair, it effectively ended their pincer move efficiently, if spectacularly.

"Damn," McQuade's voice reached me via some static on the comm. "Clear down here."

I lifted my head and scanned the area. No movement beyond the occasional operative that writhed on the ground. Some of them were in death throes. Most were already there. One or two looked like they were trying to crawl to freedom.

"Baiting the hook," I warned McQuade before I pushed back part of my cover. The movement would catch attention as would me pushing up a helmet.

Had more shooters been present and aware enough to take their shot, the helmet would get attention. Then again, maybe it wouldn't.

"No movement."

"Standby," McQuade answered. A door opened somewhere. The sound was almost violent in the quiet left by the battle's aftermath. With the litter of bodies and blood spilled over the snow, it was a scene of discarded and broken toys. "No movement."

"On three then?" Neither of us were going to move without the other clearing it. The first one up or out would be the most vulnerable.

"One," McQuade said, and I could feel him scanning the area.

"Two," I countered, moving to my knees slowly as I scanned our surroundings. The cabin had taken a beating. The roof's damage was significant. It was a pity. The building held a kind of rustic charm.

"Three." McQuade strode out front, a gun in each hand and I kept watch as he went body to body. "Are we getting takeout?"

I didn't answer right away. We'd discussed some of it. But this was a huge mess to clean up and we weren't going to be able to scrub the whole scene.

"I want to know how they're locating her." They weren't tracking us. If they were, it would shock me. We'd had the trackers removed from her, so *how* did they keep finding her?

"So takeout then," McQuade said, a faint hum vibrating along the underside of the words. "Any preferences?"

I sighted the man who came up out of the snow behind McQuade, a knife in hand. One shot and down he went. I angled it to go clean. The last thing I wanted was the bullet going through the target to McQuade.

For his part, McQuade jerked as he spun to face the now downed man. He lifted his chin, and I didn't have to be face to face to imagine the scorn in his eyes as well as the irritation.

"You're welcome," I said easily enough.

"Right, thanks mate." He smirked and I rolled my eyes.

Once he'd done a sweep of all those close by, I descended to join him. We had a vehicle to load.

More vehicles to destroy too. They'd brought a lot of hardware and firepower.

"You getting the impression they don't want her alive anymore?" McQuade asked as I emptied out the glovebox and the console on one of the vehicles.

None of the men had identification. The cars were even missing VIN numbers and I'd bet my favorite gun, the plates were also fake. The men themselves were generic, size and build suggested military. They were also from a cross-section of ethnicities.

Nothing pointed a finger in a single direction. Smart.

Aggravating, but smart.

"I don't know," I admitted, addressing his question. "Did they want her alive in the first place because of what she took? Or because of who she might have told?"

We didn't have the answers.

With a sweep of my hand, I motioned to the bodies we were going to need to deal with sooner rather than later. "This could also be here to deal with us. They've figured out she isn't alone."

McQuade let out a grunt. "I've got three live ones. You want the pick of the litter?"

I glanced to where he'd secured three men. They all had various injuries. One of them was currently soaking his shirt with blood. He wasn't going to last long. The other two were bleeding but not as heavily.

"If they're just grunts, it's a waste of time."

They wouldn't know anything more than their orders.

"True," McQuade said, scratching his jaw. "Let me do a process of elimination. You pack the truck." Without waiting for my agreement, he pulled out a rather large hunting knife and headed straight for the three men.

One of them blanched so hard, I wouldn't be shocked if he'd just pissed his pants. McQuade was in his element as he squatted in front of them and made that huge knife dance. Shaking my head, I finished my inspection of the remaining bodies and vehicles. Even if all I expected to find was more nothing, I refused to leave anything to chance.

The crack of a gun pulled me around. McQuade stared in consternation down at a body. At my look, he spread his arms. "He ate his own gun."

Death before capture? I shrugged. The more I learned about the types of people hired and the things they would do to get Patch back, the more determined I grew to end this threat. Section Five may or may not be government sanctioned, but Patch was never going to be free as long as they were after her.

"I've got two," McQuade said when I finally made it back to him. They were both unconscious, the bleeding had turned sluggish and he'd pretty much stripped them of all clothes before he dumped them into the back of our truck. There was also a dead body inside.

"I thought you said you cleaned him up before." The man had started following Locke on his last trip out for supplies. When Locke hadn't been able to shake him, McQuade met him on the road.

"No," McQuade said, rolling his head from side to side to crack his neck. "I told you I took care of it. Besides, he'll be motivational."

While the colder temps had definitely delayed decomp, the smell was distinctive.

"We need to grab the last of our things."

Then we'd need to scrub the location.

"You first," McQuade said. "Then I'll get mine." Like Locke and Patch, we had our own go bags. I repacked my rifle and made sure to bring ammunition and explosives. The mobile unit was fully loaded, but I didn't want to run low before we linked back up with them.

We also had prisoners to interrogate and they were definitely not going anywhere near Patch. When I returned, McQuade flashed me a feral smile before he jogged back inside. I stored my things in the back of the cab, well away from our prisoners under the hatch. He'd lined the back with sleeping bags and wrapped two of them up in the weather-proof ones.

It would keep them alive. Not pleasantly, but then I found it hard to give a damn one way or the other. My phone buzzed. Another alarm had gone off and McQuade came at a run.

"We've got more company."

That was a problem.

"You were right," I said after McQuade got his things inside and I fired up the truck's engine. I turned to follow the track into the woods, it bounced us all over the place, but we could cut twenty or thirty miles off the route going this way and stay hidden from air support.

"We pulled two trackers out of her," McQuade said. "Then the minute we head back toward civilization they were all over us? Had to be some kind of biochemical tracer they were using. Something on her skin that survived showers."

I grunted. "It's been over a month."

"Agreed and I think it's wearing off. If nothing else, now that we have an idea, we can look at a decon shower. The mobile unit will shield her though."

Another happy little idea he and Locke had come up with. Shielding the interior in case she was transmitting. I loathed the people after her, they were determined.

Too determined.

They were definitely the kind you killed, not just stopped. Because otherwise they would keep coming back.

"You're forgetting something," McQuade said as we bounced down the rutted track to the stream and then back up the other side. There were thumps in the back as our guests rolled around and bounced off the sides.

An explosion echoed behind us. The fireball wasn't quite visible. Though we did catch sight of the red glow after the third one.

"Timers," McQuade grunted. "Nice thinking, mate."

I groaned. "Stop calling me mate."

CHAPTER
NINE
PATCH

W e'd arrived at the "rendezvous" location earlier. The fact it took hours to even reach the rendezvous location, that was also a couple of states away from where we'd been staying, put my teeth on edge. In the time since we arrived, we hadn't heard anything from McQuade or Remington. The unease that accompanied that realization was hard to set aside.

Now, we were one of about forty different rigs parked and tucked in for the night leaving little in the way of space in between the vehicles. Though the external lights were on, strategically placed every ten to fourteen feet. The floodlights created their own shadows. The rest area was pretty buttoned down for the night. Every time headlights flashed as a car or truck exited the highway, I leaned forward.

Eventually, I needed to get out of the cab. I could head over to use the facilities, or I could...

"Fallon," Locke said as he caught my arm and tugged me around. Our breath fogged in the chilly night air and I stared up at Locke. Despite the fact that I didn't think of myself as a short woman, all three of them towered over me. "Hey…"

He rubbed my biceps, frowning.

"You're freezing."

I was? I hadn't even taken notice of it, my heart kept racing and my stomach bottomed out. I hated *waiting*. Despite the sheer amount of patience my job had demanded of me over the years, I was not a fan of it when I had no control.

None.

I didn't even have a phone I could call them on and when I asked Locke, he'd merely shaken his head. Radio silence. It wasn't just for our safety.

"I hate this," I complained.

"I know," he murmured. There was something soothing in his voice. Rather than let me go or nudge me back to the rig, he kept rubbing my arms. The contact helped to ground me even as his hands seemed increasingly hotter the longer he touched me. "I wish I could give you answers but the best thing we can do right now is stick to the plan."

A low growl escaped me and I wasn't sure who it shocked more. Me or Locke. Still, one corner of his mouth quirked up into a hint of a smile.

"That was a fierce sound," he teased. At my bland stare, his grin grew a little wider.

"I'm frustrated." Not that he needed me to announce it. As it was, I shrugged off the contact and paced away.

"I got that." He wasn't letting me get far, which was fine. I was already pivoting to head back to him. The last thing I needed to do was yell or rage

—even if it was exactly what I *wanted* to do. We were supposed to be hiding, and making a scene at a rest stop was not exactly the thing camouflage was made of.

"When you guys run ops, I'm usually in the chair, I am there if you need me. Right now, I'm nowhere."

"You are where *we* need you to be though," Locke said, the firm insistence in his voice offering me more in the way of a tether to this moment.

"In the middle of nowhere?" It wasn't quite the retort I wanted to fire back at him, but the simple truth of the matter was that I had never felt quite as useless as I was right now. I was running, and hiding. I was the passenger princess—and that was a term I hated—without the full weight of the plan.

This was where we were supposed to meet with Remington and McQuade. But what happened if they didn't make it here before dawn? Wouldn't we be noticeable if we just stayed here? I liked having a plan, as well as the backups for those plans. The only bad plan was the one you didn't take the time to make.

"Yes," Locke said slowly, curling an arm around me and pulling me closer to him. "But not quite the middle of nowhere so much as out of the line of direct fire. The last time we went into a live fire situation, you got hurt."

Hurt.

Almost as an afterthought, I raised a hand to touch the area of my temple where it was still a bit tender. The bruising there had been deep. The laceration, thankfully enough, had been shallow. It had also compromised my memory and left me with more nightmares—or maybe just new ones.

I sighed. "I know," I admitted. "I'm sorry I'm being difficult."

With a soft chuckle, Locke guided me back toward our rig. "I don't think you're being that difficult." Instead of climbing up directly into the cab, he opened a door on the side that I hadn't even realized was there. "You're frustrated."

I snorted. "Well, at least I know you can listen."

"It's one of my talents," he teased lightly with a wink before putting a hand to my elbow and nudging me up the steps that had dropped down from the door. Was this access to the back of the cab where we could sleep? He'd said there was far more room than I realized.

The interior felt... *bigger*? It wasn't until the ratchet of the stairs being pulled up and the door closed behind us that a light came on. A light and...

"Holy shit," I whispered, as the lights turned on down the long hall formed by the container we were hauling. It wasn't just gear back here. There were bunks, weapons, a workstation for me—I assumed me anyway—and more. As I moved down the narrow aisle that bisected the container, I tried to take it all in. "This is insane."

"Maybe," Locke said, turning to something on the wall near the door and a dozen monitors came to life. It gave us 360 degree views all around the rig. "But we wanted a mobile unit that would let you rest, allow us to work and still protect you. 18-Wheelers are ubiquitous on the open roads in the U.S. It might not work as well in Canada or Mexico, but we'll deal with that if we end up going that far."

That was even more insane. I twisted around to study the monitors and then he was holding out a phone toward me. The monitors on the wall were reflected on the screen of the smartphone. All I had to do was tap one of the screens to enlarge it, or pinch it to make it smaller. Logical programming. I liked it.

"Won't people notice we went inside?" I really hadn't been paying attention to my surroundings. The lack of peripheral awareness was not a good sign.

"If they were looking," Locke said. "However, we moved into the side of the truck and when I opened the backdoor, the side door on the passenger side also opened. So unless they were right on top of us, they'd think we climbed up to sleep in the cab."

What he didn't add was, like all the other rigs parked around us. Not that he needed to point it out. Trying to summon some spit to my mouth, I ended up coughing.

"C'mon," Locke said as he moved up behind me. Hands on my shoulders, he walked me forward. Then we were in front of a wall of cabinets. When he reached past me to flip a switch, I goggled at the cabinet doors sliding open and a counter pushing out. A counter with an espresso machine on it and a small fridge. The espresso machine wasn't as large as the one at the house but it was more than sufficient. "Surprise."

I twisted to look at him. The soft smile on his

lips was hard to resist. "You guys... you really meant roaming mobile command unit?"

Granted, I wasn't sure how many operations needed espresso the way I did but still.

"You needed it," he answered with a mild shrug. "What you need, you get. We've got bunks and a proper bed down here can be pulled down. We can pull out a table and chairs." As if to demonstrate, he slid round me and flipped another switch that transformed another set of cabinets.

I didn't mean to goggle but the last time I'd seen anything like this... "Tiny spaces."

He flashed a real smile at me. "You may have mentioned that a time or two."

In some Asian countries and in larger cities where the population density resulted in smaller footprints for homes, space was at a premium. They used items that could serve multiple functions for tables, chairs, and beds.

"How did you put something like this—" I stopped mid-question and met Locke's steady gaze. The deep, olive green of his eyes seemed almost opaque with all the secrets he kept housed in there. "I helped design it."

He nodded once. "Yes."

In the before time—the time after they came for me and before I was shot. The time I could no longer recall. "That's why you guys didn't tell me about this."

"Partially," Locke admitted, then he reached down to flip open the fridge and pulled out a bottle of water. When he offered it to me, I stared at it for a long moment before I took it. "We still aren't sure about pushing you to remember."

I made a face. "I'm sure."

"Fallon..."

Grimacing, I twisted the top off the bottle. "That's so weird."

"Your name?" The gentle tone turned a little more teasing.

"It's been years since anyone called me Fallon. Fallon pretty much died the day I walked. I've been Patch since then. So every time you call me Fallon, it's a jolt."

"It's your name," he reminded me. "You have a right to your name and those bastards do not have the right to take it from you."

I licked my lips. Not that I had much in the way of spit to wet them. So I took a deep drink of the water. I was far thirstier than I'd realized. I downed about half of it in short order. "Sorry," I said. "I should have offered you some."

"We have more," he told me. "Now, I'm going to fix you something to eat—not a fancy gourmet like Remy, but I'm sure I can whip something up. Then you're going to get some sleep so that beautiful brain of yours can heal."

I glanced down at the phone I was still carrying and all the monitors that showed all quiet around the rig. Then I glanced back up at him. "Are you going to sleep?"

"I'll be fine." That wasn't an answer.

"Okay, tell you what, let's make a deal." I set the water bottle on the makeshift counter then opened the fridge to get him a bottle of water. "I'll rest if you rest. I'll eat if you eat. If you need someone to take a watch, then I can do that. I'm more than capable of watching monitors."

In fact, I kind of craved it now that I'd brought it up.

Locke's eyes narrowed. "You're still healing."

"And currently, you're the only guy on deck." I rounded to face off with him. "You've been driving the rig all day. I'd offer to take over on that tomorrow, but I have no idea how to drive something this big. So, you need to rest."

"Fallon," he said with such an aggrieved sigh, I half-debated giving up the argument just so I wouldn't be badgering him.

The fact the three of them were so willing to take up the perimeter around me alternately filled me with waves of surprise and warmth. I'd been on my own for so long, it was almost impossible to imagine. Not trusting anyone had become so much simpler over the past five years.

Lonely, sure, but simpler. Maybe, just maybe, I didn't have to be alone anymore. While the desire to grasp that in both hands was definitely *present*, so was the need to protect myself.

Control issues aside, I needed to be an active part of my own life. That wasn't helped by letting them win these arguments of late. Arguments I wasn't sure how to make. Particularly when they had access to information about me that I didn't have.

The simple truth was, I may never get those days back and I could keep letting them call the shots or I could take back the control that I needed.

It was better for all of us to assert this new reality sooner rather than later.

"Justus," I said his name in the exact same tone. "Feel free to argue with me, but I am not surrendering this battle. Not this time. You need the rest. Until we rendezvous with the guys, I'm the only backup you have. Use me."

"Use you?" He blinked at me, his lips parting in a silent 'O' before he snapped it shut with a click of his teeth. Locke was usually much faster with his rapier wit. Making him speechless was an accomplishment. Truly. He flexed his hands on my biceps as he leaned his head back as though he both needed and didn't want distance. "*Use* you?"

"Yes," I insisted. "Use me."

His lips compressed into a thin line. I honestly couldn't tell if he was pissed off or confused. Then his hands tightened on my arms and he pulled me forward. Or maybe we fell into each other. Either way, his lips were on mine and they firmed in their demand.

Catching my breath became a distant thought as I fisted his shirt and he devoured my mouth. A silent little pulse of alarm rang in the back of my mind, but the rest of me just shut it off the moment his tongue tangled with mine.

CHAPTER
TEN
PATCH

T he pressure of his lips moving over mine did more than hold me captive. It made me hungry—for more. Flashes danced behind my eyelids. Another place. Colder. The warmth of his mouth and a gasp of sound—his? Mine? I had no idea.

Fuck.

I *wanted* him.

Ice cold heat splashed through me even as he pressed his lean, trim, and tough body into mine. He was so polished and smooth it was easy to forget that he was also built for all kinds of heists. I didn't stumble or fall. If anything, it was like I glided effortlessly until my back was against the steel wall.

The contrast in temperatures between his heat and the metallic cool sent another shudder through me. His tongue plunged inside my mouth. Every stroke of it invited me to open further and I wanted to suck him in deep. Drag every drop of taste from it like he was the tartest, sweetest, best Jolly Rancher ever.

As soon as the urge presented itself, I put thought to action. A low groan vibrated through him and seemed to echo inside my soul. It had been a long time...

A really, really long time.

Fisting his shirt, I fought to pull him closer. Desire leaked through the cracks in my frustration and anger. So much was out of my control. So many irons in the fire. There was what I knew. What I thought I knew. What I had to know...

And what I'd forgotten.

Them.

I'd forgotten *them*. I'd forgotten their *rescue* and my own captivity. I'd forgotten a vital slice of life and it aggravated me so damn much. Locke gripped my ass and lifted me. It shifted the angle of our kiss and I wrapped my arms around his neck.

Not once did he lift his head from mine. I only breathed when he did. The longer he kissed me, the more aware of him I became. The tingling sensation of his lips. How they went firm and then softened as though he were determined and savoring in equal measure. The scrape of stubble on his upper lip reminded me this wasn't a dream. The sharpness of teeth biting down showed me I wasn't the only one hungry.

The tension of the past days wound so tight through me, it threatened to snap. Fuck. I wanted him so goddamn much and the small voice of reason that tried to argue for patience grew quieter. Or maybe my need drowned it out.

"Do something for me," Locke ordered in breathless gasps between kisses.

"What?" I had my thighs resting on his hips, and his groin flush against mine. If not for all the clothing between us, we could already be...

"Tell me to back off," he said, his voice ragged and his control seemingly eroded. Justus Locke was one of the few "slick" operators I'd known for years. He could charm with a smile, and had a way of making even the most challenging security systems roll over for him.

"What?" The syllable burst out of me, surprise causing me to jerk back and I hit my head against the metal. Shock more than pain had me shaking my head. Locke's whole expression transformed as he slid a hand up to cup the back of my head.

"Don't do that," he ordered, the careful brush of his light fingers a gift against my scalp and bruised ego. Had I really just clanged my head off the side of the truck? I ran my tongue over my lower lip and savored the way he fixed on the motion with his gaze.

It was impossible to ignore how handsome he was or how much liquid heat filled his dark eyes. The growth of stubble on his jaw gave him a rugged look.

"Rugged looks good on you, Mr. Locke," I told him, and he let out a low groan.

"Goddammit, Beautiful. I need you to tell me to stop. To back off. Keep my hands to myself." A wry smile accompanied each suggested command.

"Nope," I said slowly, licking the taste of him along with that word off my lips. The fact his gaze seemed magnetized each time I spoke sent a thrill skating through me. "It's been a long time," I admitted.

"Fuck." He dipped, resting his forehead against mine. "Patch... Fallon... Goddammit, what do you want me to call you?"

A smile curved my lips, it lacked the reserve or hesitation of earlier smiles. For the first time since I woke in that house, trying to peer through the sooty pinholes of my memory for those lost shadowy weeks, I felt... *whole*.

"You can call me Fallon," I whispered. "If you want. I don't really know her anymore." I raised a hand to his face. "Right now, Patch seems on shaky ground."

His stubble scraped against my palm. The roughness of it was delicious. An incredible reminder that we were here, we were alive...

"The last thing you need are my demands," he said, the hoarse notes in his voice making me ache. "I'm not always a good man," he admitted. "I'm selfish. I like to take what I want. Sometimes, I like it even more when someone else has it and that means I have to steal it."

The confession bounced through me like some pinball fired in and stuck against a bumper that kept it flying.

"You... I've craved you for so long."

"I don't belong to anyone else," I reminded him. It came out a little snappier than intended but it didn't seem to dissuade Locke. If anything, his smile deepened.

"Hmm... For a while, I thought you belonged to

your work. So deliberate in keeping me in my place. Yet, I could flirt with you and you never scolded me, even if you did politely slap me down."

A laugh worked its way through me. "I didn't know 'slapping someone down' could be considered 'polite,' but I didn't mind when you flirted with me. It was funny, but we were also working. When you're paying me to protect you and help... flirting is a distraction."

He let out a long sigh and then leaned more into me. Some of the tension seemed to bleed out of him but the lightness of his lips grazed my jaw. He kissed a path to my ear where he whispered, "I have a secret to tell you... whether we were working or not, I was always thinking about you. Flirting with you is like breathing air. I need it."

My hands found their way into his hair as he rested the weight of his erection against the apex of my thighs. Not for the first time, I really wished we were in fewer clothes. "Niccolò Machiavelli once said, "everyone sees what you seem to be, few know what you really are."

Locke bit down on my earlobe and my thoughts scattered. "He also said, 'those few do not dare take a stand against the general opinion.'" The scrape of his teeth before he traced the whorls of my ear with his tongue sent another heated pulse through me.

"He didn't mean anything good by it," I fisted his hair as he began to kiss a path down my throat. "Just... don't worry about being something, just make sure you appear to be whatever it is..."

"Are you trying to warn me that you aren't what you appear to be?" The question came out so light, it sent a shiver over my skin. Maybe it was the way he sucked the skin over my pulse against his teeth. My nipples were taut, sensitive, and I swore my cunt clenched around nothing and I shifted my hips. It ground me against him and his groan gratified me more than I could admit.

"I'm saying..." Oh it was getting much harder to string syllables together much less thoughts because his hands were under my shirt. I had no idea when he'd done that or when he'd unhooked the bra. Such clever, beautiful fingers. "I'm saying that... you know the me I had to become. I think the most honest I've been about being me was when I was helping you guys."

That confession cost me everything. Wanting him? Wanting them? It was only going to complicate an already complicated situation.

"Well, your secret is safe with me," he promised, then he pushed my shirt upwards and the air seemed all that much cooler against my heated flesh. He glided his palms up my sides and I shuddered. "You really need to tell me to stop..."

"Are you asking me? Or telling me?" When his fingertips skimmed beneath my bra to cover my breasts, I was suddenly incredibly grateful to be wedged between him and the wall. I tightened my legs against his hips, holding onto him tightly. I didn't want to fall.

He nipped my lower lip, then slapped a hand against a control on the wall. There was a whirring noise as the sofa and table disappeared and a bed lowered from the wall. I gaped at it, the whole motion was smooth, nearly silent, and damn near magical.

"That's so..."

"Sexy?" He teased me with another nipping kiss to my jaw. "Amazing? Fantastic?"

"Hot," I corrected, and I twisted against him to look at the controls. It ground me against his erection again and I had to bite back a groan. Yet, I really wanted to know how it worked. It was fascinating.

"Fallon," Locke said, biting down gently over my pulse point. The sharpness jerked my attention back to him. Amusement glittered in his eyes and that well-defined, chiseled face of his with the high cheekbones and strong jawline was downright edible. I couldn't get over how intense and expressive his eyes were and right now, I was torn between drowning in them and figuring out all the fascinating upgrades inside the truck.

"Hmm?" I raised my eyebrows as he chuckled softly. "Don't take this personally, I still think you're amazing but that's..."

"Yeah, I'll give you a full tour later," he promised and then he tugged me away from the wall. His hands left my breasts, slipping around to balance me with his hands against my ass. Turning to the bed, he braced one knee against it and then locked his gaze on mine. "You can tell me to stop at any time," he whispered. "One word and I'll stop. I promise."

"Justus..." His first name slipped out. "Can I call you Justus?"

"You can call me anything you want," he murmured in a voice so soft it sent goosebumps prickling over my skin. "But I like the way Justus sounds on your lips."

It was hardly the first time I felt self-conscious and I was way too old to be shy or coy about it, but at the same time... "You are really good for my ego."

He huffed out a soft laugh that soon turned into chuckles. His humor pulled out my own laughter as we stared at each other. The amusement broke up the jagged pieces inside of me that kept grinding against each other. All the questions that haunted me about the missing time. All the shadows that crept out to torment me in my nightmares. They weren't erased, not even a little. But the laughter... It proved a balm to my soul I had no idea how much I needed.

The laughter rippled out of me and as soon as I'd tried to get it under control, our gazes would collide again and he would grin or I would—then we were laughing all over again. Finally, he fused his mouth to mine, merging our humor with a hot, tongue thrusting kiss that made me arch with need.

We landed together on the bed, dueling for control of the kiss and drowning in it together. His hot hands were under my shirt again and when he pushed the fabric up, I had to pull back from the kiss to wiggle it off and then I was bare chested cause the bra had gone with it.

All at once the moisture in my mouth dried up. The lights were still on, it seemed almost too harsh for the moment. His gaze drifted over me and I had to fight the urge to cover up. There were scars and marks all over me. My arms. My breasts. My stomach. I hadn't really thought about the fact they would be on display.

"I know they're ugly," I said, fighting for some equilibrium. "I didn't—you don't have to look at them."

Lifting his gaze to lock onto mine, Locke dipped his head until our noses touched and his breath feathered against my lips. "Nothing about you is ugly."

"Except—"

"Nothing," he said even more firmly. "Look at me, Fallon. Look in my eyes... I know beauty and art. I know magnificent pieces from the Greeks to the Renaissance. I know beauty in all its many forms. You... you are so goddamn beautiful you make me ache. I want to hide you away where nothing can ever touch you again. I want to give you a reason to smile every single day even if it takes me a lifetime to discover all the ways I can."

The unexpected poetry threatened to shred my heart. "But the scars..."

"Are scars," he said with a shrug. "They are a symbol that we survive, that we overcome, and they are a history of the path we've walked." Then as if to illustrate his point, he began to kiss his way down my throat to my shoulder. He mouthed each kiss gently, then traced some of the ruddy marks with his tongue while others he bit down around as though leaving his own.

Every single time his lips touched me, I forgot how to breathe. The ache inside of me unfurled.

"Nothing about you is ugly," he repeated his earlier statement, his hand closing over my throat.

There was no pressure, just heat. The gentle stroke of his thumb over my pulse point encouraged both the rapid beat of it and my shallow breathing even as he soothed. "Nothing. When I look at you—all I see is you."

The words wrapped around me more effectively than any restraint. "You are a dangerous man." The need for him just seemed to amplify with each syllable.

"You need dangerous men," he whispered. "But I am never dangerous to you."

With his hand there around my throat, he rose up and he continued to drink me in with his gaze. Heat scorched through all of me as he looked his fill. Unease vied with embarrassment, but each time I squirmed, he dipped his head to kiss me again.

There was something just so fucking drugging about his kisses. They sent strokes of lust to curl through my body. Everywhere he touched with his lips or his fingers sent more liquid desire to flood through me. Then he was dipping his fingers down to my pants, he hovered, his fingers tucked into the edge of my waistband.

"What do you need to say to make me stop?" The hum of command echoed beneath the silky tone of his voice.

"Stop," I whispered.

"That's my woman," he said, then he let go of my throat and hooked both of his hands into my waistband. Still, he didn't move until I nodded, then his grin stopped my heart before he swept them down and took my panties with them. My boots fell off—I'd forgotten I'd even had them on—and I had to let go of his hips.

Then I was there, sprawled on the bed—naked and bare to his view. His smile didn't diminish for an instant as he ran his gaze over me.

"Fallon?" The presence of a growl underscoring my name had my thighs rubbing together and my nipples so hard I shuddered.

"Justus..."

"I think I'm going to lose my mind in a minute and do everything I can to make you lose yours." The certainty in his voice belied the hesitation in his words. "Just remember... you want it to stop, you just say stop. I swear to God, I'll listen to you."

My heart fisted at the declaration. "I trust you."

And I did.

I trusted him.

"I want you and I trust you..."

I knew what I needed to know where he was concerned. Then Justus closed his eyes.

"But..."

His eyes jerked open at the single syllable and his gaze clashed with mine. "But?" he prompted.

"But I'd really like it if you got naked now."

ELEVEN
PATCH

T he quirk of his lips sent a bolt of
amusement through the lust in his eyes.
For a precarious moment, he seemed balanced on the knife's edge between humor and desire. To my utter delight, he swooped down to kiss
me and laughed against my lips.

Shivers radiated along my spine, sending
goosebumps to ripple over my skin. Then my hands
were on his chest and his shirt unbuttoned under
my fumbling fingers. The thicker flannel was warm
on my fingers, or maybe that was just him.

Then his shirt parted and I had my hands on his
flesh and the heat of him scorched me. He licked,
nipped, and sucked his way through the kiss as
though determined to devour me. Still, when I
pushed at the shirt it shoved off his shoulders and
then I was able to study the acres of...

"Oh my god," I whispered, pulling away from
the kiss to push at him.

"What?" Concern appeared in his eyes instantly. Until he glanced to where my fingers traced

the watercolor tattoo of a white tiger all over his left pec. You could barely see his nipple for the intensity of the image that captured the attention.

More, I was adoring the vivid blue eyes that demanded your attention.

"It's beautiful," I continued, tracing my fingers over the illustration of rippling fur. The watercolor effect made it look like the tattoo had been splashed on. "Artistic and yet alive... I love it."

"I'm glad." His husky voice washed over me. "If I promise to tell you the story behind it later, can I go back to touching you?"

The wry note in the teasing pulled my attention back to him and heat flushed my face. "I didn't know you had a tattoo," I said by way of apology.

"Noted," he said in a low murmur. "I promise to bring you fully up to speed." Then his lips were on mine and my sudden preoccupation with his tattoo drowned in a wash of need. His hands were everywhere. He cupped a breast, teased my nipple, then stroked over a hip and lifted me until he was more firmly cradled between my legs.

The denim of his jeans rasped against my skin and left me shuddering. Another light bump and the fabric grazed over my clit, the friction too much and not enough at the same time. Then he mouthed another kiss to my jaw as I forgot how to think.

Somehow, we got the rest of his clothes off. As hungry as I was to see him, he drowned me in so much sensation that all I could do was dig in and hold on. The first nudge of his cock had me going stiff and he stilled. The bite of his fingers digging into my ass grounded me.

"Open your eyes, Fallon." The rough command demanded all my attention. I hadn't even realized I'd closed my eyes. Staring up at him, I shivered as the chill left me. "It's me..."

I flexed my hand on his shoulder and then forced my trembling fingers to move his face. The rasp of his stubble scraped at my palms. His kisses had marked up my face, the warmth of it served as another reminder of where I was and who I was with.

"Do you need me to stop?" The heavy growl underscoring the words held no judgment. I didn't mistake his need for anything else. The heavy weight of his cock pressed against my cunt, the tip barely inside of me. Intimately aware of him, I shivered again. They came in waves, trailing over me until goosebumps covered me.

I searched his eyes, the raw desire in them. The fatness of his pupils filled me with a kind of primitive delight. Madness invaded his blood every bit as much as it did mine. Yet, he held himself impossibly still. He wouldn't push deeper until I asked him for it. I ached for him on so many levels and at the same time, fear eddied out to tumble against the need in me. The resulting choppier sensations left me uncertain.

"No," I said slowly. "Fuck me, Justus... I need to feel you." It was so impossible to explain. The fear, the uncertainty, and the unease did not belong here. I *wanted* him, and these stolen moments. "I want you. Please..."

He searched my eyes. The light around us left nothing in shadows, nothing hidden and then he dipped his head slowly. It was like the world slowed down, or maybe it was him, and he nudged forward. His cock pushed into me as his mouth descended.

The stretch burned in all the best ways. The feel of him was incredible. I wanted to rush him, but his grip didn't allow me to surge up or to force him to go faster. If anything, it was agony and ecstasy.

His kiss this time was a gift. Slow, almost too gentle, and yet persuasive, he nibbled my lips apart. I damn near sighed as he thrust his tongue and cock in the same moment until he seated himself so deep inside, even as I drowned in the taste of him.

"Only me," he whispered against my lips and the words had me jerking my eyes wide. Oh, Justus stared down at me, his gaze fixed on mine. It was hypnotic, delightful, and just...

"Justus," I answered in a shaking voice. Tremors rioted through me and I dug my nails into his shoulder.

"I'm right here," he said in another rough whisper. "Right here, Fallon. Hold onto me."

I couldn't do anything else.

"You with me?" I couldn't explain the wild feeling rippling through me or why I couldn't seem to calm down.

"Yes," I promised him. I scraped my teeth over my lower lip, intimately aware of everywhere we touched. It filled me and left me desperate for more in equal measures. "I don't even know why I'm shaking. But this feels so good."

Then Locke did something I wasn't expecting. He shifted his rhythm, slow, then fast, then slow again. The whole time, he studied me with a tilted head. His hair fell over his forehead in the most adorable way as he studied me. He pulled back and then thrust deep again. This time the bump of his hips to mine rubbed my clit in a way that left me gasping.

"Still good?" I swore there was a devilish gleam in his eyes now.

"Yes," I said. He gave another thrust, this one a little lighter, then another that seemed to sink deeper. He varied his rhythm until I couldn't antici-pate what he would do next.

My nipples scraped against his chest, it sent fresh waves of pleasure tingling along my nerves and then he rocked his hips and the need jolting through me demanded my attention.

I dug my nails into his back. As short as they'd been left, I needed them to anchor me into the mo-ment. Locke seemed determined to drive me mad. I wanted that madness. Craved it.

His lips were curved into a smile so wicked that I ached to know what thoughts went through his head. Yet each time a question tried to form in my mind, he thrust deeper and those thoughts scattered.

There was his body, hot, firm, and filling mine. His scorching gaze seemed to radiate some undefin-able emotion and I wanted to drown in them. His lips alternated between wicked smiles and drug-ging kisses.

Locke rolled onto his back and I found myself above him. My breasts were heavy and his cock was still thick between my legs.

"Ride me," he ordered and didn't wait for me to take the advice as he lifted my hips and then sank me down on him again. Oh, fuck...

I threw my head back as he repeated the motion and then I took over. Knees braced on the bed as I straddled him and with my hands balancing the rest of my weight with their grip on his shoulders.

"Oh..." I exhaled the single syllable as I found the rhythm and surged with it. He met me thrust for thrust. His hips surged upwards as I sank down and then he fisted my hair.

Our mouths locked in a vibrant duel that matched his body burying itself into mine. I even remembered how to twist my hips a little, to add to the sensations. Shudders danced through me as I dragged my head upward and then he mouthed one of my nipples as I ground down against him.

The pleasure expanded until I shook from it. I fisted both the bedsheets and his shoulder. It was too much, and not enough. When I would have backed off, he flipped us again. The pound of his body driving into mine pushed me further along the edge until I screamed.

Too much.

Too much.

And yet liquid heat expanded in a whirl that flooded all of me. I couldn't breathe for how good it felt. I thrashed but I couldn't escape it, Locke was inside me, filling me, and then his release set fire to me as the warmth spilled deep.

His gasps were like a symphony, matching mine almost beat for beat. My heart hammered and his breath was hot against my throat as he shuddered against me. I tried to move my fingers but I found my hands locked in his. His grip wasn't so tight that it hurt, but it kept me from flying apart into a billion pieces.

Gradually, the feel of his tongue tracing a light circle over my pulse point registered. I floated down from the wild crescendo I'd been riding. I could die happy from the drugging weight of Locke's fierce kisses. Then he was raining gentle kisses over my cheeks, and my eyes.

Inch by inch, I came back to earth and when I opened my eyes, I found him studying me with so much emotion I should have fled in that moment. It was raw, naked, and punched me with a fist so powerful I couldn't breathe.

No one looked at me like that.

No one.

"Justus..."

"I'm here," he said, his voice thick and lazy, infused with something that struck me almost like a purr. I'd have given everything I owned to record that sound so I could listen to it forever. It was beyond anything I'd ever imagined.

Not that I should have ever imagined being in his arms or feeling him fucking into me. Yet, here we were and I couldn't lie to myself. I wouldn't.

I'd had the occasional fantasy. Locke was a beautiful man and that one tumble already had me hungry for more.

"Hi," I whispered and his smile softened.

"Hey." He was still inside of me, his cock softened, but slowly. The heat and the dampness were there. He'd come inside of me and... "Oh, shit."

He raised his eyebrows.

"We didn't..." I could kick myself. "I have an implant. Or I did." Pregnancy wasn't an issue. "But I don't know if it was safe for you..."

"The doctor did panels," he soothed in the kindest of tones. "You are clean sweetheart, but frankly, I'd risk infection to be with you."

I wrinkled my nose until I saw the spark of laughter in his eyes. "That's gross."

"But funny," he teased and then he nibbled another kiss to my lips. "Don't worry, I'm clean too. I can get you my medical records if you need."

"Except you weren't..." Reality crushed the beautiful moment, and I groaned. Closing my eyes, I tried to shove it back out. The last thing I wanted to be talking about was this.

"I have you," he said again in that silky voice that demanded I believe him. "You aren't going to hurt me, and I won't hurt you."

I clung to him, tightening my arms around him. That—I needed to hear that. An unexpected sound penetrated the bliss and the rattle of something at the door had Locke jerking upward. I barely had time to register the door was *unlocking* then McQuade and Remington were just there.

They were alive and safe. That knowledge filled me with joy, right before it crashed headlong into the information that Locke and I were tangled together, naked, and you couldn't mistake it for anything else.

From the expressions on their faces, neither man seemed to make any other excuse for us. Their hooded, yet burning gazes raked over me as their lips compressed.

"You're here," I whispered, torn between embarrassment at being caught and thrilled that they were actually here.

Then they turned those heated *glares* on Locke.

TWELVE

MCQUADE

ody disposal had never been my favorite task, but it was a practical and necessary one. Our prisoners hadn't known much. They were grunts, working a grunt assignment on a need to know basis. Clearly, they hadn't needed to know. How unfortunate for them that their employers considered them that disposable.

Why else keep them out of the loop? What they didn't know, they couldn't reveal. Course, it could also mean they had an expected fail rate. For that, I was fine. If they considered sending anyone after Patch was a lost cause, then *good*. From this point forward, I was sending their people back in pieces.

We'd left them a pretty fucking clear message back at the house we'd used. The bodies stacked like cordwood should send them a signal. Come for her at your own peril. As it was, I was torn between heading down to Louisiana and firebombing that location after we data-mined it, then going on to the next.

Remy hadn't seemed opposed, however, he did

point out that we needed to wait for Patch to remember. She had to be a part of the op.

I got it, I really did. But... "I don't want her to remember that part." When he frowned, I'd just given him a look. "We can meet her a hundred times. I don't care if she remembers we came for her. We can make new memories. But if she remembers her captivity, she remembers the torture, and she doesn't deserve that."

While the British fucker remained skeptical, I couldn't agree to her remembering her incarceration. Sure, would I like to have some of our progress back? Yes. But could I wait for her to truly trust me again? Also yes. Particularly if it meant she didn't have to relive that trauma. Her nightmares remained littered with it.

Those screams killed me, so did her begging. But her whimpers? Those just left me wanting to slaughter any and all who had ever hurt her. It was going to happen. Just a matter of time.

Once we finished, we were free to get on the road and meet them at the rendezvous. If we weren't there by dawn, it would be the second one.

We had a few hours. Of course, the skies decided to help us with potential tails and surveillance by opening up. The icy rain came down in sheets. It didn't turn to snow, which was a blessing and a curse, but Remy didn't seem to be troubled by the low visibility or the crappy road conditions.

Good. The need to put my eyes on her and know for certain she was fine burned in my gut. Impatience was a good way to die on an op. So was longing. Yet, here I was, suffering from both. I just—

"We're here," Remy said and it jerked me away from the needy direction my thoughts were going. It was damn near two in the morning. I squinted at the clock. No, that said three. Fuck. My eyes were gritty and I'd kill for a shower, but all of that could wait.

"They could be asleep," I warned, not that Remy was an idiot.

"Agreed, but we have codes for a reason." Practical son of a bitch didn't quite smirk, but I heard it there in his voice. If he weren't so fucking useful in a fight, I'd be tempted to just dump him on the side of the road. We pulled into the packed rest area, passing all the trucks pulled off onto the shoulder of the road because the interior slots were all taken.

The mobile unit blended in pretty damn well. We were both scanning, but we didn't spot it right away. Maybe we did too good of a job.

"There." It was near the end of the row, but not so close they were exposed. The rain began to slant sideways and the pellets of ice tapped against the windows. We still needed this vehicle, at least until we transferred what we had to the mobile unit.

"Parking first."

Agreed. Not that I said anything. The entirety of the rest area seemed silent, frozen in time. The rain turned even more into ice. I dragged on a jacket with a hoodie and pulled it up before we climbed out of the car.

Remy led me by two strides as we crossed from the car parking to truck parking. Even the lights on near the toilets and the information center seemed like isolated islands in the darkness.

The rumble of engines idling at low offered the only other sound to accompany the ice plinking against the trucks. I'd caught up to Remy as he circled past the truck next to theirs. Good plan, we didn't want to draw attention to the mobile unit. I scanned the front windows, and the vehicles around ours for cameras.

Nothing jumped out at me, but our cameras were also camouflaged. Paranoia, Patch used to preach at me, was a terrible way to live. It was a good way not to die, I'd always quip back. I had no idea how intimately aware she truly was of those facts.

Not for the first time, it occurred to me that I really wish I had known sooner. I'd always been fond of her. Grown to like her more and more over the time we'd worked together. Enough that I made a point of calling her to check-in, even if I didn't really need her for a consultation.

Talking to her always made me feel better.

Being close to her was even far more preferable to that. Two quick scouts and we were at the door. Remy opened the keypad and entered the code to let us in. I was shaking ice crystals out of my hair and beard when the smell of sex hit me.

Sex?

I wasn't sure if it registered with Remy in the same instant though he mirrored my actions. I'd already shrugged my jacket off, but caught it with one hand as we circled the first of the faux walls to stare at the bed, it had been lowered for use. And it was definitely in use.

The low-lighting did nothing to hide Patch and

Locke entangled atop the sheets. Not one goddamn thing on them was covered. While I wanted to take time to inspect every inch of Patch's skin, I couldn't quite choke out the rage that geysered through me.

What the fuck was he doing?

Her eyes widened as she stared at us. "You're here..." The husky note in her voice was pure sensual overload. I wanted to wrap myself up in the voice that had saved my sanity and my life more times than I could count.

As tempting an idea as it was, I couldn't shake the fact she was wrapped around Locke or the swollen state of her lips and the red marks on her cheeks betrayed the kissing. The scent alone told me all about the fucking.

I switched my glare to Locke, largely because not even my rage at him was calming the erection stiffening in my pants. Patch was every inch the beautiful woman and there was something absolutely hypnotic about her freshly fucked expression, tousled hair, and raw voice.

It was enough to drive a man to pure madness and kill the son of a bitch who had his hands on her.

"Gentlemen," Locke said by way of greeting like he wasn't sprawled there with his wet dick, caught with it literally in the sweetest jar. He eased away from Patch and dragged a sheet up to her. "Give her a second, why don't you."

The last few words held a semi-hostile note. I wasn't impressed, nor was Remy. Neither of us moved.

"Guys..." Patch's inquiry tugged my attention

back to her. Far more powerful than the lure of a siren, the need to answer her had me taking a step forward. "You're all right, right?"

Her marked up cheeks seemed to pinken deeper the longer I stared at her. I swallowed the bitter pill of anger and shook my head. "We're fine." I could lie to her with my words, but not the rest of me. Her brow tightened as if she understood. Instead of holding up the sheet, she dropped it to scoot off the bed.

Fuck my life, she was all curves from her hips to her breasts to the way her tummy belled out a little. Nothing hollow or too taut for her. There were muscles, but she wasn't all muscle. So much softness to wrap around a man.

No matter how hard I tried to keep my gaze on her face, there was no way I could resist sweeping a look over the roundness of her breasts or how puffy her nipples were.

Goddamn it. I was going to kill Locke.

"We're fine," Remy said abruptly, echoing my statement with a great deal more calm and elegance than I could or wanted to manage. He stripped off his oversized coat and moved to her. "Here..."

She eyed him then the long coat that reached his knees and would probably drop to her ankles. Rather than argue, she twisted to give him her back and let him slide the coat onto one of her arms, then the other. The dark material draped her, hiding that sumptuous body from my sight.

Not that I hadn't already memorized so much of it I could conjure the image with a single thought.

As it was, Locke was pulling up his pants when I returned my attention to him.

"All clear?" The inane question irked me on a primitive level.

"We wouldn't be here otherwise," Remy answered and for once, I let the fucker have it. His cool, accented tones held far more control than I possessed at the moment. Far more. "Do you really think we'd be careless with her safety?"

The fact the question not only dismissed Locke for asking in the first place, it slapped him for what he'd done—fucking her and forgetting that he was supposed to be guarding her. We'd just walked right up and onboard, he'd not known we were here until we came in.

"And you don't even have a fucking weapon handy." The realization burned like acid in my gut as I spat out the words. Then Locke had a gun up and pointed right at my head.

"Think again," he advised. "Just because I don't like the damn things doesn't mean I can't use them."

I took another three steps forward until the muzzle of the gun was right at my forehead. Gaze locked on his, I practically dared him to pull the trigger.

"And you could reach it while you were fucking her?"

"Obviously." Disdain practically crawled through Locke's voice. "I wanted her to have all the pleasure I could give her. The gun being handy didn't prevent that."

Smug.

Arrogant.

"John," Patch said in that low, husky voice of hers. I cut my eyes to the left but I didn't back off from the gun. I really didn't fucking like Locke right now. The uncertainty in her eyes sliced me open from sternum to throat.

I was scaring her.

Goddammit to hell and back.

"It's fine, Sugar Bear," I soothed her. "Why don't you get our resident lordship to show you the bathing facilities, such as they are. Then you can get dressed and we'll bring you up to speed on everything."

A frown tightened her brow and she didn't take those storm gray eyes off of me. "I can... but you're angry."

"Never with you." It was true. I'd never been angry with her. Even if she gave herself to him. That was her choice. I'd never begrudge him. Locke, on the other hand, was a fucking idiot for burying himself so deep in the prize he forgot to watch out for her.

"C'mon luv," Remy said, holding out an arm. "We've got a bit of a clever workaround I think you'll like."

"I don't want to leave them to fight."

"We're not going to fight," Locke told her and he took the gun from my skull and put it away. Better him than me to say it.

Still, she hesitated. No way she believed Locke, or me for that matter. That was fine, I could earn her trust. Finally, she licked her lips. "I could use some water."

"Good girl," I murmured. "Let Remy look after you."

I waited until he ushered her around another faux wall, his soft words to her carrying for a moment. The nice part of the design was we'd used sound dampeners on purpose. Harder to listen in if we didn't let sound escape. When I was sure they were another room away, I slammed my fist toward Locke.

I'd give the little prick credit, he batted my fist to the side and dodged the follow-up blow. The third, an uppercut, lifted him off the ground. He hit the bed before he bounced and rolled off of it.

With a tumble, he was back on his feet and instead of the gun, he had a pair of knives in his hand. I nodded slowly. That was better. Maybe he was more prepared than I'd cared to admit.

Maybe.

"I told her we weren't going to fight," he warned me.

"I didn't." I said then shrugged. "Next time you want to get your dick wet, you make sure you have backup present who can watch out for both of you. We could have been anyone coming through that door, there you would be, ass in the air, balls deep in her sweet cunt and what?"

A blade flew across the room and slammed into the wall just behind me. The whisper of its passage brushed my cheek and it wobbled there, so close, he could have offered me a shave.

I studied the blade for a moment then met his challenging gaze. "Fine. You still wait until you have backup."

CHAPTER
THIRTEEN
PATCH

As grateful as I was to see them both, the last thing I expected was for them to choose that exact moment to appear. Riddled with embarrassment, I clutched Remy's coat a little closer to me. It was still warm from his body. Even better, it was satiny soft on my skin.

Behind us, McQuade and Locke seemed almost eerily silent. Chewing my lip, I didn't say anything as Remy guided me around to an area near the back of the truck. He touched a switch that released another wall to fold out. This one looked more like an ornamental privacy screen. The frosted glass offered an occluded view.

With a light touch, Remy nudged me around the corner into the square of space that had been created by the privacy screens.

"You installed a shower?" The drain on floor had been a clue, but the fact there was a nozzle above with a rain head on it gave me pause. I couldn't help but gawk at all of it. "How? This is a truck? Where do you even keep the water? How do

134

you recycle it? Is it potable? Or just useful for showering? Can you even *heat* it?"

I had a hundred different questions and Remy's soft chuckle drifted around me. I pivoted to find him watching me with a small smile on his lips.

"What?"

"You're quite adorable, luv," he murmured.

I wrinkled my nose, uncertain that I cared for that description.

Not an ounce of apology reflected in his expression. "You are even more adorable with this frown crinkling right here."

He lifted a slender finer to trace the space between my brows. The light touch sent shivers up and down my spine. I wanted to erase the frown but the effort only seemed to make me frown harder.

When a chuckle escaped him again, I scowled for real. His chuckle turned to a laugh even as his eyes warmed further.

With a sigh, I gave up the effort.

"Am I really annoying you?" Genuine curiosity inhabited his voice.

"No," I said, instantly irritated with myself for giving him that impression. I lifted my chin to meet his gaze. "Truly, I'm not upset and you aren't annoying me."

The last thing I wanted to be was coy. I'd been a bit hesitant to lock gazes with him, more out of fear of seeing the judgment or disapproval that seemed to radiate off of McQuade. Yet, staring in his eyes now, all I saw was real concern. Before I could offer another word of assurance, however, I spotted the bruise shadowing his jaw.

"You're hurt." I closed the distance, and grasped his chin with light fingers. He didn't resist when I tilted his head to study it in the light. The bruise stretched from his jaw down to his throat.

Now it was his turn to raise his brows. "What was that for?"

"Kissing it to make it better."

"Oh, well, in that case..." He rolled his shirt up to show me another bruise on the side of his forearm.

At his glance, I wrapped a hand over his wrist and pressed a kiss to the newly revealed bruise. His skin was warm and the light sprinkle of hair along his skin tickled my lips.

"Any others?"

The corners of his mouth quirked a bit higher. Reaching for the two buttons on his shirt, he opened it from his collar to his sternum. The bruise on his pec was easily the size of my fist. Entertainment and curiosity gave way to a fresh wave of worry and anger.

I put a hand lightly against his chest as I closed that distance between us and I kissed the edge of the bruise, then the center, and across to the other side of it. The steady pound of his heart beneath my fingers reminded me that he was here.

"You're a sniper," I scolded him. "How did you let them get—"

I never finished the question as he fisted a hand in my hair and tugged my head back. Then his mouth fused to mine. The liquid heat from earlier flamed back to life. My heart threatened to combust as Remy leaned into me. The tilt of his head to mine had me drifting backwards and then his arm banded around my middle.

He hauled me upwards with such ease, it made me dizzy. His tongue swept through my mouth, as if determined to lick up every nuance of flavor and I abandoned any pretense of keeping his coat closed as I wrapped my arms around his neck.

The injuries left me with so much to worry about, but he was here, safe, and in my arms. I drank in all of him that he shared. Renewed hunger flared in my system, I trailed my fingers into his hair as my scalp lit up from the tug he applied.

The only thing keeping my legs from wrapping around his waist was the dampness I was keenly aware of, but then my thoughts scattered as he sucked against my tongue. The steel band of his arm kept me tethered to earth as his kiss sent me soaring higher.

Biting at his lower lip, I delighted at the very low hum of a growl he released. It was damn near a purr and I bit him again. The sound rumbled against my chest and my skin lit up as currents of electricity danced over every part of me.

When he sank his teeth into my lower lip, I groaned. Then he was kissing a path to my throat. The smoothness of his skin was almost a revelation. I traced my fingers over his jaw. It was silken, hot, and demanded to be stroked.

The scrape of his teeth over my pulse point made me vibrate and then he stilled utterly. I wanted to protest. I damn near dragged him closer, but he'd gone so very rigid.

"You need to clean up," he whispered against my throat. Every syllable a hot tease of the delight he'd already shared. "Then rest."

My heart stampeded and my breath came in sharp pants. The earlier satiation was gone and I *wanted* with a visceral, and violent need. "I don't want to rest."

No sooner did I give voice to the protest than I slapped at myself for my greed. He wouldn't have said anything if he didn't need it himself.

"I'm selfish," I whispered. "Sorry."

"Never apologize, luv," he said in a soothing voice even as he mouthed a damp path of kisses to my ear. "I mean it. You never need to apologize to me."

Still, we clung to each other and the coat was open and my breasts were against his bare chest. When he dipped his gaze downward, his lips quirked upward again.

"Though if you want to stay like this, I hope you don't mind me looking. You really are beautiful."

An entirely different type of heat swarmed through me. My cheeks scalded, and I swore even my ears burned. There was something in how these men looked at me. I wasn't so insecure I wasn't aware of my own attractiveness. Nor was I so vain as to expect it.

No, it had less to do with that than *who* it was looking at me. Remington was a beautiful man and he made me feel so damn beautiful when he stared at me like that.

I had no idea how long we'd stood there and indulged ourselves, but he was right. I needed to clean up. We needed to get back to McQuade and Locke. I needed to know if they were all right.

In the same breath, I didn't want this moment to end anymore than I had the time spent with Locke. Sighing, I closed my eyes and tilted my head back. I needed to get my breathing and my heart under control, not to mention my hormones.

I was not the only one taking longer, slower breaths and then with the kind of gentleness one might show a kitten, he set me on my feet. Not that he released me. The coat still hung wide open and the cooler air was so damn welcome against my flushed skin.

The lightness of his grip remained on my hips until I opened my eyes and met his gaze. The amusement in his expression was utterly indulgent, and more than a little smug. It was the latter that chased away the self-consciousness.

"I'm glad you're here," I told him.

"Even if we interrupted?" No criticism, just real interest.

I wanted to shrug that off, but I wasn't sure I should. That said, I wouldn't run away from it. "I had sex with Locke."

"I noticed," he said with a wave of his hand. "Absolutely your choice, luv. As long as it was your choice."

I blinked. "Of course it was my choice." Locke would never...

"Good."

"Good?" Now I was confused. "You don't mind?" Not entirely the question I meant to ask.

"It has nothing to do with whether I mind or not," he informed me in that so very proper voice. "It's about whether you enjoyed it and it was what you wanted."

Yeah. Still confused. Based on some of their reactions—hell based on their *glares* when they arrived, that didn't seem right.

"Am I chuffed?" Remy continued, then shook his head. "No. I'm a possessive man. I want you for myself."

I wasn't sure which declaration knocked me sideways more. Could you freeze a moment and just keep it forever? This might be one that I wanted to preserve.

The amusement in his smile deepened. "Did I shock you?"

"No," I said slowly, then gave myself a little shake. "Yes." I shrugged off his coat, the contrast between the cooler air on my bare skin versus the overheated mess I was becoming seemed the far lesser of two evils. "You aren't upset?"

"Patch... nothing for me to be upset about. Do you feel better?"

"After the sex?"

"Yes," he said patiently and I had to fight the urge to facepalm. Had I managed to absolutely disintegrate my brain? Apparently.

"Yes," I exhaled the word.

"Then I'm happy enough for you." He traced a finger over my shoulder and then turned me to face the wall. "I'm going to exhibit some absolutely stellar restraint by showing you how you can wash. The water will be warm. Not cold. Not hot. And you have to press the button to get thirty seconds' worth and wash in between."

The explanation, so rational and patient, settled my jagged nerves more than I cared to admit. Or it did until he traced his fingers down my spine and leaned in to press a kiss behind my ear.

"Just know, when you and I have sex, I really want you to enjoy that too."

CHAPTER
FOURTEEN
LOCKE

The shower installation was a huge hit with Fallon. She'd returned with a smile on her face and a fresh flush to her cheeks. Remy prowled behind her like a silent guardian. Each time his gaze landed on me, he'd go unreadable.

Frankly, I couldn't tell if I needed to watch my back or just make the most of my time with Fallon. The Brit was a sniper after all. I'd probably never know what hit me. There were worse ways to go.

Then Fallon would look at me and the harsh glare of reality softened. The strain around her eyes was gone and the tightness to her lips had relaxed. If nothing else, sex had definitely taken the edge off.

At the same time, it left me hungry for more. By unspoken agreement, we slept for four hours, then had a planning session. We left the big bed to Fallon and I took a bunk nearby, so did Remy and McQuade. As we had at the house, we all took turns on watch.

I got the first one.

Fine.

When it was time to get my two hours, it went by in the blink of an eye. Not even the coffee Remy pointed me toward seemed to touch the sandpaper in my eyes, much less the fuzz around my brain.

The lack of sleep would be the death of all of us if we weren't careful. At least my morning view included a deliciously rumpled Fallon, cradling her coffee mug in hand as she stared at the map Mc-Quade had spread out.

"So," McQuade said. "We didn't get much out of our invaders because they didn't know much." Annoying, but practical, his tone suggested.

"Except, we may have figured out how they kept finding you."

Fallon snapped a look up at Remy and he gave her a gentle smile. "Are you going to share?"

"Yes," McQuade said. "Injectable isotope. I've heard about it..."

"Slow decay over forty-eight hours, not harmful, and hard to scan for without the proper equipment." Of course she knew what it was. "But I've been at that house for a week and based on our discussions, for a few weeks before that... Why now?"

"I've been thinking about that," Remy said before McQuade responded. "The isotope is likely gone, but we'll want to scan for it regardless."

No arguments from anyone on that subject.

"You were likely injected while they had you, probably updated it—a failsafe."

Her nose wrinkled.

"It took us more than two days to secure the house," I said. "They had to have used a tracker to get close and then stay close..."

Fuck.

McQuade met my gaze and nodded. "All they had to do was get a tracker on a car or on one of us. The smart thing would be to make them slough off or activate one at a time, so we wouldn't find them in a simple sweep. They used us to triangulate."

"That's a lot of work," Fallon argued. "A hell of a lot of work, not to mention the risk to keep track of me. The fast decay, bouncing trackers. Unless..."

The moment she said unless it was almost like you could see the processing reflected in her eyes. She'd thought of something. Hands planted on the tabletop, McQuade stared at her steadily.

As rough and ready as he came off, he was a master of patience with Fallon—rock steady. Dependable. His punch earlier had fucking hurt. At the same time, he hadn't been wrong.

No, he hadn't been wrong in the slightest. When she'd noticed my new bruise the night before, she'd frowned at the explanation I offered. I'd deserved the blow and that was enough for me. While she seemed like she would object, Remy distracted her.

"Skimmers might have caught the call..." There had been no word from her contact since the meetup went to hell. McQuade was sure whoever they were, they'd been dead before the meet. "But if they'd already tagged me to the house, they could have tasked a satellite to keep an eye on it."

No sooner did she say that then she shook her head.

"Overkill." No, it wasn't. Her concentrated frown seemed to say she'd evaluated the statement and discarded the idea immediately. The interplay of emotion dancing through her expressions fascinated me. "No, not overkill. But the cost of resources seems exponentially out of balance with the return unless the information I encoded is more critical now than it was then."

All at once, she was talking to herself and not us. She pushed away from the table, her gaze and mind a million miles away, then she whirled to face us.

"I need to do some research."

"Your system is onboard and ready to go. We have enough power for the juice, but if we go too many hours we'll need to recharge it." McQuade folded his arms, a content look on his face.

"My system?" She frowned. "It's very annoying that I helped with any of this and I can't remember it."

"Trust the source, luv," Remy told her. "You set up the specs and got everything on board. Locke brought your tower with your hard drives from the house."

I had. "Yeah, let me grab that."

"Wait," she said, before focusing on McQuade and Remy. "Did you get anything else out of them?"

"Not really." McQuade shrugged. "The tracking data was what they had. The idea they knew about the house but didn't move on it bugs me."

"They were waiting for her to get the files," I

said. Son of a bitch. "Once she was out of their hands, and they had the tag, they had to keep someone on her. On us. Once they had the location and a solid fix, they sat back and waited. They wanted you to bring the information to them. Or at least get it to where they could lay hands on it."

"It's digital," Remy countered, skepticism rifling over his words. "How would they know when she collected it?"

That was an excellent question. Fallon stilled, head tilted. For all she had trusted us, she hadn't revealed this part. She told us she strip-mined it all. Damn impressive, but not where it was or how to get to it. Was it in a physical or virtual location? Both? Neither?

If it were a physical location and she had issues with remembering *how* to get it, I'd take care of it. Virtual location? That would require her, specifically.

"They wouldn't," she said slowly. "Not until I acted on what I took. Not until I'd done what I said I would do. Then they would try to intercept."

Fallon's eyes went distant, the chilly look didn't belong on her warm, animated face. If anything, it seemed downright alien. Then, I'd never really been able to "see" her while she worked. Maybe it was how she processed.

"I threatened them," she continued in a voice that was almost too quiet. "I threatened them with more than exposure. Shadow ops only work if they can remain in the shadows. Governments hate to admit that they are running them, so when they are exposed—"

McQuade snorted. "Exposure means scorched earth. Disavow the identified players. Senior officers fall on their swords, and if they are jailed—well, that's the cost of doing business." Disapproval echoed beneath each word. "It's clever and stupid in equal measures."

Remy folded his arms and merely shrugged when McQuade shot him a look. McQuade seemed like a lifer, so I had to wonder what made him leave that life behind. Particularly since what he did now was basically the same job—only he worked for himself.

That, I understood on a visceral level. I didn't do acquisitions for others unless I approved of their reasons for wanting something. For me, it was never about the money. Okay, to be perfectly honest, it was never about *only* the money.

"The exposure would cost them their investments in time, budget, and manpower," Fallon continued, tapping a finger against her plump, still kiss-swollen lower lip. Swollen from my kisses. Possessiveness slid through me. I wished I could just kiss her again and table the rest of this discussion.

Sadly, not an option at the moment.

Later, I promised myself. Definitely later.

"That's not all it would cost them though," she said. Lips pursed, she paced away from us, then back. The restlessness around her had transformed from chaotic energy to something far more laser-focused. The intensity of it demanded all of our attention. "International relations with allies could be forever damaged."

Allies?

Remy raised his brows. "Do you know everything in the files?"

The harsh, cold reality of that question left my bones aching. If she knew it all...

"Yes." No prevarication or play. Nothing coy or dismissive. If anything, she was blunt, hard, and direct. "Enough to be a threat, but without the files themselves, I'm just a crackpot conspiracy theorist and easily dismissed and painted into a corner. Like so many others before me."

"But you have the files," McQuade seized the thread. "That means you know the names of those involved..."

Well, shit... "You would also know who we might be able to trust with the info if you have to take it public. Cause if we go public with it, all their reasons for going after you evaporate. They are exposed."

"Yes," she said, only this time it was far softer. "They would also lose any rationale behind trying to be quiet about it. At that point, assassinating me could just be a drone attack if they wanted."

"Retaliation," McQuade said in a tone that suggested he agreed with her conclusion. "Right now, they *need* you alive cause they don't know that you haven't set up a failsafe. You die and it goes public. You go missing for too long, it goes public— *son of a bitch...*"

The lack of anything resembling surprise on Fallon's face told me she'd already reached that particular opinion.

"They let me go," she said. "They wanted me to escape."

Assholes. Except...

"You might not have made it if we hadn't been there." She'd been struggling so hard.

"Maybe," she said. "Or were they the token resistance I wouldn't have identified as token because I was drugged up, exhausted, in tremendous pain, and ready to believe anything... who says you didn't scoop me up before their scoop team could—the team that had been set up to play my savior."

I raked a hand through my hair, but it was Remy who looked grim now. "Operatives running as civilians. Someone to offer you a ride. Another a doctor..."

"We fucked up their plans." Aggravation gave way to a kind of feral glee in McQuade. "Fucked them up good."

A smile flirted around the corners of her mouth. "The truly frightening part of all of this, is how good of a plan it was. They truly could have gotten me."

"Except, even when we first rescued you, you didn't tell us where the information was." I hated to rain on anyone's parade, but it was the simple truth. "You didn't trust *us*. No doubt exists within me, you wouldn't have taken their bait."

"Agreed," Remy said firmly. "With that in mind, don't tell us. We're not asking unless it becomes something you think we need to know."

"As much as I hate it, I also think that's wise." McQuade nodded. "Give us a list, Sugar Bear."

"A list?" She raised both of her eyebrows.

"Yes," Remy said, as though picking up the thread. "We need a kill list. Eliminate the potential threats until those that know about you are gone. Then they can't threaten you anymore."

Though she didn't dismiss it completely, she did frown. She was thinking about it. When she flicked a look toward me, I shrugged.

There were worse plans.

"Whatever you want to do," I told her. "I'm in."

FIFTEEN

"*We need a kill list.*"

I turned that statement over several times as I settled in behind the computer screen. The fact I "knew" all the logins and security challenges quieted some of the earlier unease. I tended to use a series of different passwords for different things. They followed a pattern, but it was a kind of pattern that usually only I could follow.

The squirrel code worked for me because I would set the passwords based on my mood. The only set of codes I could have used for this particular setup had to be tense and annoyed. Kind of like when I was PMSing. Sure enough, the codes worked.

Four layers of encryption. Each layer required a new passcode. The first set the pattern for the rest. No single one I used formed any kind of phrase. They were the result of gibberish, or mental rhymes I created based on the numbers, letters, and symbols. I used all of the above along with varying the upper versus lower case letters.

If nothing else proved what they'd told me, the fact my codes were here, unfiltered and ready to work, did. Did I test to make sure that it wasn't just *any* password being used? Yes, yes I did. It wasn't about not trusting them, so much as not being able to fully trust myself.

Midway through doing a full system check, I paused. It really wasn't them that I didn't trust. Somewhere in all of this, I had begun trusting them. If I hadn't, I'd never have gone to bed with Locke. My body hummed at the memory. There was a distinct, sensual ache between my thighs and I had to fight the urge to clench everything.

It had been long enough since I'd been intimate with anything beyond a toy, that I'd forgotten how good an enthusiastic round of sex could leave you. Endorphins for the win. Follow that up with Remy's hedonistic promise and the intense look in McQuade's eyes and my core temperature seemed to rise.

Rubbing a hand against the back of my neck, I tried to blot out all the arousing images cascading through my mind. I needed to focus on the tasks at hand.

First task... track down Section Five. They were the ringmasters of all my problems. It wasn't just the employees of the organization. Many would be a great deal like I'd been, fooled into believing we were working for the country. It would take too long to convince them otherwise, or I'd attempt that.

If I hadn't discovered the discrepancies and started to put the disparate puzzle pieces together on my own... Would I have believed anyone else bringing me this story? As much as I hated to admit it, I didn't think I would.

I sighed just before a single drag-step alerted me to someone behind me. Glancing up, I found Remy's even gaze resting on mine. He also had a cup of coffee in hand. The smell of it wrapped around me like a lover and I indulged in an inhale to savor it.

With care, Remy set the large mocha—oh the chocolate was heavenly—with its rich foam and cream atop it, down on the desk next to me. I wrapped my hand around it and let the warmth chase away the apprehensive chills rippling through my system.

Pulling up a chair, Remy joined me. He didn't have a coffee of his own, but then he did prefer tea. "I hope you guys installed a kettle on board."

"We did," he said easily enough. "I'll make a cup in a bit."

I sipped the coffee, then chased the whip cream off my lip with my tongue. The heat in Remy's eyes tracked the motion and sent another shudder through me. "You should get some sleep."

"You first." The volley was easily returned. While I might have not had a lot of sleep, I suspected that neither Remy nor McQuade had gotten any at all.

"I sent McQuade and Locke to take some rack time. Three hours..." He consulted his watch. "It'll be dawn by then. One of them can drive and I'll get some sleep in."

That still seemed like a long time. Rather than comment, I took another sip of the coffee. It was— I closed my eyes and just let the coffee fill me. It was damn near perfect. Not too sweet, more than warm enough to get rid of the ice reality left in its wake.

That and it was just *good*.

"Want to tell me what the really long sigh was about?" Remy asked when I finally stopped making out with my coffee. I was more than half-done. It definitely tasted like more.

"Thinking about how stupid and foolish I was," I said. "I know we need to track down these heads of Section Five. You guys want a list. Finding the directors will be harder than the worker drones. I flirted with the idea of turning one of the drones. But I wouldn't have believed anyone bringing me this story. It's too far-fetched and wild. It sounds like something from television or a movie."

"That doesn't make you foolish," Remy chastised me lightly.

"It does when it's based on blind loyalty."

"You *trusted* them," he said, pressing on as if I hadn't disagreed with him. "In the field... you have to trust your handlers. Your eyes in the sky. You have to give them everything and put your life in their hands."

The intensity in those words arrested me and I twisted to look at him. All I found in his eyes was a kind of dedicated solemnity.

"Working in intelligence is the same way. They

recruited you when you were young and impressionable."

When I would have argued, he covered my hand on the coffee mug with his.

"You were young. You were in college. They courted your intellect. When you are being sought for the very skills that could bring them down, you don't look for a trap. Why would a shadow organization bring in people who had no idea what they were doing for real?"

It wasn't an unfair question. Letting go of the cup, I clasped his hand. "I just—I hate that it took me so long to see it. How much blood is on my hands because I did what they asked of me without question?"

"Did you do it with no question at all? Or did you wait until they'd given you enough evidence to trust that you could believe them?"

This time, the sigh that left me seemed to deflate everything. I cut my attention from him to the screen once more. It scrolled through the interior programs I had running. Sniffers to make sure nothing had been installed that I didn't want, as well as details on the drives I'd connected.

Yes, I had set up the system. Didn't matter, I always verified everything now. Triple verified if I could.

"I don't want to fall into another trap," I admitted without looking at him. "The holes in my memory could be one, easily. You guys could be another. Except..." I didn't sigh so much this time as pause to regather my thoughts. "Except I do know you."

Now I looked at him again.

"I know you and McQuade and Locke. I've known you for years. The three of you didn't know each other. You never worked jobs together. Except on very rare occasions, you have not been in the same cities on assignment or otherwise."

"So what does that tell you?" He'd begun to stroke the side of my hand with his thumb. The action soothed, but it also helped to keep me grounded. I probably shouldn't be leaning on them so much, but the last thing I wanted to do was pull away.

I chewed the inside of my lip, trying to examine it from all angles. "You met because of me."

"Correct," he said with a single nod.

"You guys are only working together because of me."

"Also correct."

A faint smile curved my lips. "You don't much like each other."

To that, Remy shrugged. "What I know about them? I like. McQuade will die for you. He will also kill. That makes him a good ally. Locke—"

The hesitation now seemed far more pronounced.

"Locke?" I prompted.

It was his turn to give a faint smile. The lighting cast his face half in shadow. It was as though I saw both sides of him, the dark assassin and the cheerful man who enjoyed dry teasing.

"Locke is not a killer. He has no interest in becoming one, but he goes right into the fight if given no other choice."

Now that intrigued me. "If he is given a choice?"

With the faintest of snorts, Remy turned my hand over so he could trace his thumb over my palm. "During our hunt for you, we needed to gather information from an installation. McQuade and I were going to go in, take it by force. Locke went to relieve himself, but didn't return immediately. Instead, he just let himself into the building, got the drives we needed and got out without a single shot fired or anyone noticing."

The grudging admiration was harder for him to hide. The description also sounded so much like Locke. "He loves to pit himself against security systems, the more challenging, the better. His mind never stops working, and he could sell sand to a desert dweller with his charm."

"You care about him," Remy said softly. "Don't you?"

"Yes." That wasn't so hard to admit. Even when I thought to soften it or at least bury it, I didn't want to. "I care about all of you. That makes you dangerous to me."

Eyebrows raised, Remy gave a sharp, negative head shake. "None of us would ever harm you."

The absolute conviction in that statement told me more about his trust in the other two men than anything else. In his opinion, they would never hurt me. They would protect me. They would keep me safe. Not him. Me.

They were so very dangerous for me.

Particularly when I wanted to lean into the devotion. I studied the way he stroked my palm.

"Too much?" The question tugged my attention upward once more.

"No. Yes. I don't know." Each answer came out definitive until the last. Amusement crinkled the lines at the corners of Remy's eyes.

"As long as you're sure."

I chuckled. "I'm not sure of much. I'm struggling between what I *want* to believe and what I *can* believe. Then there's all of you."

"What about all of us?" The steadiness in his voice eased away another of my concerns. Maybe it was the accent, the crispness in it just seemed refined and yet no nonsense. At the same time, I could listen to him all day.

"I do know you," I said softly. "I've worked with all of you for years."

"But?" he prompted, still drawing slow circles against my palm. The contact eased away the tension and left pleasurable shivers to trace through me.

"But that relationship has always been predicated by having a phone line and sometimes more than one ocean between us. It's different to be with you now."

That might be putting it poorly.

"Different bad? Or different good?" Before I could respond though, he nodded to my coffee. "And don't let that get cold. You don't like cold coffee."

I wrinkled my nose at him. Not that he was wrong. I really didn't care for cold coffee in the slightest. "Different, I'm not sure yet." Still, I picked

158

up my coffee with my free hand. The warmth penetrated my fingertips and reminded me of how chilled I'd grown. "But..."

I paused to take a sip, while also turning my answer over in my mind.

"Not bad," I finally admitted. "Definitely not bad. I may not know what to do with all of this—all of you." That wasn't entirely true. After having sex with Locke, and Remy declaring he wanted me to enjoy having sex with him, I had a few ideas.

The problem, however, was that no matter how great sex was—it didn't fix everything. It could only up your endorphins and maybe give you time to figure things out. Worst case, it just delayed the resolution.

"You don't have to make any decisions at the moment." The gentle acceptance in Remy's words and voice buoyed me.

"Not totally true," I said, meeting his gaze.

"As true as it needs to be right now. No one is going to force you to make any decisions you don't want to make or aren't ready to make. No one *will*." Or they would deal with him.

I squeezed his hand in wordless thanks. "I need to get back to work." As lovely as this discussion was... "We can't let them keep setting the tone." So far, I'd been fighting defensively.

"No, we can't." With that, Remy dropped a kiss on my head. "I'll bring you more coffee in a bit. Two hours, no more than that. You also need to sleep."

I made a face at him.

"Please," he added. "You need to rest or we are

all going to worry more." All the fight went out of me.

Fine. "Two hours," I promised, then pulled my hand from his grasp and turned to face the monitor once more. I could do a lot in two hours.

SIXTEEN

REMINGTON

Three days after reuniting with Locke and Patch, we found a rest area along a desert highway to park and settle in. It was late, the weather outside had shifted from cold to considerably warmer. Though the temperatures would plummet when the sun went down. McQuade and Locke had alternated turns with the driving.

Once parked, Patch took over any local cameras, looped their feeds, then did a full scan. We were the only trailer parked here and a pair of cars that had been there when we arrived, left shortly thereafter. With the all clear, we opened the ramp and I drove the SUV down. We'd parked the vehicle aboard as soon as we caught up

Locke slid into the passenger seat as McQuade closed up behind us. I didn't wait for Locke to buckle his seatbelt before I hit the accelerator.

Our first identified target was a little over an hour away, where the desert met the mountains. My comm hummed to life.

"Comm check," Patch said, her voice soothing

in my ear. The past three days had seen her come back to life. She'd been healing before, but she thrived now. The work, the hunt, the search—it was all doing her a world of good.

"Copy," I said easily.

"We're all clear here," Locke added. "Try to get some rest while we get into place?"

"I will after I finish my follow-up searches." The hint of impudence in her tone reminded me that she was retaking control of her daily choices. We could coax, but she didn't follow orders. Something, I suspected, the others enjoyed as much as I did.

"Let us know if there are any changes," I said before Locke could scold her. She had to put up with McQuade while we were gone. He would be far more likely to pick her up and dump her into her bed. To keep her there, he would pull the power supplies to her equipment and refuse to give them back until she slept.

"Will do. Be safe." Laughter edged the biting note beneath her words. I'd bailed Locke out and she let me do it. A soft click indicated the line was still there, but it would remain quiet unless we or she activated it.

"She isn't sleeping enough," Locke muttered.

"She won't while she has so much on her mind." Or while nightmares continued to plague her. Not that she'd said anything about that being *why* she preferred to be up, almost round the clock, on her computers. "You know as well as I do that she will not let go of this until she's solved the whole puzzle."

"Doesn't mean I have to like it."

No. It didn't. I couldn't say I much cared for it either. However... "This is her life," I reminded him. "Her battle. She has been in this particular fight far longer than either of us. She needs to do this and we need to let her."

"Just like that?" Locke shot me a look of intense dislike. Whether it was for my statements or me didn't really matter right now. It all came from the same place—the desire to protect her.

"No," I said, keeping my tone even.

One thing my training had taught me was to reserve my anger and passion for when they were necessary. At the moment, it wasn't necessary. His frustration wasn't even with *her* much less me. It was the whole situation.

"Not just like that. You have to know she will do what she needs to do. We can fight her, which will only make it more difficult for her to achieve her goals, or we can support her by eliminating the threats she uncovers."

Locke said nothing for the next few miles. If I read him right, he was chewing my statements up and trying to find a counter for them. His lengthy sigh was an answer all of its own.

"I kind of hate you right now," he said without an ounce of real heat.

"Go right ahead." I shrugged. "We have another forty-some odd minutes for you to deal with your feelings, then you need to pack them away for work."

"Thanks," he scraped the word out in a dry tone. "I appreciate it."

I hadn't missed the sarcasm underlining the words. Still, I grinned, and said, "You're welcome."

His snort was the only response.

An hour later, I eyed our target. It was an obscenely large wood cabin style mansion. They might label it a house, but it sprawled over the side of the mountain and fit against the trees as if it had been grown there. That took considerable effort and funds.

In addition to the home itself, there were a pair of generators hidden from view on the far side, as well as a garage to house the vehicles. The home was likely as self-sustaining as they could make it. A good bolthole.

Not good enough.

Flat against the earth, I studied the visible egresses. Two main doors on the first floor. The plans Patch had dug up said there were two more in the back.

One was into the garage itself, the other onto a deck where you could slip off to the side. Being tucked to the mountain made all elevations accessible to the ground depending on where you were.

Locke had begun his path around the house to the rear. Even out here, most people kept lighter security on their back doors than their front. It was like they assumed even intruders would prefer to come in the front doors.

A soft beep in my ear told me Locke was in place. I tapped my comm twice.

"Talk to me." Her voice wrapped around me with the softness of a lover and the confidence of a partner. A grin tugged at my mouth before I could suppress it.

Professionalism meant no distractions. Still, I savored the experience. I hadn't realized quite how much I missed these intimate little moments, even if I shared it with Locke and most likely McQuade.

"We're in position," I informed her. "I have eyes on the home. Are you ready to receive?"

The car was parked two miles to our south, but there was a booster there to take the signal I sent. The satellite signal wasn't perfect, but it would do.

"Give me eyes." The crisp order resonated and I switched on the specialized scope attached to mine.

"Transmitting," I murmured as I began a slow scan of the building moving from east to west across the face of it.

"Hold," she said and I locked on to what I imagined was the living room area. "I count three in residence on the main floor. Two heavily armed. The third is seated, no visible sign of weapons."

I gave her a minute, I couldn't see what she was seeing. She had to be our eyes.

"Two are definitely there as guards. To protect or restrain the target? No idea. They are positioned at seven and one from the main door. Copy?"

"Copy," I said, committing the details to memory.

"Continue scan."

We repeated the pause each time she located another person. Thankfully, there were only four others present in the house. Two were likely servants of some kind. The other pair might be bodyguards on a break since they were horizontal and on the second floor.

"Can we get eyes inside?" Her question held just a hint of teasing.

"Is that meant as a challenge or an insult?" Locke retorted.

"Yes to the former, not so much to the latter. But we've all been taking a bit of a break..."

His snort in response carried an eloquence of its own. "I'm ready to move. I have three ingress points on the second level. They didn't wire the bathroom window for security." Disapproval underscored the amusement in Locke's assessment.

Careless.

The pause between the information and her response elongated.

I didn't hurry her, nor did Locke. There was something almost elemental in the comfort I took from her studying our options. She'd map out the various paths, identify the pitfalls, and estimate the varying chances of success based on each choice.

The woman was exceptionally gifted. It was also why I trusted her calls. She never moved on one without some certainty and if she had a less than optimal outcome, she didn't let that stop her or us—she just informed us of the hazards.

"Locke, you are cleared for first ingress. Your task is to identify and paint the targets on the second level *only*. Once we clear those, you may proceed to the first floor. Understood?"

"Understood. Going radio silent. Thirty seconds."

"Copy," I exhaled along with her acknowledgement and moved my site to the second floor.

Mentally counting it down, I was ready for my first target. The scope lit up with the laser tag.

"First target acquired," I said softly.

A moment later, a laser lit up a second target.

"Second target acquired. Clear the field."

Five seconds later, Locke said, "Clear."

"Clear to fire," Patch said a beat later. It took no time to take out the first and second targets. Two bullets each. The distance suppressed the sound of the gun more effectively than the suppressor. The noise cancellation in my ear comms protected my hearing.

"Targets down," I reported.

"Confirmation?" Patch wasn't distrusting me, she was making sure nothing popped up to surprise Locke in the house. I could cover him, but we wanted one of these guys alive. So better to minimize the collateral—for *now*.

"Confirmed," Locke answered a few seconds later. "Remind me not to piss Remy off."

"You've survived it once," I informed him. "You'll be fine."

"Focus," Patch said, though a chuckle threaded the word. I'd made her smile.

"At the stairs, going silent to get to the first floor." Locke didn't wait for our acknowledgement, he just went quiet. I moved my attention to the main floor where the other three targets were located.

The drapes were open, but a sheer covered the glass. I wouldn't be taking the shot through the glass. While no glass was truly bullet *proof*, there were varieties of bullet resistant.

Those made it challenging, but not impossible. You had to plan for the time to take down the resistant glass with multiple shots. However, in the time it took to take down the glass, your targets had time to escape and shift position.

I had a .50 cal with me. As useful as the heavier firepower was, it added some limitations to accuracy. Since we needed one of these assholes alive, I'd prefer to keep that margin of error smaller.

Two beeps.

Locke was in position.

Another two beeps.

Locke was ready to move.

He waited for me, however, and I did a slow sweep with the specialized scope.

"Target one acquired," Patch told me and I marked it mentally before proceeding. "Target Three, no joy here."

The target we wanted to take with us. I moved to the next corner.

"Target two acquired."

I returned to target one. "Confirmed," she said in a tone that made me want to kiss her. At my sweep past target three to target two, she added a second, "Confirmed."

It would take me a full second and a half to move from target one to target two.

"Be ready to take down target two if he moves," I told Locke. "Clear the row."

Two beeps. An acknowledgement.

"Ignition in five," Patch began the countdown. "Four, three…"

Everything faded as I prepped for Target One.

On one, the glass exploded outward. The two charges Locke had put into place decimated the glass, cracking it at all anchor points, letting its weight and gravity do the rest.

I fired, eliminating the first target before he even finished coming into view. The second target was moving for the third, but Locke appeared in the visual.

"Hold," Patch said unnecessarily, because my finger was already off the trigger. The second guy went down with three sharp slices and a series of swift stabs. For a guy who didn't like the fight, he was damn useful in it.

I was back on target three, he had a gun in his hand.

He didn't need the hand to answer questions.

I fired, the bullet would shatter his wrist if he was lucky, but probably sever the whole damn thing if he wasn't.

"Target three down," Locke said, kicking the weapon away. "Fuck, that's messy."

"He'll live," I told him. We didn't need him to live that long, so the target's comfort was completely secondary. Besides, if he'd gotten the shot off, Patch would have been upset. I refused to give her more reasons to cry. "Secure him. I'm on my way."

CHAPTER
SEVENTEEN
PATCH

Fifteen minutes after they cleared the guards, Locke and Remy removed the target from his home. Cleanup would take too long and setting a fire would likely create more problems. There were too many trees around the dwelling.

"Leave it," I said after studying the scene via their cameras. "Let's tap their lines and I'll pull a trace on any calls they get." Pregnant silence greeted the statement. "Yes, I'm aware it's fishing, but it doesn't mean we won't get a nibble."

They didn't argue, but I did catch Remy's thoughtful gaze in Locke's camera before they split up to tap the cell phones and the land lines. They were gloved and Locke wore a tight cap. We didn't want to leave any DNA traces. Remy, on the other hand, didn't have to worry about his nonexistent hair, but he'd put on a dark cap too.

As for the target himself, one William Henry Mackintosh, he was still alive though currently unconscious and bagged for transport. The original plan had been to question him there, but cauterizing the wound where his hand used to be resulted in him screaming until he passed out.

The man had lungs.

Oddly enough, the vague pangs of guilt these types of jobs used to leave me experiencing were absent at the moment. Mackintosh was linked to Section Five. He was the architect. At least, that was the information we'd retrieved.

Memorizing a list of key names from the data I'd pulled helped identify him when the guys asked for a list of people to kill. No doubt existed within me. Mackintosh would not be walking away from any of this.

The only decision he was in control of was how fast or slow he got to die. If he answered our questions directly and without bullshit, he'd get a quick death. That said, I didn't expect him to cooperate. At least not easily.

"Found you a present," Locke said quietly and I flicked a glance to his screen. The door he'd opened accessed a computer room.

"Oh, you delightfully sexy man," I said with a slow smile. "Do you still have my thumb drives?"

"I do. Which one do you want me to plug in? Red? Or blue?"

"Red first. Download all the encrypted files. Then blue, that will leave them with nothing to work with." I checked my watch. "You have about seven minutes left on the clock. If you can't get it all downloaded by then—blow that room."

It made me a bit sick to think of the lost information, but we had priorities. Mine included getting my guys out of this and in one piece. They were already taking all the risks. I didn't doubt they weren't the best at what they did, I'd been with them on far too many jobs to question their skill or their talents.

I also valued them for far more than their professions. At the six minute mark Locke, along with Remy, left the house behind, their package in tow. They would hike back down to their car, the location staging amended for the "attack" they'd suffered. What clues had been planted would detour, at least for a while, whatever trackers were sent out.

Hopefully by the time they had anything actionable, we'd already have the answers we needed. I tracked the guys all the way back to the SUV. Once they had Mackintosh loaded and got on the road to return, I'd let myself relax then. As it was, adrenaline still sang in my veins.

"It went smoothly then?" McQuade asked and I glanced to where he leaned against the wall, arms folded. For the majority of the operation, he'd drifted in and out, followed the conversations and brought me coffee.

The reminder had me glancing at the now fresh cup steaming on the table next to me along with a sandwich. Right... "I promised to eat as soon as extraction was done."

One corner of his mouth lifted in a hint of a smile. For all his roughness, McQuade was far gentler than he let anyone else see. I had no idea why I was so special, but I appreciated it. He was a big guy, the copper in his beard seemed almost wiry in the light, though there was a hint of silver and white peppered through the darker shades.

Raising my hand like I was a scout, I said, "I know, I promised. I will dive right in as soon as—"

"Transport secure," Remy said in his beautiful voice. It was almost like receiving the most practical of roses, distinct yet sweet. "Package in the boot and we're on the road. ETA Ninety minutes. Confirm?"

I pressed down a button on the keyboard. "Confirmed. Drive safe." Ending the transmission, I leaned back. Now, all I had to do was keep a lookout for their approach.

Pushing away from the wall, McQuade placed the sandwich and coffee in front of me after nudging the keyboard out of the way. I could still reach it, but his priorities were clear.

"Pushy," I reminded him.

"I can cut the sandwich up into triangles if you want," was his only response. Though I didn't miss the flash of humor in his eyes.

Shaking my head, I wrinkled my nose at him. "I said I would eat." Then to make a point, I picked up the sandwich and took a healthy bite of it. He nodded and then retreated from my "office" space.

I washed down the bite with a long swallow of coffee. The ham and cheese was probably a simple sandwich, but it was also delightful. The cheddar was the perfect sharpness and the ham a bit salty. Still, I don't think I'd eaten a kinder meal before. The coffee, however, was the best.

Eyes closed, I took a deeper drink of it. Sweet, foamy, and rich, it enhanced the bite of the coffee's bitterness at the end. Smooth with a kick, just the way I liked it. When my eyes opened again, McQuade had come back with his own sandwich and coffee.

Instead of standing over me, he pulled up a chair and took the spot opposite my side desk. It let us look at each other while we ate. "I thought about chips," he said. "Then I remembered when you dumped the Pringles crumbs during that firefight."

Pringles crumbs?

I paused with my sandwich halfway back to my mouth. Firefight? Pringles... Surprise flickered through me. The moment the memory presented itself, however, I was glad I hadn't actually taken the bite, I would have choked.

"Thought I'd forgotten that," McQuade teased. "Hadn't you?"

"No, I just—I haven't thought about that in a long time." Like years, really. "That was our first year working together. Why do *you* remember it?"

"You cursed so colorfully and creatively," McQuade said with a shrug, the amusement still thick in his voice. "You also called me a McQuackadoodle and that lingered."

My face flamed at the reminder. Now *that* I had forgotten. "You were laughing at me." Not that it was much of a defense.

"Sugar Bear," he deadpanned. "I was taking fire from three different locations and I still needed to finish the retrieval. I didn't much care if your keyboard crunched when you typed and you were throwing out directions amidst all the cussing."

Nose wrinkled, I gave him a helpless little

shrug. "To be fair, I was more worried about losing connection with the keyboard or worse, losing sight on you in the middle of that fight. Both could have gotten you killed."

It was the first time I'd experienced genuine fear for one of my contractors. I took a bite before I let even more information out.

"I'm not complaining, Sugar Bear," he said, putting a hand on my wrist as I chewed. The light touch trapped me more effectively than a shackle.

Of all of them, McQuade didn't shy away from touch, or invading my space, or even teasing me about my memory. It was all normalized around him. They were all gentle and caring in their own ways. I loved Remy's cultured gentleness and Locke's sophisticated teasing, but I also craved Mc-Quade's blunt effortlessness.

"I was afraid," I told him, confessing the long kept secret. "I hadn't been doing the operator job for long. You were one of my first long-term clients and I thought...you might end up being one of my last if I got you killed."

I set the sandwich down with my free hand, then retrieved my coffee. Then I turned my wrist under his hand and let the weight of his palm settle against mine.

"The ambush hit when I least expected it—I know now that makes sense and I look for those types of traps, but... I hadn't really seen that coming then." They'd caught him in a crossfire while trying to close in on him from behind.

The only available exit for him meant going right between the sides firing at him. He'd have been exposed, the chance for success? Minimal. Every moment he lingered there, the greater the threat to loss of limb if not his life.

"You didn't show our panic." The assurance didn't help *now*, but it did make me smile. "You were so fierce and your cussing so damn heated that it took my mind off the situation."

"Liar," I said, though the softness in my voice robbed it of any sting. "You never stop thinking." Sipping the coffee, I enjoyed the flash of surprise flickering through his expression before he shook his head.

"I think you vastly underestimate your appeal, Sugar Bear. You also didn't stop thinking. In fact, you were the one who then decided to blow that transformer a block over."

A kernel of pride fluttered through me and popped like it had just hit the hot oil. "I gambled."

"You won," he countered. "What makes you a good operator, what has always made you the best at what you do, is that you don't stop thinking. You look for solutions that may only have a ten percent chance of working, the bet the odds no one else will see it coming."

The compliments buoyed me. "You're just biased."

McQuade laughed. The sound came right up from his belly and seemed to shake his whole body. It was a vibrant, deep, and masculine sound that threatened to sweep me away.

"Considering how many times that brain of yours has saved my ass? Yes, I'm one hundred percent biased. You are the goddamn best at what you do, Sugar Bear. You got it, you can flaunt it."

I wanted to roll my eyes and shake it all off. The level of pride in his statements, and the embrace each one offered just added to my embarrassment. At the same time, I treasured every single word.

"Tell me the truth... how many operators did you have before me?" I didn't want to fish for compliments, but I was genuinely curious. Another swallow of coffee and I tapped two keys on the keyboard to switch the monitors to exterior cameras. A couple of tractor trailers had pulled in out there.

One was parked a few slots down from us. The other was already pulling out. There were two cars on the far side. One a family and the other just a single driver. Looked like they were stopping for a bathroom break. So far, no one appeared to be "working" the information station inside.

I imagined they had a cleaning staff that came out periodically. If we still had company when the guys got back, we'd have to relocate so they could get back aboard with the car without drawing attention.

"Two," McQuade said and I snapped my attention back to him. "I did one mission each with them. They weren't my people. Then I got you... third time's the charm."

"Seriously?"

He shrugged. "Personality conflicts. Not everyone appreciates me for the charmer I am."

That did make me smile. "You are pretty perfect."

He gave my hand a squeeze. "Thanks for noticing." Only his attention wasn't on me now, it was on the monitors behind me, I twisted to watch a dark SUV enter and begin a slow drive toward the parking slots.

Too slow a drive.

The rasp of metal on leather told me he'd freed his gun from the holster, but he hadn't let go of my hand.

"Wait," I said, tracking the car as it all but crawled toward a parking spot. Dark SUV didn't have to mean government or reclamation agents. It didn't have to mean anything.

Still, when it finally pulled into a slot, I swore my nerves had been pulled too taut. Then the driver's side door opened, and a woman exited the vehicle at a dead run for the bathroom.

Relief spilled through me like water being released from a drain. The rasp of metal on leather told me he'd put the gun back as we tracked the woman's mad dash for the facilities. Then I glanced back at the car. No other passengers were visible.

"Give me a closeup on the bathrooms," McQuade said and I split the screen, keeping an eye on the cars while I switched to the camera on the bathroom doors. There wasn't one inside the bathroom and we all needed boundaries.

That was definitely one for me.

One by one, the other cars left, but it took our friend in the SUV a *long* time to leave the bathroom. While McQuade stayed fixed on it, I scrolled through the other angles to make sure we hadn't lost track of her.

By the time she finally emerged, however, I

wasn't the only one blowing out a harsh breath. She looked pale and sweaty. Her walk back to the car was almost pained. Road trip and upset bowels were not a good combination.

Despite the lightness of our earlier chat, neither of us relaxed even after the SUV finally pulled out and returned to the highway.

Just fifteen more minutes and the guys would be here.

Fifteen more minutes and we could put miles between us and this place.

Why did I think that we were asking for a lot with fifteen more minutes?

CHAPTER
EIGHTEEN
MCQUADE

William Henry Mackintosh expired three hours and forty-seven minutes after he arrived courtesy of Remy and Locke. It took a little under thirty minutes for him to regain consciousness, then another twenty of him screaming before he passed out again. Finally, at the ninety-minute mark, we got him awake and talking.

Granted it was another couple of hours for the gibberish to be translated into English, after which I put a bullet in his head. It ended his suffering and mine.

Irritating man.

Locke skipped the questioning by moving up to drive. We didn't invite Patch into the interrogation. She didn't need to see this. Thankfully, she didn't ask so we got to avoid that fight.

Remy and I bagged the body up silently. The plastic layers on the walls made cleanup straightforward. I stripped off the plastic body suit that kept his blood off me. Once everything was bagged and stored, I checked my watch.

"We still need to find a place to get rid of him." One drawback of being on the move constantly. We were going to have to make use of multiple dump sites. We were still in Nevada and heading south again.

"We've got some options in Arizona," Remy said before opening the door to the soundproof room where we'd worked. I was a half-step behind him. The door closed with a pressurized hiss. It required a code to open it.

I didn't try to fool myself that my sugar bear could get in there if she wanted. I just had to trust that she didn't want to. "Who do you know in Arizona?"

To be fair, he'd trusted my sourced support in Colorado. While I didn't expect it from someone with his pedigree and background, I could probably trust it. The real mistake would be assuming he didn't have contacts of his own.

"I know quite a few people," he said, a faint smirk on his lips.

I swallowed my snarkier response as I caught sight of Patch scowling at her computer screen like it had betrayed her.

"Problem?" I asked, bypassing Remington even as he also headed in her direction.

She spared an almost distracted look at me. "No, I was examining the infrastructure of Mad Dogs' various enterprises. They have diversified in this damn near elegant pattern, and it's pissing me off."

"How is it elegant?" I moved to lean against the corner of her desk where I could see the screens she studied. "Businesses are businesses."

"Yes, and no. All businesses, even super-secret government shady ones, leave a paper trail. It's how they get caught. You can pretend you don't exist all you want, but purchases have to be made, buildings inspected, and taxes paid."

Taxes. I snorted. "You'd think even the government could avoid that one."

She shot me an amused look over the edge of her glasses. I hadn't realized she even wore them. Apparently, they were for long hours focused on the computer.

"No one screws with the IRS. Not even the U.S. government itself." Her droll tone was at odds with her humor, though she sobered swiftly. "While Section Five might have begun as a government operation, I don't think it's stayed that way. In fact, I have a feeling it's a hellish set of nesting dolls that took advantage of top secret status to build a profitable information network under the umbrella of national security."

I turned that nugget of information over.

"Any evidence or just a gut feeling?" I didn't doubt her instincts, but actionable intel was always best. It made my gut burn to think we didn't get as much out of Mackintosh as I would have liked.

"Gut feeling," she admitted, leaning back in her chair and rolling her head from side to side. There was a distinctive sound of clicking as if she'd popped her neck. I didn't miss the faint grimace that flickered across her face.

Straightening, I settled a hand against the back of her neck and began to work the taut muscles. They were locked up hard. "Tell me—" I spared Remy a look where he stood not even two feet away. "Tell us about the gut feeling."

Not answering immediately, she let her chin drop toward her chest as I continued the slow massage of the cramped muscles. A low groan escaped her and I accepted it for the encouragement it was.

"It's just... *fuck* right there." The low, throaty sound was definitely something I wanted to spend more time coaxing from her. "I didn't realize how sore my neck was..."

Another sigh, but she leaned into the massage so I kept the pressure steady and worked the area where the muscles seemed to be loosening.

"Mad Dogs is incorporated as Mad Dogs Inc, literally. The company itself is just a holding company. An umbrella corp that allows multiple shell games to be played simultaneously via a network of businesses from MD Professional Resources, that provides office support, to MD Outfitters that provides equipment for hiking and extreme sports."

Another little sigh left her. Those low sounds were the most unexpected aphrodisiac.

"Office support—they're looking for industrial espionage?" Remington's elegant, if irritating, accent put the brakes on my personal fantasies. Not that I could indulge them at the moment.

"Possibly," she said, lifting her head to look at him even as she leaned into my touch.

"That would make the Outfitters the wet work contractors and more." I didn't need her to confirm it, but it made perfect sense. In fact, it made almost *too* much sense.

It was the outsourcing and the outfitters that had gone for her. Who had held her. I locked eyes with the assassin and read equal intent in his gaze. The tempest of anger in the air sizzled against my skin, but like me, he locked it down as we looked at Patch.

"Yes," she said, leaning more into the contact with my hand. I shifted the massage to stroke the column of her neck. "That's the problem. While they all exist under the same umbrella, they don't share any kind of visible network or staff ties."

So they filed different paperwork. I didn't see a problem with that.

"Also, there are at least eight other 'MD' operations that have been incorporated or dissolved over the last fifteen years. The most recent one to dissolve included a complete shut down of the whole structure. On the surface, it looks like they filed Chapter 11. Restructured the debt and the assets until the organization essentially vanished as a new 'MD' took over."

"I presume there is something about this most recent one that bothers you," Remington said slowly, his tone conveying more than anything else the careful weighing of what she was and wasn't saying.

When she tilted her head back to rest against my hand, I stilled. The fall of her hair over my wrist tickled the skin. I was glad I'd washed up before touching her. The long sigh escaping her seemed to resonate with me.

"They apparently liquidated the operation a little over five years ago." No emotion colored those heavy words. Over five years earlier...

"You believe they liquidated the operation you worked for," I said, matching her tone evenly. I wouldn't shy away from that grim reality. No matter how personal this was for her, and I didn't make the mistake of thinking this wasn't personal, but *she* hadn't done anything wrong.

If they shut it down and scrubbed their employees, that was on them. Most black site operations, especially an off the books, private one that avoided answering to any kind of government oversight would find a few bodies a lot easier to deal with than any questions.

"Yes," she said, then swiveled back to the screen. She pulled away from contact with me as she scooted forward. You could practically see the shields going up around her. Her screens switched, information scrolling as she accessed their histories and paperwork.

I skimmed it, but I kept more of my attention on her than what was on the screen. What she'd found upset her more than she was willing to admit. Based on the way Remington tracked her motions, I didn't doubt he read the same into her response.

If it was another target, we'd deal with it. But I didn't think this was strictly a target or an information deep dive. Clamping my jaw closed, I forced myself to wait her out.

"I was trying to figure out what the hell Mad Dog had to do with Section Five... A cluster of operations based around a label like 'mad dog' doesn't fit. Even if it started as a government sanctioned black op that went off books, why 'Mad Dog'? Why sound like a liquor? Or a motorcycle gang?"

Now emotion bled into her voice. Irritation fluttered between each of the words—no, not irritation. Disgust. Something about the whole thing truly disgusted her.

"What did you find?" Remington maintained a kind of cool presence I wished I could offer. At the moment, I'd like to split a few skulls open, starting with the guys who'd made her feel this way. It wasn't what she needed from me right now though, so I kept my temper locked down.

If the fucking Brit could give her the kind of steadiness she craved, then I'd back his play. She stilled at his question, then shifted her gaze toward him. I could almost feel the tension spilling off of her and adding to the earlier turbulence.

"MadOg," she said, pronouncing it "Mad Dog" as we'd been calling it, but then she spelled it out. "M-a-d-O-g."

I still wasn't seeing the connection. They'd skipped the extra D, made it sounds like Mad Original, but that didn't seem like the point. Or was it...?

"Five letters," Remington said, seeming to hone right in on it and she snapped her fingers then pointed at him.

"Section Five." With that, she hit two keys on the keyboard and a wealth of information populated the screens. The keyword seemed to all be MadOg. Still mad dog, but not. The MadOg, the one she'd worked for, was listed as a failing operation.

Everything had been liquidated, even the equipment sold along with the real estate.

She'd taken their secrets, then vanished before they could silence her. To cover their own trail, they shut it all down. Afterward, they erased all the witnesses. Cold-blooded, ruthless, and efficient.

All three of her screens began to fill in with more and more connections. Umbrella was not the right term. It was more like an iceberg. An iceberg where far more of it was below the surface. You only saw a sliver of the truth.

"It's a web, a violent, bloody web that focuses on profit and loss. To keep their books balanced, they have no problem going into the red. They'll bathe in it if they have to." The chill in her voice didn't belong there. I dropped my gaze from the intricate maze she'd uncovered. The darkness in her eyes pulled at me.

"It's not your fault," I said. Maybe she wasn't ready to hear it. Maybe she would never be ready, but I'd say it every damn day until she believed me. "What they did is on them, not you."

Head tilted, she closed her eyes. I could almost feel her shutting me out. Tugging her chair backward, I swung her around.

I had to brace my legs as the truck slowed. I wasn't sure if it was traffic or if Locke was pulling off for a break. Right now, the only thing that mattered was Patch.

"I know you don't want to hear that," I continued and crouched in front of her. I didn't want to loom over her and intimidate her into believing me. I could do that, but it was pointless. Instead, I gripped the arms of her chair and locked my gaze on her face, practically willing her to open her eyes.

"If I hadn't taken the information to blackmail them into leaving me alone..."

"You did what you had to do to survive." I believed that with every molecule of my body. "You could have gone to the media or warned your coworkers. Sure. They would still have shut you down and all those people would still have been scrubbed. The only difference is you would have been scrubbed with them. At least in the best case scenario."

That jerked her eyes open and she frowned. "Best case?"

"Yep." I kept my hands on the chair and not on her no matter how much I longed to drag her into my arms and hold her. "Best case. Cause worst case, they would have painted you as the bad guy. Wrecked the life of every single person you knew. Your family, your friends, your neighbor, the local dog walker. They would have painted you with a violent brush. In the end, you'd have no idea what was real and what wasn't."

Fear edged out grief, but neither could stop the anger surging into her eyes. *That's it. Get pissed, Sugar Bear. Get mad. Those sons of bitches will cheerfully fuck you over. We're not letting them do that.*

I wanted to shout it all from the rooftops, but she wasn't ready to hear that yet.

"In the end, you're just another crackpot. An out-there conspiracy theorist that resurfaces as an urban legend now and then. It's even better than plausible deniability for them. Because they'd have already debunked the rumors of their existence by proving you had no idea what you were talking about."

Every word I said seemed to generate even more fire in her eyes.

"I hate them," she whispered.

"Me too," I said and now I put a hand on her knee.

"As do I," Remington added his hand to her shoulder, then met my gaze over her head. She'd given us a kill list whether she realized it or not. I nodded once.

MadOg, or whatever they wanted to call themselves, were living on borrowed time. Still, neither of us said a word. It had to come from her.

She had to be ready to face the next step.

It didn't take her long. "How do we stop them?"

Not that I'd had a single doubt about her. My sugar bear was a fighter.

CHAPTER

NINETEEN

PATCH

Tracking MadOg took us from the desert of Nevada towards Texas. A small town settled somewhere between Hill Country and the Gulf of Mexico. Hours of research and two satellite hacks later, I knew not a hell of a lot about Juniper, Texas.

The town had a population of 2,145 people as of the last census. Over the course of five years, three Silicon Valley companies relocated to Juniper, bringing with them a huge infusion of cash to promote the population boom.

Combined investments added three new subdivisions to a town that had all of one main road—Main Street—with a barber, a grocer, a beauty salon, a veterinarian and the town doctor, who worked out of the same building as the mayor. The doctor and the vet took turns serving as the medical examiner.

It was like something straight out of a movie, or maybe a CW teen romance show. Even as I dunked on the idea mentally, I knew damn well I'd absolutely watch it. The town only had one school, and most of the high school age kids took a bus to a town forty minutes away for classes.

If the middle of nowhere had a name, Juniper would be it. The place made me itch. I didn't sleep that much even when the guys got cranky about it. Real rest proved elusive, not with the dark dreams that kept haunting me.

When it wasn't shadows grabbing for me to drag me under it was attacks from actual monsters, like a giant alligator crushing the engine and beginning to tear into the vehicle I was in.

McQuade helped, but even his presence couldn't drive them away. We had too much to do and I needed to know more about Juniper, the MadOg operations there. While I'd only linked one of the companies to MadOg, I suspected all of them were but I couldn't find the link to prove it.

All I had was my gut instinct. It was that gut that tied itself up into knots as McQuade, Locke, and Remington worked out their plan to surveil the town and its inhabitants. We'd save the new company campuses for *after* they got a look at the town.

With only one car, they couldn't arrive in town separately. They'd debated it, the pros and the cons. Pros, they could gather different information with different approaches.

Cons? They would be separated and it would be harder for all three to return here in case of an emergency. That led to another debate, did all three go or did one of them stay here?

Eventually, the argument circled back to the beginning. They all noticed different things and had different specialties. That meant for the most efficient manner of information gathering, all of them would go.

It was early afternoon when they left. The truck was parked at a rest stop about ten miles out of the town. The new subdivisions were another five miles south and two miles east. The company campuses were solidly on the other side of town.

I double-checked their comm connections and nodded at the weapons the guys had left me secured within easy reach.

"Be safe," Remington ordered before he gripped my chin, tilted my head back and kissed me solidly. It robbed me of all breath. His flirty wink made me happy that I was seated.

No sooner did he back away than Locke took his place. He gripped the arms of my office chair and swooped in for a kiss that was all teeth and tongue. My hammering heart seemed to triple its pace.

Where Remy's kiss had been as sweet as the tea he drank, there was the solid bitterness of coffee and the hazelnut creamer that Locke preferred to flavor his kiss.

Heat flushed through me and scorched my face. I probably looked like a boiled lobster as I turned my attention to McQuade who'd watched as both men kissed me.

"I'll be with you boys in a minute," he said as Remy and Locke seemed ready to wait. They eyed each other, then him before Locke focused on me. I waved them off. McQuade wanting a moment of privacy was fine with me.

Frankly, I craved it myself. Having all of them

watching me as they each delivered their kisses unlocked a whole new kink. Now was definitely not the time to give into that particular desire. It definitely wasn't the place.

McQuade didn't move until Locke and Remy vanished around the divider that separated my office from the other living spaces. Once they were gone, he closed the distance between us and reached for my hand.

With one light tug, he pulled me up and plucked the headset off me with his free hand. The wild heat from earlier still scorched my face. When I stumbled a half-step, McQuade steadied me even as I caught myself with a hand pressed to his chest.

"Sugar Bear," he said, his voice dipping into that low growl that made me shiver. I couldn't look anywhere else but him. The magnetism in his gaze kept me in place even more firmly than his hands.

My throat went dry and the slam of my heart grew even louder in my ears. "John?"

Where his voice held command, mine was far less certain. I'd grown so used to their presence even as it baffled me to lean into trusting others. But I'd meant it when I told Locke that I trusted him.

Somewhere along the way, I'd discovered a real trust for them and their motives. They asked me for nothing, other than a list of targets. They never had to come and look for me, yet they had. The guys had other work, jobs they did and rather than hurry this along, they'd put the rest of their lives on hold for me.

Digging my fingers into McQuade's chest, I

used the steady thump of his heart to slow my own. He said nothing, his gaze riveted on mine. It was like we were falling into each other, this slowly decaying orbit with one or both of us at the center.

Collision was imminent. I could feel the stroke of his gaze over me when he glanced at my lips. Despite the lingering caress of his attention, he still didn't move. Need splintered inside of me. I fisted both hands into his shirt. I wasn't sure whether I dragged him down to me or pushed up to meet him. Maybe I did both. His mouth crashed into mine.

The ferocity in his kiss left me dazed. He slid an arm around my waist and lifted me. No more stress on my neck tilting it back to gaze up at him. The softness of his beard alternately teased my skin and rasped against it too.

Thrusting my tongue against his, I savored the delightful tease of dueling with him. Every move I made, McQuade mirrored. If I bit at his lip, he nibbled mine. If I swept my tongue in to taste him, he devoured me. I wanted to pull the tie from his hair, so I could sink my hands into the thickness of it.

"Sugar Bear," he growled against my mouth. Desire pulled taut in my belly even as shivers cascaded over my skin.

"That name is growing on me," I whispered in response. I felt more than saw his smile.

"Is that so?"

"Hmm-hmm." Another kiss. "You need to go."

"Yes," he agreed, kissing me again. "I do."

"Be safe?" It was as much a request as an order.

"You too," he retorted. Another biting kiss and

then he put me on my feet. Thankfully, I didn't embarrass myself by stumbling on weak legs or falling on my ass. "Sugar Bear." He winked.

I ran a finger against my mouth, still tasting him, as he went to follow the guys. Still trembling, I dropped back into my chair and retrieved the headset he'd plucked off. The sound of the car starting filled the interior, then they dropped the ramp and drove out.

The external doors were already closing, sealing with a hiss. One finger stroke brought up all exterior cameras. We were still in the clear. The SUV appeared briefly as it drove away.

Blowing out a breath, I concentrated on getting my pulse under control. No more distractions. I needed to get ahead of them. Small town or not, it had some cameras. Not everything was wired—rude on their part. The guys had some equipment to drop for me depending on the availability.

Headset on, I took a sip of coffee before punching in the code to connect to their comms.

"Patch online."

"We're receiving you clearly, luv," Remy said, a smile in his voice. It was odd how comforting I found the sound. The familiarity of it settled in my bones.

"Want us to pick you up some souvenirs while we're in town?" Locke asked.

"Hmm, not sure this place even has a gift shop."

"Just means we need to be creative," Locke said, there was no mistaking the suggestiveness in his voice. "I can be quite creative when required."

I snorted.

"Focus," McQuade said with a rumble. "Let Sugar Bear work."

"You tell him, Sugar Lips," I retaliated. "Though, we can multi-task, you know."

Silence greeted my statement and I had to suppress another smile. Having all three of them on line might be normal, but having them on the same line was definitely new.

A snort of laughter finally echoed down the line as McQuade said, "So that's how it is?"

I grinned. "Yes, that's exactly how it is."

"We'll check in with you once we get to town," Remy said, amusement salting each word.

"Understood, Patch out." I cut the line. They could initiate the next contact. For now, I worked on getting into whatever systems Juniper had that were connected to the net.

Funnily enough, the cafe and the grocery store had the easiest to access systems. What security they had in place was utterly pitiful. Then again, their information wasn't precisely top secret either.

The grocery store had three cameras. Unsurprisingly, two focused on the entrances located in front and back. The third on the grocery till itself. Not much appeared to be going on in the building. So I set that to one side, then brought up the cafe.

Interesting... the cafe had six cameras, including one pointed at their oversized walk in cold pantry and the freezers.

Had problems with employees taking food? Maybe the boss was just big on the overkill. I could appreciate it. Even better, one of their cameras pointed out onto Main Street. It gave me a better view of the sleepy little town.

Foot traffic appeared heavy, and there were four men meeting just outside what was the mayor's office. What I wouldn't give for some zoom and enhance. The fact they had cameras at all was amazing.

Beggars could not be choosers. The pixelization made identifying the men tricky, but I screen captured as much of them as I could, then brought up a program to try and clean it up. It could extrapolate data based on what features were clear.

Not perfect, but I had a photo of the mayor online as well as the other town personnel. It would take some time to see if any of these guys were him. The more information I could gather before the guys got there, the better.

Once I had the cafe camera feeds locked down, I took a good look at their town hall building. It seemed distinctly odd that they didn't have any cameras for me to hijack. Stranger still that there was better security and overwatch on the cafe than the mayor or sheriff's office.

What about their local jail? Wouldn't they need something there? I was still puzzling over that when my comm beeped and I clicked in to connect with the guys.

"Talk to me..."

CHAPTER
TWENTY

LOCKE

J uniper, Texas was hot, dusty, and almost a
cliche in how small it was. As advertised, there
were a handful of buildings lining the dusty
main street. The street itself boasted cracks and
potholes that you'd think they could fix easily
enough—it was only one road.

Apparently not, though. Most of the buildings
were a max of two stories. Made sense, they didn't
need more space. The largest building was the
school...

The fence around it had plenty of holes and
tears. The playground equipment was sad and
faded. It was also completely empty of children. I
checked my watch as I studied the school from between the general store and the local laundry that
was also a bait shop, and boasted a Notary Public
on staff.

A bait shop meant they had to have fishing
somewhere. But I hadn't seen any water on the way
in. Maybe it was somewhere else. What I had seen

was dust. More dust. Some rocks. Dust. The occasional hay field. And dust.

McQuade bumped my shoulder as he passed me and I fell into step behind him with Remy following me. We'd snagged attention when we'd pulled in at the diner. Leaving the car there had been a choice. There were also cameras set up on the front and back. Patch would keep an eye out on us and the car.

Bells hanging on the door rattled and rang in the most discordant fashion. It was definitely not the right note. Kind of like the town itself. The whole place rubbed me the wrong way.

We split up. I was sliding listening devices into place as I checked out the merchandise. One under a shelf here. Another on the edge of a display there. Places where we could maximize the coverage.

McQuade headed back toward the freezers and Remy kind of drifted along in my wake. Like McQuade and me, Remy wore jeans, a t-shirt, and boots with a baseball cap over his shiny bald head. Keeping silent had been my suggestion.

We were already going to stand out, strangers in a strange land and all that. His accent would be a great big red flag waved at a bull. No, we'd keep that in our back pockets thank you very much.

The man at the register stared at me as I wandered about. I looked at everything but didn't pick up any one item. Instead of reacting to the hard gaze of the clerk, I focused on getting my devices into place.

The store was a lot bigger inside than I expected. There was also a counter for a pharmacist, but the sign hanging there said Closed, and to find Earl at the Vet's office if it was an emergency.

I could barely suppress the shudder that wanted to crawl through me. People in small towns wore lots of hats, but I was pretty sure this might be my definition of hell. Give me my big cities with their noisy streets, pollution, street vendors, hawkers, and street performers working their hustle between buildings that blocked out the sun.

Anonymity was like candy and I craved it. Fading into the woodwork was a fuckload harder in a place where everyone knew your name, your business, and probably your secrets.

No. Fucking. Thank you.

"Can I help you find something?" The barest hint of a Texas drawl feathered over the words.

Dressed in the brownest uniform I'd ever seen —brown trousers, brown shirt, brown jacket, brown cowboy hat, and for fuck's sake, a brown tie —the deputy eyed me with a kind of suspicious friendliness. That was a challenging combo. I wanted to give him two points for the effort.

"No, thanks," I said, adopting a bare hint of the same drawl he'd used. When manufacturing an accent, it was always better to not lay it on too thick. Besides, Texas was huge. I could be from just about anywhere. "Just trying to make a list in my head. Forgot to make one before we left."

The click at the end of my statement was a little tsk. The first time I'd heard it, Patch had been scolding me for moving too fast. She just did this little click with her tongue at the end of the scold.

I kind of liked it.

Fit this character I was playing.

"Might help you remember more to write it down," the deputy said, some of his friendliness sanding away and leaving only the suspicion. "You just passing through?"

"Uh oh," Patch murmured in my ear. "Someone doesn't like you."

"Maybe," I said, as much for her as it was for him. Hell, the quick smile touching my lips was definitely all about her. "Might stick around a while. You never know."

"Is that right?" The deputy eyed me like I'd kicked his dog or something. Kind of insulting. I didn't kick dogs. Might kick this asshole if he didn't fuckoff.

The man shifted his gaze to behind me. Remy had already let me know he was there with a faint drag of his step. This was a recent development. If we were all going to be living in such close quarters, he and McQuade needed to make sounds when they walked. They were too damn quiet and I was going to end up stabbing them or something.

"Could be," I said, giving him a smile that was all teeth. "Thanks for asking, Deputy. I always appreciate a friendly town." *Also, you can go suck a dick*, I finished in my head.

I circled round him, not giving him too wide a berth, but not invading his space and moving on to the next aisle.

"What about you?" The deputy stepped in front of Remy, stopping him from following. "You just passing through with your..."

Patch sighed. "His name is Leroy Jenks Wilson.

He was born and raised in Juniper. His daddy is the sheriff, and he's got 'bully' written all over him. Lots of petty shit with the law in the big cities, nothing locally."

Daddy probably cleaned it up.

"His father probably swept it all under the rug. It's a place where everyone knows everyone else. He's got power and he isn't afraid to exercise it."

"You don't say," I murmured, then pivoted as the deputy jerked his gaze to me.

"What was that?"

"Robbie there can't talk," I told the deputy. "He can't say what he's doing here. Though, you could probably hazard a guess that since he's with me, he might be passing through. He might not."

I was all smiles, and very friendly.

"He don't look like he's got something wrong with him." It was official, I would like to add burying Leroy Jenks here in the desert sooner rather than later.

He was fucking annoying.

"Son," McQuade said, his voice deeper and gruffer than I'd ever heard him before. "Maybe you should walk along before you give a man who served his country any more grief."

McQuade just stepped right into the deputy's space, blocking him from Remy. The deputy wasn't a particularly small man, but he wasn't anywhere near as tall as McQuade and had to be at least thirty to forty pounds lighter on the muscle.

I had to wipe the smile off my face before I started to grin like an idiot. Deputy Wilson actually paled and there was just the finest sheen of sweat on his brow.

"I didn't see a uniform," he said, not quite stuttering the words. "You have to understand, Mister..."

"Sir," McQuade corrected him, his expression could have been carved from granite.

"What?" Deputy Wilson stumbled to a halt.

"You called me 'mister,' the correct address is *sir*."

"Yes, sir," the deputy said almost automatically. "Sorry, sir."

Not laughing took every ounce of my effort.

"Better. Now son, maybe you should just go on about your day and your business. You clearly have a job to do. We're just here to get some supplies and take a look around the town."

None of which was a lie.

"Might even head over to that nice diner where we parked. Been stuck eating their grub for the last few weeks. Always ready for something better."

"I see," Deputy Wilson absolutely floundered now. He'd lost the thread here, utterly surrendered it to McQuade's authority. I could feel bad for the little shit, but he was a little shit. "You might ask Ms. Nora about the pie. She always makes a fine cherry pie this time of year."

"Well, I haven't had a fine cherry pie in a while," McQuade answered. "I'll have to do that. Thanks, son. Now... don't let us keep you any longer."

We didn't move though. McQuade's posture made it clear that *we* were not going to be the ones who surrendered the ground. Deputy Wilson here would be the one who walked out.

The standoff, or what it was, lasted for another thirty seconds. Deputy Wilson could not hold McQuade's gaze, he kept shooting a glance at me or Remy then tried to go back to McQuade.

The beads of sweat on his forehead increased and one slid down his cheek. Finally, he jerked off his hat and waved it at himself like he was too warm. "Well, if you have any questions... I'll be around at the sheriff's office most likely. We're a tight little town."

"Sounds good." McQuade still didn't move or back off. The deputy retreated a step, then another, before he finally turned on his heel and stalked out of the little store. The discordant jangle as the door slammed echoed through the place.

"Nicely done, Sugar Lips. Maybe I should call you Sugar Tongue."

I choked and even Remy wore a hint of a grimace, but McQuade was all smiles. "We'll discuss that later." The unspoken "Sugar Bear" hung off the end of the sentence.

"I look forward to it. I'm picking up all the new mics. We need to add more cameras. So let's finish up in here gentlemen and you should probably buy something since you chased off the deputy."

Yeah, I felt *real* bad about that. Not rolling my eyes, I lifted my chin toward McQuade. "You find anything we need?"

"A couple of items," he said, his thoughtful gaze sweeping the place. I didn't wonder too much about what he saw. The store itself was tidy, if dilapidated and aged. The linoleum had definitely seen better days. The shelves had taken on a gray cast, though they'd likely been a cream color at one time.

Whoever looked after this place definitely cared about it. The stock was stacked in neat rows and it was all managed with a kind of rigid tidiness I could respect. Yet, all that work couldn't erase the weathering of time marching through the space.

If they made enough to keep it operational, it didn't likely leave much over for improvements. Probably had to make due with what they had and for years, just cleaning probably did it.

The cracks in the linoleum betrayed more than just age. It betrayed fading to obscurity. Shaking off that melancholy, I headed toward the produce section. It wasn't the best, but it all looked fresh.

There was no meat counter, but the sign said you could leave a message for the butcher about the cuts you needed. He only came by twice a week. Small towns gave me the damn hives. Remy continued in my shadow, though he paused at a display and pulled a snow globe off the shelf.

Weird place for one. The circle left behind on the glass said it had been there a while. It was mostly dusted, but you couldn't get it all if you didn't move the items. The piece inside the snowglobe was a miniature Texas and a tree.

Remy thrust it at me and I gave a little shrug. Sure, why not. A couple of new shoppers came in as we gathered some random items—bread, Ding Dongs, a *box* of exceptionally cheap wine, batteries cause they were always useful, and a couple of paper maps that were at the register.

The clerk glanced from me to McQuade, but his gaze just slid right over Remy. For his part, Remy just kept quiet and his gaze wandering. No doubt he'd heard the part about "Robbie" not being able to talk.

When the clerk rang up the total, I didn't say a word about the markup on the items, kid was not that slick. I just peeled off a few twenties and paid for it in cash. I even dropped some pennies into the little dish for those who might be short.

Items bagged up, we made our way out. Not even four steps along the path that would take us toward the beauty shop and barbers, I could feel the eyes on us.

More, I started tracking the placement of people. A guy hung out on the porch of one business, rocked back on two legs of his chair. Another worked on a car on the street—or at least he pretended too. He had the hood up and was unscrewing the carburetor cover.

The little town was being awfully precious about their secrets. A man left the sheriff's office across the street, strolling out slowly. His hat was low, hiding his eyes, and he was dressed in the same shitty brown. He was older and boasted a paunch that came from one too many beers while eating a bit too much grease.

Deputy Wilson's daddy no doubt.

"Boys," Patch exhaled softly, the whisper of her voice like a blast of fresh air in the growing oppression of the hot and humid air. "We have three cars incoming, and there's a fourth one that just pulled into the diner and parked right next to the SUV."

"We got their attention," McQuade said with a satisfied smile.

We had at that. But even as I kept my head on a swivel, there was a question chewing on me. It was almost lunchtime. Why couldn't we hear kids playing over at that school? And where were the women? Kids meant women, right?

"Come on," McQuade said, slapping me on the shoulder. "I'm in the mood for some cherry pie."

"Be careful," Patch admonished.

"I'm always careful," McQuade said, adding a little swagger to his steps as he led the way back up the street. If we were gonna be watched, he was apparently determined to put on a show.

"No," Patch said. "You're not. But I've got eyes on you."

That... that relaxed a lot of the tension this place had pulled taut in me. We had Patch's back and she had ours. This place might hold the next clue to find the bastards after her.

Cherry pie was beginning to sound *really* good.

CHAPTER
TWENTY-ONE
REMY

The diner held a half-dozen customers. A couple of farmer types holding up space at the counter. Another pair at a back table with a game of checkers in front of them. The waitress was just putting on another pot of coffee as we walked in.

Every eye in the place seemed to be on us. The man in the booth nearest us had a newspaper open in front of him and the crossword half-filled out. He studied us carefully. The only one watching without making a show of it was the bearded black man four seats back.

He had his head down, hands wrapped around his coffee cup and a book open that he wasn't reading. I couldn't quite get a read on his age, the beard offered some camouflage for his face and the lowered eyes meant I couldn't quite see the lines around his eyes.

Everyone else made no pretense of openly studying us. The door to the back opened, letting out steam and the smell of frying grease. The cook wanted to get a look at us too.

The waitress finally turned toward us. Dressed in a powder blue shirt dress uniform with a cute apron over the front that had definitely seen better days. She had salt and pepper hair, aged lines marked her face from too much time in the sun. The pinched look to her mouth wasn't remotely encouraging. The cool assessment in her eyes told me a great deal about how she was taking our weight and measure.

Giving her our back would be a mistake. Noted.

Three facts about Juniper presented themselves in the eerie tableau of the diner. The waitress was the first woman we'd seen since we got here. Not counting her, not a person in the place appeared over forty. Though her time in the sun may be hiding her age.

"You are open, right?" McQuade was asking because the waitress hadn't moved or said a word. It was like he jolted them all back to action with the statement.

"Sure are. Grab yourself a table and I'll be over in a minute."

"Thanks." McQuade swung his head briefly to meet my gaze. He didn't like this place anymore than I did. It was full of bad sight lines. He cut a glance to Locke once then back to me and I nodded.

I'd take one side, McQuade would take the other. We'd watch each other's backs and keep Locke covered. With that in mind, I followed him to a booth closer to the black man. McQuade might have continued past him, but I tapped the table once and he pivoted.

I slid in on the side that would let me look past McQuade to the man who glanced up so briefly, I nearly missed it. His eyes widened a fraction when his gaze struck mine. He hunched his shoulders a little more and frowned at his book.

Filing the behavior away, I leaned back in a stretch and identified everyone in their place. The waitress hustled over with the menus and slid them onto the table. "Breakfast is over, but I might can talk Big Bob into doing some bacon or something if you want."

"That's fine," Locke said, his voice so smooth and easy with the drawl he'd picked up off the deputy. Useful skill, but also creepy. "We heard a rumor about cherry pie and how fine it is."

The hard lines around the waitress's eyes relaxed a fraction as she smiled. It took me a moment to register it, but she was blushing. All Locke had done was say something about pie and smile.

McQuade hid a smirk with a cough. "Yeah," he added in his gruff voice. "The deputy told us not to miss out. That you made the best pie in the county."

"An endorsement like that," Locke said as he picked up the thread, "definitely must be followed."

"Well," the waitress said pulling a pen from behind her ear before she smoothed down her skirt. She wore a name tag that read "Janice." "As it happens, we baked up fresh pie today and they've had just enough time to cool."

"What are the chances we can get it with a

scoop of ice cream?" Locke put his hands over his heart like he was just begging for it.

"Pretty good," she answered, then gave his shoulder a slap with her little order check book. "Flirting will get you everything."

He chuckled.

"Well, Janice," Locke said smoothly. "May we get three cups of coffee. We're all big fans of coffee and pie with a little ice cream to cut the sugar."

Bloody prick. I didn't scowl at him. I was not a fan of coffee and he damn well knew it.

"I'll get that for you right now..."

"Hey, Janice..." One of the guys in the back called.

"Wait your turn, Tony, I've got real customers here." She didn't even look in his direction. "Let me grab your coffee then I'll go get that pie for you."

"Thanks, Janice."

He wasn't even laying it on thick, it was just natural charisma. Started making sense how he waltzed in and out of places.

"Have to admit, I'm impressed, Justus." The warm compliment in Patch's words made me wish I'd been the one doing the charming. "Don't let it go to your head. The waitress is calling someone in the back. I'm trapping the line so I can trace it. Watch your backs."

And just like that, we were all back to work. The man behind McQuade stared at us again. He yanked his gaze away swiftly when I caught him. The others in the place were making a point of not staring, but not this guy.

Did he know something? I wasn't getting a bad

vibe off of him. If anything, I got *worried* more than anything else. That concerned me more than anger or claiming territory like the deputy had been doing.

Janice was back with our cups of coffee, sugar was on the table in a huge jar. "I wasn't sure if you fellas liked cream or not, so I opened a fresh carton for you." She slid the silver pitcher onto the table. "Be right back with that pie." She gave Locke a wink.

Her pleasant expression melted as she swung away. The hard-eyed look she gave our neighbor sent a warning along my nerves.

The man was already closing his book and picking up a hat from the seat next to him. He was on his feet before she was behind the counter again. After counting out a few bills hurriedly, he left with the book tucked under his arm and the hat on his head.

I tracked his progress as he headed down the street. I tapped against the table, it was a quick morse code.

"Yes, I can," Patch added. "I've got eyes on him. As long as he's in range of the cameras. Am I looking for something specific?"

That was a harder question to answer. I tapped out a no, but just to keep watch.

"Understood."

Having her in my ear was a comfort. All the work we'd done over the past few weeks, it had been the three of us while we watched over her and let her heal. Nearly losing her on that first op had cost us.

Cost her.

But having her in the chair, even if it was a whole new chair, was the kind of reassurance I didn't even know I wanted to have. Then we got to see her when we returned. It was better than our past.

So much better.

Janice was back in no time with the pies and ice cream. She gave me a frown. "Don't like the coffee hon?"

Not reacting proved easier than I thought. Coffee was not my favorite, but I could make it tolerable. I signed a swift message that the coffee was fine, I was waiting for the pie.

Bewildered, Janice turned to Locke, but McQuade said, "It's fine, Janice. He just likes to eat something with his coffee."

It was a rough translation. I added a couple of teaspoons of sugar and some cream to the bitter brew as Janice hovered over us. The itch in the back of my shoulder blades increased.

Should we even be eating this pie in this sketchy little town?

Locke seemed to have no such objections as he took a big bite of the cherry pie with some ice cream. "Oh, this is fantastic." He practically groaned the words. I somehow doubted it was as good as sex, but Locke was convinced.

Janice gave him another blushing smile and I finally took a sip of the coffee. Disgusting crap.

"Coffee's not so bad," Patch told me. "You just need to find the way you like it."

I tapped I liked it when it came in a tea bag and had boiling water poured over it.

Her rich, warm laughter settled me. Janice was still hovering. She looked at McQuade expectantly, so he also took a bite.

"This is pretty damn good." It was a rough compliment from a rough man. Janice was all smiles, then she looked at me.

I didn't pander to her. I just took a sip of my coffee and ignored her. She stared for another minute, then her gaze slid away. Yeah, it was uncomfortable to be ignored. One of us should stay clean of the pie in case she put something in it.

"I'll be right over there if you boys need anything," she said, finally excusing herself.

"Janice Harrold, age forty-two, she's lived in Juniper her whole life. Single. Was engaged when she was nineteen, but her fiancé went in the army, married some girl back at his base, and had Janice on the side when he came home. She only found out when he told his parents he was expecting a grandchild."

Sympathy lived in Patch's voice. I could understand why. It sounded like she hooked up with a shitty guy.

"She never left Juniper. She's worked in that diner since she was fifteen. Still lives in the house she inherited from her parents and drives an old model Ford truck. It's a piece of shit, but I bet it would be a sweet ride if she could afford to fix it up. Her income and outlay are pretty standard for a small town waitress. She makes enough to cover her bills, and nothing else. She doesn't have any extravagances that I can track down. Pretty clean medical record, no significant debt there..."

"Sounds too good to be true?" Locke asked as he took another bite of the cherry pie. If it had a poison in it, it wasn't fast acting cause he wasn't dead.

"Maybe," Patch hummed, but Locke was right. She was having trouble with some part of it. "I want to keep looking into this. But she called the sheriff's office, by the way, she wanted to make sure Sheriff Nelson knew there were some new folks in town."

Did she now?

I swallowed another mouthful of coffee. The sugar couldn't do anything against the bitterness, no matter how valiant the struggle.

"What did the fine gentleman have to say to that?" McQuade hid the fact he was asking a question by covering his mouth with his cup.

"Told her he knew, and to get the hell off the phone and back out there to watch you. He wants to know where you go and what you do." She didn't like that anymore than we did. "How do you boys feel about baiting the hook?"

"Depends on what we're using for bait," McQuade said in a tone that dictated quite clearly that we would *not* be using her.

"Mark Reynolds is the guy you have me watching, Remy," she said, blowing right past McQuade's stern tone. "He's relatively new to Juniper, moved there about two years ago. Keeps to himself, has a place over the barber's, little apartment. He's currently sitting in there staring at our SUV in the parking lot. His angle isn't good, and he's got his curtains mostly closed, but I'd say he wants to talk."

Sounded like it to me.

"Since you boys have an audience, why don't you split up? We need more cameras and I want to know which of my three bachelors they are interested in the most."

Her three bachelors?

I smoothed away the smile before it could form. She was having fun and I would never begrudge her this, whether she was teasing us or not.

"Sounds like a plan," Locke said, finishing his pie before he eyed mine. "You gonna eat that?"

I just stared at him.

"Fine, I'll take it for the team. But if I keel over dead, just appreciate my sacrifice."

I rolled my eyes and I wasn't alone in that. Splitting up was a good idea. I tapped a quick message on the tabletop.

"Agreed," McQuade said. "We'll send you to the bathroom, then we'll head out front."

I nodded once. I wanted to go see Mark Reynolds. He was worried about something. Was he worried about us or for us?

Definitely a question worth asking.

By the time they finished their pie, I was ready to hit the toilet. They rose and I left them to head to the back where the doors were marked for cowboys and cowgirls.

How quaint.

Inside, I appreciated the fact that it was clean. I took care of business, washed my hands, and then went to the window. It was a decent sized one and opened up to face the back.

"All clear," Patch told me. "Everyone is watching Locke and McQuade out front."

I couldn't hear them, she must have switched the channels on our comms. "Make sure you loop me back in with them if they get into trouble, luv."

"Will do."

I opened the window and let myself out. Closing it behind me took no time. I used the buildings for cover and moved along the back of them toward my destination. How lucky for me there were wooden steps leading up to the apartment above the shop.

Very convenient.

"Hold," she warned me before I cleared the next to the last building. The heat was a slug in the face after the coolness in the diner. The whole place just *felt* wrong. It was hard to put a definition on the why.

But it reminded me of those towns back in the fifties and sixties, where Soviets trained their operatives to blend into America by immersing themselves in the culture. Rumors of their little American towns were popular spy stories and showed up in plenty of media.

I didn't think this was housing Russian spies, but they were hiding secrets.

A lot of them.

"You're clear, go straight to the stairs. They have

a couple of cameras back here, but I've hijacked them and put them on a loop."

I grinned. This was what I loved about her. She was always thinking three to five steps ahead.

"Let's go see what Mark knows, yeah?"

TWENTY-TWO

MCQUADE

" I 've got eyes and ears on Remy," Patch told me. "I switched channels so he can focus on his target. What trouble would you two like to get into?"

"You have a high opinion of my plans," I commented, digging into my pockets for a crushed pack of cigarettes. I didn't smoke anymore. I used to, but I quit. Now and then though, it was a habit that came in handy.

Like now, standing under the hot summer sun, when I wanted to be a distraction. Locke gave me a piercing look, but I ignored it for now. Two of the cigarettes were crushed beyond usefulness but the third one was mostly intact.

I jammed it between my lips then patted myself down for a lighter. Fuck, what had I done with mine?

Locke flicked open a Zippo and lit it with two smooth motions. He held it up for me and I got the cigarette burning.

Mouthing it was shit and it tasted worse, but it

served its purpose. I took a drag and then blew the smoke upward and away from Locke.

"Thanks," I said, then slid on a pair of sunglasses. The light seemed to be even more intense. Or maybe that was the addition of eyes on, and off, the street. I leaned against the side of the SUV while Locke affected an equally bored, and waiting expression.

"Since when do you smoke?" My sugar bear didn't usually call me out like that, so I figured she was due an answer.

"I started when I was sixteen, gave it up in boot camp, picked it back up again in my first war zone. Kept it up until I retired from active. Then decided to abandon it." I toked in another mouthful of smoke, then blew it out like I'd inhaled it. At this distance, they wouldn't notice.

"So we're smoking now to give you a reason to just stand in the parking lot?"

I grinned. "Checking us out, Sugar Bear?"

Locke snorted. "She can check me out any time she wants."

"Focus," I muttered and Locke chuckled. "Right, time to give them a headache. Go check out the vet's office. Get some bugs in there for Sugar Bear."

"Where are you going?" Locke rolled his head from side to side and dropped the bag from the grocery store in the back of the car.

"To take a walk to the far side. I want to check out what's on the other side of the sheriff's office and the mechanic's garage."

Locke gave me a sideways stare. "That's a hike if you get into trouble."

I smirked. "Didn't know you cared."

"I don't," he retaliated. "I'm just not a big fan of running."

I snorted.

"I have him, Justus," Patch comforted him. "I have you too. Watch your backs, and don't get dead."

"Yes, ma'am," I blew out the last bit of smoke before I ground the cigarette out. "Call me Sugar Lips again?"

Laughter drifted down the line. "Maybe after you brush your teeth."

I could do that.

The walk took me past several buildings we'd already visited and tagged. The sheriff wasn't standing out in front of his office anymore. But I made no mistake of thinking they weren't watching me. There were more locals out—some sweeping, others smoking like I had been and still more just sitting and watching.

Older guys could do that in small towns. It wasn't creepy at all. There'd been some towns like this back when I lived on base with my parents. Dad got moved, we moved with him. Some of those little towns had their own rules, a practical fiefdom.

They didn't like newcomers, but if you showed up, they beat the rules into you and you kissed the ring they wanted you to kiss. Unless the locals were fewer and farther between, then the brass ring might just be there for the taking

Yeah, this shit felt all too familiar and I hadn't been a fan of it then and I wasn't a fan of it now. I was almost to the mechanic's shop when I spotted him. The glimpse I'd gotten earlier seemed damn familiar.

That mother fucker being here changed the game.

"Don't freak out, Sugar Bear," I said quietly. "Running silent for a bit." Then I shut off the comm before she could respond. Not the most politic, but right now, I didn't want her as a part of this conversation.

Not with this asshole.

Not even by third hand proxy.

"John McQuade," the older man said as I approached. He stood there, practically at parade rest. His hair was still trimmed to military standard and his manner expected—no demanded— respect. "It's been a long time, son."

"Not long enough," I said, not bothering to add the "sir." He didn't deserve the respect. Not from me. Not from anyone.

"John, John, John..." He practically tsked. His men weren't quiet. They kicked up a lot of noise racing at me from behind. The retired general's expression didn't shift one iota from its bland smile as his guys hit me from two sides.

I took the hits, rolling with them. Right now, I wanted the information I could get out of them. Sometimes, you just had to take a hit.

"Bring him inside," the general ordered and the beating stopped almost immediately. Not that it was much of one. Fuckers had steel toed boots and they didn't use them. Good for me, but damn stupid on their part.

Each one grabbed an arm and lifted me up. I

played dead weight, forcing them to do all the work as they dragged me inside. It didn't take long for them to remove my gun and hang me from the ceiling in shackles.

As techniques went, not bad. Definitely not efficient though. The strain of my weight would eventually dislocate my shoulders. In a few hours maybe... could take a whole day.

Once I was strung up, Abdias Stone, retired general and all around lunatic, strolled up to me. He had a cigar in one hand and he sported a new scar on his face. Almost improved his ugly ass mug.

"It seems we have a bit of a problem, John," he said, almost conversationally.

"Well, if you're looking for a light, 'fraid I'm all out. But if you find one, I got cigarettes in my back pocket."

Stone's expression hardened. With a careless wave, he sent his goons toward me again. The big guy on the left had a wicked left, but his right was ass. Probably a shoulder wound, a tear... I could work with that. Every other blow managed to knock the breath out.

Second guy was a lot leaner, shorter, and all muscle. He had solid punches and he knew where my kidneys were better than I did. Probably gonna be pissing blood after this.

Better make it worth that.

"Enough," Stone said, and the men backed off immediately. Well trained little soldier boys. Yeah, I was never that trained. Following crazy because it gave you an order and had rank didn't make it any less crazy.

I twisted, my toes scraped against the floor of the mechanic's shop. The smell of old oil and grease gave it a familiar air. But then so did the cordite and sulfur. They weren't just working on cars in here.

"John," Stone said again. "I don't really want to spend a lot of time inflicting pain on you. I don't want to spend any time on you at all."

"That makes two of us. So, why don't I just head back to my car and we can go back to pretending we don't know each other."

The mad general gave me a small, thoroughly insincere smile. "That doesn't really work for me."

"It was worth a shot." I didn't try to stabilize myself. Instead, I just relaxed my muscles. The bruises along my abs and back were gonna hurt like a bitch. Better to give it a break for the moment.

"Of course, and I would have been insulted if you hadn't asked. Just as you would have been insulted if I allowed you to do so." He sounded perfectly reasonable, conversational almost. We might as well be discussing our plans for a meal. "Now that we've gotten the pleasantries out of the way, I need you to answer some questions for me. You will cooperate."

"Despite all evidence to the contrary?" I leaned to the right and spat out a wad of blood. I'd cut the inside of my cheek apparently.

"You always were a stubborn boy. It disappointed your father, you know."

"Yeah well, he and I have been disappointing each other for nearly forty years. Why break from a good thing?"

"I thought you might have learned something

since you left the military. Abandoned the path your father set for you... true patriots exist, you know. Not all are relics of a bygone era. Like your father...like you *used* to be.

"I used to be a lot of things. Haven't turned bat shit crazy this week. Still time, I suppose."

Stone didn't look impressed. Instead he gestured with his unlit cigar. "I am aware of your extra curricular activities. Your unsanctioned missions into enemy territory. Your work with refugees. You could be doing more for your own country, you know?"

I snorted, then asked in the boredest tone I could manage. "What do you want?"

"What I've always wanted, a safe and secure country once more. I want to take it back from all the enemies who've invaded. It's not a straightforward war anymore, son. Now we bring them here. We save them, bring them in, house them, cloth them, and give them funds. We let the enemy in because the enemy has learned our greatest weakness."

"That we're cuckoo for cocoa puffs?"

The general waved his hand and his guys came at me again. The pummel of their fists threatened my ribs this time. Yeah, that wasn't working for me, I gripped the chains with my hands and caught the little guy with my legs.

Too late to help himself, he realized what I was doing. I locked my legs around him, squeezing the air out of him and with the right torque—I snapped his neck. He dropped unceremoniously and the guy with the weak shoulder retreated.

Hey, look, some fear in his eyes. Smart. Fear might let him live longer.

The general gave me a benign smile. "You are the best. Like your father. You know he and I planned all of this together... Sadly, he doesn't see that by letting in more and more of our enemies, we are literally trying to destroy ourselves from within. The people who want to defund us or shrink the military budget—worse criminalize the police and take all the guns. Who defends us then, John?"

There was crazy and then there was this guy. "Thought you and my father had a falling out."

"Difference of opinion. I know we can do something, he doesn't think that because we can, we should. Still, he helped me to build the apparatus."

Section Five.

I had no idea how he covered his crazy from the military for so long. Then again, he called his operation Section Five, maybe he was on to something. Stone wanted an ear in every household, and he wanted his finger on the pulse of every person, good or bad, because their job was to defend against all enemies foreign and domestic.

In his opinion, sometimes you had to crack a few eggs to make an omelet and if freedom is that omelet, then he's willing to crack all the eggs. My father was a hardass but he wouldn't promote this. Protection yes, but Stone was insane.

So much of what happened to Patch began to make more sense and it pissed me off. Stone's phone rang and he paced away to answer it. I couldn't catch if he said anything. He finished the call swiftly, then turned to look at his surviving man.

"Deal with him. I want him softened up. I'll be back later." Then he strode out of the garage.

Fuck.

The guy with the bad shoulder looked at me and I looked at him.

"You want to do this the easy way or the hard one?" I meant it. I wouldn't be in these chains much longer. I could practically read the understanding in the guy's eyes.

"You gotta make it look good."

"Not a problem," I promised.

Still, he hesitated, and I almost had one wrist free. Finally, he swore and crossed to where I was. He loosened the chain so I landed on my feet and then he undid the shackles.

"There—"

I slammed my fist into his bad shoulder and his mouth opened in a soundless scream before I shut him down with an uppercut.

He dropped like a rock.

A rush of footsteps had me spinning just as I retrieved my gun from the feckless wonder at my feet. Locke and Remy stared at me.

"You're fine..." Locke said. "We came to..."

"Save me?" I grinned. "Good job. I'm all safe now."

At least, I was until we got back to Sugar Bear.

CHAPTER
TWENTY-THREE

PATCH

"Don't freak out, Sugar Bear. Running silent for a bit."

Then he shut off his comm.

He. Shut. Off. His. Comm.

No explanations, no brainstorming, just that message followed by dead silence as he clicked off. A part of my brain registered the conversation Remy was having with the man from the diner. The man really wanted Remy to leave. He was all but begging him to go, because if he was caught talking to an outsider it could go badly.

Another part of my brain tracked Locke's interaction with the vet. The man was almost too genial, too easy going, and too—"good ole boy"— was the only description I could come up with. But like Mark Reynolds in his little apartment over the barber shop, Dr. Townsend was not enthusiastic about having any conversation with Locke.

"So, you can handle cattle and horses, but not ferrets?" Locke was asking in a voice filled with genuine curiosity. "We've got dogs and cats too, but the ferrets—I worry about them."

When he'd started the questioning, the vet had tried to answer him directly and get him out of his place. But the more he tried to brush off Locke, the more questions Locke came up with. The minute he brought up a chinchilla though, I had to shake my head.

"Look, you don't understand," Mark Reynolds was saying to Remy. "This whole town is bad news. Just get your guys, get in your car, and get out of here."

"You don't know us, but you seem to know why we shouldn't be here." The measured tenor of his voice encouraged confidence. Or maybe it was just that I liked the sound of it.

Locke had already dropped a couple of well-placed cameras, allowing me a better look inside the veterinarian's hospital. It was pretty straight-forward from what I could see. I split my attention between that screen, the main street still visible on the other cameras, the glimpse I had inside of Reynolds' place via the street camera so I could keep an eye on Remy and his target, while I scanned the others to find McQuade.

He'd said don't freak out and then just *vanished*. It was irritating me. The town didn't seem to have a lot of surveillance installed. At least not where *they* didn't want to be looking, which suggested the cameras were placed in areas the people who ran this town thought they were needed.

Food for thought.

It could mean there was nothing to see, and at

the same time, too much to see. Every answer yielded more questions.

So many more questions. A dull headache flared behind one eye. I rubbed a hand against my forehead, trying to massage my temples without dislodging my headset or losing track of which camera angle I studied.

McQuade was out there and he was running alone, without me to watch his back. While it was hardly the first time, I didn't care for the lack of notice. At least when he went quiet before, I had a clock to count down or I could track him.

This...

"Mr.—" The vet interrupted Locke's soliloquy on the relationship between mental health and pygmy goats. I needed to ask him about that later. He seemed to know a great deal about the creatures.

"Eregion," Locke said smoothly. "Linden Eregion, but you can just call me Linden."

I almost choked. That was straight out of *Lord of the Rings*, here was hoping the doctor hadn't heard of it.

"Mr. Eregion," the man's easy drawl seemed less easy and *far* more strained. "I have clients with patients I need to see. As you can tell, my office staff has the day off, so I really need to send you on your way, and get back to work."

"Well, why didn't you say so? Don't have to get testy." I could *hear* the smirk reflected in his words. "Just trying to be friendly."

The doctor didn't quite manage to mask his glare, but I took advantage of his direct look to screenshot his face, then put it to work on a secondary search. Something about him was bugging me, beginning with his absolute lack of digital footprint.

It just wasn't normal.

"I don't know you," Reynolds was saying, the man's guarded voice betrayed a distinctly Eastern seaboard accent. Mid-Atlantic? "I don't want to know you."

No, more northeast. Not New York. Boston?

"Tell me what has you afraid," Remy said, seemingly unmoved by the man's urgency. Unfortunately for Mr. Reynolds, Remy could be furious and his pulse would barely blip. His self-control and discipline were crucial to his work.

Did make reading him frustrating.

But I was getting better at it.

"Why?" Reynolds demanded. "I'm trying to do you a favor. I don't know what the hell is going on with these people. They could be cartel, or criminals, aliens, or just some people whacked out on happy juice trying to form their own cult."

That was a lot to take in. Locke was on his way out of the vet's office, whistling. "Can you see Mc-Quade?" I asked him before I could even think twice about it.

"Nope," he said, switching from whistling to humming. "Need me to punch him for you?"

Surprise bubbled up at the offer and I laughed. "No, I just— Never mind."

He was running quiet. He was a grown man. He could handle it.

I apparently couldn't, but he could.

"Remy is getting some conflicting info from Reynolds. Head toward the barber so you're in place for extraction. We need to get in the sheriff's office." Yes, it was stream of consciousness.

"I don't mind getting arrested for you, sweet, but I think we should wait until later. This town probably closes at sundown. I'll get you all the eyes and ears you could want."

"You might be on to something." It wasn't a bad plan. I switched to the screen where I could see McQuade's comm, it was in standby mode. Not connected.

Annoying man.

"The problem," Reynolds was saying as I tuned back into the conversation and continued paging through all the angles I had on the town. Where the hell had McQuade gone? "The people in this town ain't playing. I came here to follow up on a story..."

"You're a journalist." Remy's cool tone masked his personal feelings but I gritted my teeth. A journalist could be in a lot of trouble here.

A lot.

"Yeah, I am and you have fed written all over you, only you're British, so maybe you're a foreign operative. Either way, you don't need to be here," Reynolds told him firmly.

"By that logic," Remy replied. "Neither do you."

"I have a job to do. A job I'm going to do. Now, they're watching me which means they know you came up here..."

"No, they don't," Remy told him, and I caught Remy's movement as he shifted to glance out the window before drifting back. It was just a shadow, but I knew who it was. I had to give Reynolds credit, he didn't look like he was talking to anyone.

"They have eyes everywhere."

"So do I," Remy said. "They won't know I'm here. What are you investigating?"

The man pulled out a tape recorder. "If you get to ask questions, so do I."

I chuckled. "I like him."

"I like you," Remy said, echoing the sentiment.

"We can't read him in. Not enough info. But I'm running him now."

I flicked a look at the clock. It was closing in on forty-five minutes since McQuade told me to not freak out.

"Liking me isn't answering my questions," Reynolds said.

"No, it isn't. I'm not entirely sure what to do with you."

That last was a question for me. Locke was making his way down the street. "Still no eyes on him?" The question asked me a lot of things. Was I worried? Did I want him to find him?

"No, Remy disengage with Reynolds. Leave him in play. We may have compromised ourselves with him but I don't think so. I'll keep fishing. Join Locke, McQuade's gone missing and we don't have eyes on him."

Frustration scraped through me. Where the hell was McQuade? Remy left Reynolds as silently as he arrived. I could track him, but I was also scrubbing their surveillance so they couldn't see him.

At fifty minutes, I activated a ping to hit McQuade's comm. If it was off, it would still send a signal back. I could triangulate using the signals and that part of town.

"The town isn't that large," Remy said as he linked up with Locke. "Which way did he go?"

"Mechanic's shop." I answered in unison with Locke. It was also where the ping returned from. "I don't have eyes, so I can't see what you're walking into. They have no cameras there, or if they do they are *well* shielded against intrusion."

Irritating, but if they did have them, I'd find a way to crack it.

"We can handle it, luv," Remy said, his voice soothing some of the rougher edges of my worries. "Don't mind McQuade, he's a cantankerous prick, but he can handle himself."

Yes, he could. It didn't mean I had to like it.

Silence relayed down the line. Then Locke said, "We've got a car pulling out from behind the shop, it's heading south and away from town. I got a picture, but couldn't catch the plate."

Oh, please let McQuade not be in that car. But I kept my words locked down, not trusting myself. The conversations with the vet and Reynolds may not have netted much, but they had served as a distraction.

"Watch your backs." The nearest camera I had to their location was rapidly losing them. I couldn't help them if I couldn't see what was there.

What was with the cameras on this side? Most of the town had flimsy security but this side was battened down tighter than a skif at the CIA.

"Got him," Locke said, but the tightness in his voice had me digging my nails into my palms.

"He's—fine." I couldn't get a read on Remy's tone, was he amused? Annoyed? Or just observant?

"You're fine..." Locke said, as if belatedly agreeing. "We came to..."

"Save me?" McQuade said, the sarcasm ever present in his voice. "Good job. I'm all safe now."

Anger struck a match inside of me. He was fine...

"Status?" It came out far more clipped than I cared to admit.

"Bruised, still ugly, and definitely not the best personality," Locke offered his assessment. "But he took out two guys here. Getting photos for you."

"I've got some info," McQuade was saying—to them. Not to me. To them. Because he hadn't turned his damn comm back on. "We should probably blow town for a bit. We might be compromised..."

"What happened?" Remy asked.

"TLDR—someone recognized me. I recognized them. We need to go. I'll fill you in later."

I tapped one nail against the desktop as I continued to scroll the images through town—there they were. They were moving at a relaxed, if brisk, pace back to the car. McQuade walked with his hands in his pockets and his chin down.

The air backed up in my lungs as they got closer to the car and I could see them on *our* cameras. Bruises marked McQuade's face. There was blood on the corner of his mouth.

His comm was still off.

Then they were in the car and Remy took over the driving with Locke sliding in the back. McQuade was up front.

"We're secure," Remy said. "On our way back to you."

"Brief us now," Locke said. "She can hear us and she's already working on a dozen other threads."

McQuade sighed.

Yes, briefing now meant he'd turn his comm back on, not that I couldn't hear him via theirs. But he couldn't hear me and he had to know I wasn't going to put up with that. If he didn't know, he was going to find out.

I waited.

The click as it came back online echoed in my ear. McQuade blew out a breath. "Online, Sugar Bear."

I stared at the screen.

Then back at the town. "Then brief the boys," I suggested, fighting for a professional tone. "I'll have my report for you when you get back. Going silent."

I shut it off before he could say anything. Shut all of them down, then yanked the headset off. My heart hammered so loud, it echoed in my ears and my hands were shaking.

Worse, I couldn't decide if I wanted to cry, throw up, scream, or hit something. I pressed the heel of my hand against my eye as my head thundered with every beat of my pulse.

McQuade had gone silent and had been in some kind of fight. He'd been recognized. Recognized someone who was there. But he'd been running alone.

He could have been killed.

The more my thoughts chased around in circles,

the worse my headache got. Doors swung both ways, you could open and shut communications. He'd been offline... anything could have happened.

I'd just gone offline when...

No sooner did my mind go there than it retreated. I shoved away from the desk and headed for the little kitchenette. I retrieved a bottle of water from the fridge and pressed the icy plastic against my suddenly flushed face.

I had no idea how long I stood there, how long I fought to get the shallow breaths to deepen, and to stop panting. I was still there when the alarm alerted me to their arrival. The slam of the car doors echoed through the silence. Their footfalls, a soft shush of shoe on the metal floors and then quieted more when they hit the rubber mats that lined everything for traction.

Then they were walking around the corner, McQuade in the lead. I had no idea what I was going to do before I did it, but when he grinned with his bloodstained lips, I saw red. Then I threw the water bottle as hard as I could and it smacked him upside the head, bouncing once before he caught it.

Locke and Remy froze in place and McQuade stared at me. "What the hell?"

"Apparently, I needed to *freak out.*"

CHAPTER
TWENTY-FOUR
PATCH

S till holding the bottle of water I'd hurled at him, McQuade eyed me. No smile touched his lips, nor any teasing expression on his face. Good. I wasn't kidding.

This *wasn't* funny.

"All right," McQuade said slowly, his guarded gaze fixed on me. "We good now?"

Are we good now?

Are we...

My headache surged as I clamped my teeth together before I said anything more.

McQuade set the water bottle down on the little kitchenette counter as he took a couple of steps in my direction. Neither Remy nor Locke moved. It would almost be funny, if anything about this situation was laughable, how still they'd both gone.

"I get that you're pissed, Sugar Bear. But it was important for me to get this info."

His next step put me in arm's reach and I took a step back and to the side, retreating, but also regrouping. Arms folded, I fought to keep my expres-

238

sion neutral. Probably failed at it, because right now, I was *anything* but neutral.

McQuade exhaled a long breath. "Tell you what. Let me debrief. I was filling the guys in but you disconnected before I could read you in."

My stony silence would just have to serve as all the permission I was going to give him. I absolutely did *not* trust myself to speak.

"I know who was behind your kidnapping. I'm eighty percent certain I have the right person, whether they were the driving force of it or they were merely following orders—it was *him*."

I was very happy for him to have found the answer. It might have been useful if I'd been in on the conversation. Still, I kept it all battened down tight. I was in danger of losing control on all fronts.

That wouldn't be good for anyone.

"His name is Abdias Stone, he's a former general. Storied legend in a lot of circles, with more redactions in his file than commendations." McQuade planted his hands on his hips as he continued speaking. "He and my father served in the same unit when they were younger. That kind of thing leads to lifelong friends. It did for them, for a time. I give my father a lot of shit, but he has limits. Section Five was about at the edge of what he would sanction for national security. Abdias Stone wanted to take it a hell of a lot further."

Considering what I'd been pulling out of Section Five and MadOg, it sounded like he already had. Was he the poison pill in the agency that deviated from its primary mission?

"He's here. He's got people working for him,

former military from the look of them. Probably washouts, cause they weren't really up to my standards." He gave a careless shrug as he motioned to his face. "I let them beat on me while he asked his questions. You can learn a lot about what people are up to if you let them direct the conversation."

A flicker of amusement skated along the edges of my irritation. I was familiar with the technique. The gleam in his eyes seemed almost hopeful before he folded his arms. No, I was not ready to forgive him this particular transgression.

"Can you access the information you took? I know you said it would be tricky, but I want to nail this son of a bitch. My gut knows it's him, but we need hard evidence."

"If she does," Locke said, interrupting for the first time since the debrief began. "It could make her far more vulnerable."

It would make all of us vulnerable. They wanted it back in hand if possible or destroyed if not. I could make copies though. So many copies. Send it around the world. This wasn't the kind of evidence that sent people to jail.

No, this was the kind that derailed careers, forced Congressional hearings, and scandals. Someone would fall on their sword and take the heat, then it would all be quietly mopped up and everyone would get back to work.

I used to believe in fairy tales, but I was a hell of a lot more pragmatic now.

"She's vulnerable now," McQuade said, evenly, not taking his gaze off of me. "You are, Sugar Bear. You're the best at what you do and we wouldn't have gotten *this* far without you. I'm not asking you to present the evidence to the world, I just want confirmation. I'm happy to take him out right now, the suspicion is enough to make me scrub him off the board. Trust me when I say he deserves it."

"But he wants to make sure you're safer if he does it," Remy said, adding his own thoughts to the mix. "I can't say it's a bad plan. I wasn't planning to put any of your captors or former employers in jail anyway."

"Nope," McQuade said. "I want them scratched off permanently. Dead men can't come after you again."

My throat closed at the absolute conviction in their voices. Even more at the passion filling McQuade's eyes. He meant it. They all did. The emotion clawing its way through me wouldn't be denied.

Eyes burning, I turned away for the first time since they'd entered. Hot tears splashed onto my cheeks before I could stop them. Pressing a heel of my hand to my right eye, I fought the overwrought reactions shattering what little control I'd managed to cobble together.

It was like someone ripped open all the compartments where I'd shoved my fear, my loneliness, and the what-ifs from my life before, and they were spilling out everywhere. Walking away from that existence had been the hardest thing I'd ever done.

I'd *survived* it by building a new identity and these three men had become vital to me. Their survival, getting them through their missions, being there for them...

It *mattered.*

I was rapidly losing the struggle against the worry that surged past the barriers I'd erected. Tears slid down my face and I couldn't get a deep breath. Hands closed on my arms and McQuade dragged me back against him.

He was just there, surrounding me like an impenetrable wall and the sob I'd been trying to smother broke. Jagged cracks spread like spiderwebs through the dense ice I'd tried to use to keep the world away.

"Sugar Bear," he said, the growl in his voice giving way to something far softer. I'd never wanted to grasp onto something so much in my life and I shouldn't. "I'm here," he said and the weight of his cheek pressed against my temple as he kept me wrapped up tight.

"We're going," Remy said, and it seemed to come from a great distance. "You have this?"

Something taut inside of me snapped.

"I have it, and her. Figure out the Reynolds guy."

"I don't know if—"

"Fuck off, Locke," McQuade snarled the order, the hot tears pouring out of me seemed to slash at the cracks, melting the ice. "I have her. If I think—" All at once he cut himself off, then he was lifting me upward and I couldn't even see him for the tears blurring my vision. "If she asks for you...I'll get you."

The last was a concession, even I could hear it. But I couldn't get the sobbing to stop. The ragged emotions were done being bottled. They kicked open every compartment, scattering their debris everywhere.

Facing McQuade abruptly, I realized our heads were almost on the same level. No, he was carrying me. I wrapped my arms around his neck and dug my nails into his shoulders.

"I've got you," he said, and it gradually sank in that he was saying it over and over. When he sat down, he parked me in his lap. Not even his coaxing could get me to lift my head from where I cried against his throat. "I've got you."

Bit by bit, he let me cry and just rubbed slow circles against my back. My eyes were swollen and sore, my nose kept running. I had the hiccups and I was all snotty. I hated this. Trying to wipe at my face with my sleeve, I couldn't seem to get any of it to dry.

"Here," he said, grasping my chin gently when I would have tried to look away. With care, he dabbed at my eyes and my nose. The fabric was much softer than the scratchier edge of my sweat-shirt. "Sugar Bear..."

The long sigh had me swallowing another set of sobs. The handkerchief he had was cotton and the more he dabbed at my face, the clearer my vision grew. I almost laughed when he wiped my nose.

There was something so deeply moving about how he stared at me. This giant of a man was so big, and he filled every space he was in. Yet, in this mo-ment, he wrapped all that size around me and it didn't make me feel small at all.

It made me feel *safe*.

"You going to look at me again?" The quiet

question pulled my gaze up to meet his. My eyes really hurt. "There she is..."

He seemed to be searching for something, but I really had no idea what. The release of so much emotion left me—aching and empty. Like I'd lanced some wound and now it needed to heal.

Concern tightened his expression.

"I hate crying," I admitted in a voice better suited to a croaking frog. "I always get swollen eyes and a shiny nose, I look *terrible*."

"No, you don't," he said, lying at me with a straight face. "I mean, the nose might be a little shiny, but it's not like Rudolph shiny."

I blinked at him.

"And the eyes? Well...maybe if you were really into the makeup thing, you'd have these black smudges, but right now they just look a little red and puffy. The stormy gray there makes me think we just got caught in a thunderstorm."

Now I just stared.

He raised his eyebrows. "Too much?"

"I have no idea what to do with you," I admitted.

"Anything you want, Sugar Bear. Especially if it will make you feel better and not cry anymore."

I snorted, which was damn hard with my sinuses all stuffed up and he offered up that handkerchief all nice and polite.

"You maybe want to tell me what's going on in there?" He touched two fingers to my temple then pushed some of the hair back and tucked it behind my ear.

"I don't know," I said, being as honest as I could be. "I didn't even expect this until it happened."

"Okay, well let's try it this way. What happened?"

The bruises on his face were darkening from the red marks to something more blackish-purple. They just added to his fierceness. The longish hair that he'd had pulled back from his face earlier, spilled around him now, kind of like a Viking, and his beard had felt soft whenever he rubbed his cheek against my temple.

Nothing about this man said gentle, caring, or kind. Nothing. Not his voice. His physical presence or the brutal, sheer violence I knew he was capable of, and yet... he was also the man who came in to hold me when I had bad dreams and would stay awake to chase them off when they came.

He was also sitting here with me in his lap. While I didn't think it was possible to make himself small, he was doing something.

"You went—you went off comms. You didn't give me any time, you just shut it off and you were in a no camera zone. I couldn't see you. I couldn't back you up." Every word was like pulling out a piece of my own soul and slapping it down. "I'm compromised on every level. I can't do my job if you don't let me, and I can't watch out for you when you go off book."

I licked at the salt on my lips. A tear escaped from the corner of my eye and slid down my cheek. I could barely feel it but his gaze traced the path.

"I hate this—it's not like you haven't done it before. In the field, in far more violent situations, you go in alone all the time but you were out there..." I swallowed that hard lump in my throat. "You were out there without Locke or Remy or me... and you got *hurt*."

"It's just a few bruises," he said, dismissing it and I punched his shoulder. Fuck he was so damn dense. The blow hurt my hand and I had to shake it off. "Sugar Bear... don't..."

"Don't what?" I demanded as he caught my hand. He pressed a kiss to my protesting knuckles. His beard teased my skin. "Don't freak out?"

He winced. "Clearly," he said slowly. "I could have handled that better. But really, I'm fine... It's not like I got shot or anything." The chuckle was there, just beneath the words. Faint, but present.

I yanked my hand out of his and I slapped his shoulder. That still hurt but not as bad as my knuckles had. "It's not funny. I couldn't *help* you. I didn't know what was happening and all I could do was *wait* and when I finally couldn't wait anymore, you were already hurt."

The fleeting smile on his face registered as he caught my hand, but he sobered. "Sugar Bear —*Fallon*." It was the command on my name that quieted the emotion that was boiling up again. "I was fine. I knew what I was doing. I'm sorry I didn't give you more warning. You're right, I should have. Hell... I could have probably taken you in with me."

That...that *helped*. "But you didn't."

"No," he said slowly. "I didn't. Because Stone is an ugly part of my past. He's fucking crazy. The worst kind, because he's a damn true believer of his idiocy. Fanatical. I didn't want him anywhere near you, not even second hand."

I swallowed around another lump. "But I can't protect you if I'm not there and I'm not going to judge you by the people in your past. I worked for them, remember?"

"Yeah," he said slowly, his voice deepening again. "I know you did and I know they hurt you. You didn't know you were working for them. The trouble is, I saw the problem. It took me time to put distance between me and them, but I did know. I just walked away instead of fixing it."

The tangle of emotion housed in those words trapped me.

"I didn't do anything to stop it, Sugar Bear. If I had...maybe you would never have been dragged into all of this. Maybe... maybe you would have been safe. That's... that's on me. I should have done something. I didn't then, I am now."

"Maybe I wouldn't know you right now," I pointed out. "Or Locke or Remy."

He grumbled. "I don't care about them so much."

"Yes you do," I countered. "You like baiting them and fighting with them."

"Don't tell them that," he ordered, not denying it.

"I won't," I said. "Your secrets are always safe with me."

He fisted my hair suddenly and his gaze pinned mine. "I know they are, but you need to understand I'm always going to choose you. You first. You need to be safe. Nothing else is as important as that and if I have to burn the whole fucking operation down, and my father with it, I will. You matter more than anything."

"Together," I said, trying to not face the depth of that confession or what it did to me. "We do this together, John. We have to. I know there are things that I don't remember... I am seeing some of it. Images. Feelings. They're right there, like on the tip of my tongue and then they slip away. But secrets and lies, they destroy everything they touch. You can't do this without me. If you cut me out—I'll leave."

I met him glare for glare.

It wasn't an empty threat.

"We do this together," I told him. "That means I'm with you. Every step of the way. You want to put me first, that means you have to let me help. Because it hurts too damn much to be left out and if anything happened to you..."

My stomach dropped. It made me sick to even think about it. But I held his fierce stare and then he dragged me forward and kissed me. The hard pressure of his mouth on mine demanded a response and I bit down on his lip before he thrust his tongue at mine. He tugged my head back.

This wasn't a duel or a fight. This wasn't even a battle of wills. It was passion, pure, hot, and blinding.

"Goddamn it," he whispered against my lips. "You're not going to take no for an answer."

"No," I told him. "To any part of this. I want you. I want to be there... I'm in or I'm out. Which is it?"

My lips tingled, my heart hammered, and the

tears that had slid free earlier dried under the ferocious heat pouring off him.

"In," he snarled and then he flipped me around until I was on the bed and he was over me. I didn't even know when we made it here or where the guys were.

I didn't care right now either, because John pounced and he blotted out the rest of the world.

CHAPTER
TWENTY-FIVE
PATCH

A knife slid up the inside of my sweatshirt and split the fabric in two. I blinked a little stupidly at the gleaming blade then up at John's intent expression.

"You're cutting my shirt?" Granted, the answer was likely obvious, but I couldn't quite wrap my mind around it.

"I am," he said, almost agreeably. The cool steel of the blade's flat side teased a nipple before he sliced through my sports bra. The fabric peeled away almost effortlessly. I bit my lower lip as he seemed singularly focused on his task.

The air against my flushed skin made me shiver, more in anticipation than cold. The slices to the bra left it in several strips of fabric and my breasts bared. Then he dispensed with the sweatshirt similarly.

A blush spread over my skin at the smile on his lips. The possessive gleam in his honey brown eyes had me reaching for him. He didn't object to my hands on him, but he didn't abandon me for a moment. If anything, he spread his legs as he knelt over me and began to slice off my pants.

"I could just take them off," I told him, but his grunt in response made me laugh.

"I'm having fun..." He glanced up at me, then winked. "Since we bought you these clothes, I'll be more than happy to replace them. Or you can go naked, I'm not fussy."

"Oh... you're not?" I dared him. A slam of a cupboard in another part of the truck reminded me that we were hardly alone. As big a space as they'd created, it was hardly private.

Then the smooth side of the blade glided down my abdomen as he cut through my pants. "Don't worry about them," he told me, the metal seemed hot through my panties as he glided over the pubic mound to my thighs. "They don't mind." Then he pitched his voice louder. "You guys are good, right?"

My mouth fell open and I stared at him.

"Yes," Remy answered, his voice gliding through me like a caress all its own. Then he was just *there* glancing around the room divider. The very *thin* room divider. They were literally right there.

Blazing heat scorched my face and my skin. I was torn, I wanted to hide from the hunger in Remy's sweeping gaze. He didn't stare at me, but he also didn't avoid looking at me.

"Keep watch, yeah?" McQuade continued. "I'm going to be distracted for at least an hour."

Goosebumps raced over my skin.

"You can do better than that," Locke called. "Or is that your age talking?"

"I'll deal with him," Remy said before McQuade could respond, amusement tinging each word. Then he seemed to focus on me and when his gaze and mine collided, he held it for a long moment. His words from before whispered sensuously against my ear... *Just know, that when you and I have sex, I really want you to enjoy that too.* Maybe he heard it too because he nodded slowly. "Enjoy yourselves."

Then he was gone and my gaze riveted up to where McQuade watched me. The smile he wore softened everything about him, blurring away the harder edges. "Feel better?"

That seemed an odd description for what just happened but... "Yes," I said. "I never want to seem like..." How did I say this?

"That you're leaving them out?" McQuade suggested before he dipped his head and caught one of my nipples against his teeth. The hard suction was so sudden and unexpected, I arched my back and gasped. The sound escalated as he nibbled against the hardened tip, before stroking the cold blade over my too hot skin.

My thoughts scattered as a bolt of pure lust struck. It dragged from where his mouth connected with my breast and seemed to pull the liquid heat all the way from my core. Squeezing my thighs together, I writhed under the sensory overload of his caresses.

I didn't know what to focus on first. He abandoned the first nipple and the air was almost brutally cold. The skin pebbled even tighter and then he had the blade right there and I let out another

252

cry as he sucked my neglected nipple into his mouth.

The cool steel was everywhere, like the heat of his mouth. He never slipped, never cut, but the stroke of it over my skin was unlike anything I'd ever experienced. He left my nipples to kiss a path to my throat and then his mouth fused with mine.

Fierce, nipping kisses, followed by a long, drugging one as his tongue dueled with mine. I could barely grasp one wave of sensation before he washed me in another. What the hell was he doing? I dragged my fingers down his denim clad thighs, trying to hold on.

His beard alternated between silky softness and rasping abrasion where he kissed me. Pleasure and pain, magnified by the way he ravaged me. Then that dangerous mouth moved down my chest, paying particular attention to my breasts, then my stomach.

When he reached my soaked panties, he killed me by rubbing his nose against them. "You smell fucking fantastic, Sugar Bear. All hot, and wet, and desperate..."

I fucking felt that way. I pushed up onto my elbows, and forced my eyes open to stare down at him. He rubbed his cheek against my abdomen and then down to my thigh before moving to the other thigh and coming back up.

There were little scrapes of red from his beard marking my skin. Everywhere he touched left me more desperate for him. My pants were gone, so were my shoes and my socks. All that was left were my panties.

When my gaze locked onto his, he began to smile and the gleam in those honey brown eyes backed all the air up in my lungs. He didn't look away as the blade slid under the fabric. The caress of steel was a sensual promise I wanted to pursue.

The slices were so clean, I didn't even hear them. Just one moment I had panties and the next they were gone. It left me bare to him. Not once did he look down, he held me captive with his eyes as he dipped his mouth.

One kiss above the pubic bone. Then another to where my thigh joined my hip, then the other side. All at once my thighs spread like a butterfly and he grinned.

"Ready?"

It was a dare and a request all at once. The earlier tears filmed my eyes all over again. He wanted me on board for every part of this.

Nowhere else I'd rather be.

I nodded slowly. "Ready."

Thought became action and he devastated me with a carnal kiss as he buried his face between my thighs. The beard was pure softness, tickling my skin. His tongue was all demand, as he lapped at me. The stroke from entrance to clit left my mind a buzz of competing emotions.

I fisted the blankets, trying to hold onto my sanity as he traced his teeth ever so lightly along the labia, then against my clit itself. It was like he pushed me for more and nothing kept me still.

The pressure was exquisite torment. A sob tore out of my throat. Then another cry. It was a battle to not pull away or grind against his face. He was ruthless in his hedonistic assault.

The tension pulled tighter and tighter. His hand clamped down on my hip, holding me in place as he sucked, nipped, and licked at me. I was twisting against the blankets when the first orgasm crashed into me.

I shuddered and sobbed through it. Part of me pleaded for him to stop and the rest of me wanted more. The pressure was unrelenting and then it spiraled me into another series of cries.

Riding those waves, I crashed to earth when he pulled back. In my blurred vision, his damp beard gleamed briefly before he reached behind him to drag off his shirt. Then his jeans were gone.

The heavy, red-veined cock thumped against his belly. It curved almost like a scimitar, the thick tip practically purple as it strained. I never thought of a dick as having personality, but the thickness and length were so perfectly him.

When I would have pushed myself upward, still shaking, McQuade shook his head. "No, Sugar Bear," he said in that low, rough growl of his. "You touch me, and I'm going to blow like some pimply faced teen confronted with his first pair of boobs."

That—image—stopped me cold and I was caught between wild laughter and the shuddering quakes still rocketing through my system. "Okay..." The word came out far more shaky than I liked.

He chuckled, low and decadent. "Just answer a couple of questions."

I nodded, not trusting myself to speak.

"Can I flip you onto your stomach?"

Could he... well... "Yes?" It came out a question, but more because I wasn't sure why he was asking that. His grin was all teeth and feral. It had my cunt clenching in anticipation.

He didn't ask his second question before he gripped my hips in his big, callused hands and then flipped me onto my stomach. I got my hands under me as he dragged my hips back and then I got the answer to the question I hadn't really asked.

Excitement and impatience swirled through me as he teased his cock against my soaked cunt. A glide through my labia until the head bumped along my clit and then back again.

"Fuck, your ass is incredible." He palmed one cheek and gave it a hard squeeze. "I like having something to grip, Sugar Bear."

The words were utterly undoing all semblance of control I'd managed to regain after the cascade of orgasms.

"You had a second question?" Fuck, when did words get so damn hard.

"Yes," he said, then he bit my shoulder. It didn't sting so much as feel like a possession as he settled his teeth into the muscle. I closed my eyes. Like the knife earlier, and the way he'd rubbed his beard against me, he was marking me.

Would he carve something into my skin if I asked him to?

That image was heady as hell and came from the dark cavern inside of me where my memories seemed to hide. Did I want him to mark me more? Carve himself into my skin?

Even as I shied from that answer, I could hear

256

myself sobbing and pleading earlier as he took me apart with pleasure.

Yes, I did want him. I wanted everything he would give me.

A hand landed against my ass, the slap hot and stinging. It forced a startled yelp out of me as tears sprang to my eyes, not from pain so much as surprise. He massaged the heat out and then he nipped my earlobe. His whole body curved over mine, a shelter and a shield. His cock throbbed between my legs and I was rocking against him, a slow, beckoning motion.

"You with me again, Sugar Bear?"

"Yes." Not a question this time. "Did I miss a question?"

His low, delighted chuckle would live in my head forever. "You did, but I'll ask it again."

I licked my lips, tilting my head back so I could see him from the corner of my eye. Heat radiated off of him, and I was burning up with a fever thanks to the way he traced his hands over me.

He touched me everywhere. His cock nestled between my legs. His chest against my back. His hand teased along my abdomen to my breasts. Lips teasing my ear, he stroked his free hand along my side. All caresses and kisses, and soothing motions and I moved, teasing his dick and myself.

"Ask," I said. "Please..." Because the man was driving me mad.

"Do you like to be watched?"

I heard the words, but my brain stuttered on the meaning. "What?"

"I know you watch us..." Another bite against

257

my earlobe. "You always watch us and I love that you do."

A shudder rippled through my belly and I clenched my thighs, gripping his heavy cock as I rocked and he let out a groan of his own.

"But do you like to be watched?"

I didn't really have an answer to that. Maybe that was why my next words startled me. "If I know who is watching..."

Yes. That was true. I didn't try to overthink it or strain my mind.

"I think I would like it...if it were you or Justus or..."

"Me?" Remy asked and his accent wrapped around me like a new lover and I lifted my eyes to find him leaning against the divider. His arms were folded, but his eyes blazed with so much passion, it was like a fire racing across the room to consume me.

"Yes," I said, elongating the syllable as I sighed. "I would love to be watched by you."

John's hands firmed on my hips and then he filled me in one brutal stroke. His cock was huge, and it didn't seem to matter how soaking I was, it was an intrusion. The penetration took him deep and I forgot how to breathe.

My gaze fixed on Remy's as John hooked a hand around my throat. He wasn't strangling me, he was gripping me with one hand on my hip and the other on my neck and then he set a savage pace.

Every thrust struck deep, sending sparks through my system. It was like his mouth was on my clit all over again. Instead, he was all ferocious motion, a feral coupling that demanded everything from me. Each time he bottomed out, I whined a little more.

I didn't even recognize the sound of me. I was right on the edge when Remy abandoned the divider, and then he cupped my chin, keeping my gaze before he kissed me and swallowed my screams as John let go.

The hot jet of his release flooded inside of me. My inner walls fluttered and convulsed as I came again. What breath I had, Remy robbed me of and then he pulled back, licking his lips as he stared into me.

John still throbbed inside of me, hard and heavy. Remy looked at me like he could eat me alive. I could never have imagined this and I didn't want anything to puncture the moment.

The sweetest torment, suspended between the two of them. My body was bound to John's and my gaze to Remy's. I had no idea how long we existed in this moment, but I never wanted it to end.

Suddenly boneless, I collapsed and John moved with me and so did Remy as he knelt. My eyes were open and fixed on my beautifully dangerous assassin even as my wild and brutal mercenary held me like something so precious to him.

"Still with us?" Remy asked and I nodded slowly.

"I don't want to be anywhere else."

The trust I'd realized with Justus existed with Remy and John too. It had from the beginning, whether I'd been ready to accept it or not. Something dark and cold whispered from the back of my mind.

It wasn't all pretty. Hell had swallowed me before they'd come to find me.

But they *had* found me.

That was enough for me. No matter what else happened, they found me and we were together. I had no idea where this went or how this worked, but—

"Hate to be a buzzkill," Locke said, sliding around the divider. "We've got movement."

The cold reality of what awaited us when we were done meant we had to finish the mission first. I closed my eyes, and extended a hand toward Locke. When he slid his palm over mine, and gripped my hand tight in his, I soaked up the connection with all of them.

"Okay..." I said, getting my breath control back. Interlude over, we had work to do. "Talk to me..."

CHAPTER
TWENTY-SIX

REMY

S hadowing Stone from Juniper north and east to San Antonio then onward to Austin took little in the way of skill. When Locke announced he was on the move, I'd pulled myself away from the absolute beauty of a sensually wrecked Fallon to check the camera angles.

None of us were her, but she'd shown us enough to be dangerous. The man was in a car and moving out of town at speed. Even if we got the rig started and on the road immediately, it was wildly conspicuous and definitely not made for a high speed pursuit.

Tactically, I was the best to go. I had the best chance of keeping him in sight from a distance. I could also get mics and other cameras in place. McQuade and Fallon were in the shower.

"I'm going," I told Locke. "I'll keep comms on standby. But I'd rather not be transmitting if he's got a jammer or interceptor on board."

"You should probably wait for them," he advised, but I shook my head.

"This is the right plan. It might take them a moment to see it, but they will. Catch up when you can, the car's tracker will help with that too."

Not waiting for his response, I dropped my go bag in the backseat, and started the engine even as I lowered the ramp. I pulled directly out and the ramp was already closing before I accelerated away from the rig.

We'd moved the truck from a rest area to a shady spot on a dirt road about five miles north of Juniper itself. A full scout of the area had shown little to no traffic, no residents, and a small chance of someone tripping over the vehicle.

The longer we stayed in a public area like the rest stop, the more likely we were to arouse suspicion. Considering the reaction of the sheriff's deputy? I was right.

McQuade's actions, as frustrating as they'd been for Patch, had kicked the hornet's nest and revealed a particularly nasty stinger. As I accelerated toward the highway we'd tracked him to, I kept one eye on the moving dot on my screen.

Not even ten minutes on the road and there was a beep in my ear. I tapped it once. "I will apologize later if this proves to not be the right call. However, you needed a moment to regather yourself..."

Watching her fall apart had been a kind of heady eroticism and I looked forward to seeing it again as much as I did making it happen.

"And," I continued when she didn't take advantage of my momentary pause to interject anything. "I wanted to give you that time. Right now, we want to track Stone to wherever he is going.

Could it be a distraction to pull us away from Juniper?"

By "us," I meant McQuade, yes it could be. Another reason for me to take point and let them stay where they were.

"I agree, it absolutely could be. Stone was recognized. That said, Stone also recognized McQuade. He doesn't know me—not yet. I make my living by not being seen. I can do this for you, for us, and you can work on deep diving everything. Let me gather the information my way, while you gather what we need, your way."

That was as close to asking permission as I was going to get. If it came down to choosing between putting her in harm's way or removing the obstacles before they could identify her again? It was not a choice.

Her soft sigh told me the battle was won without a single shot being fired. "I hate that you are being very logical about this."

The huskiness in her voice was a pure delight. I'd always found a kind of epicurean charm in her voice. The pleasure and tranquility I found with her in my ear compared to nothing else I'd experienced.

Now, I could add hedonistically stimulating. My dick had been hard from her very first gasp as McQuade took her apart on that bed, and that was just listening to them. The erection, however, was not going to prevent me from doing my job.

I'd gotten to savor her desire and her release. That taste promised that she was more than worth waiting for.

"I'd apologize, luv, but I did think about this as I

was leaving. Juniper is too small and too remote to be a 'coincidence' and based on what Reynolds was saying, there's definitely more going on there than is visible."

I accelerated onto the highway and flicked a glance to the dot on the map on my phone. It took some talent to hit a moving target accelerating away. Fortunately, Locke noticed him on the move soon enough for me to get into place. It meant letting him pass me, but I tagged his car. After, it was just a matter of closing the distance on Stone kept me in range of the signal. All I needed was to see his car, then I could fall into highway driving.

Americans were very fond of their road trips. More, they were very similar in how they drove. Those who clung to the speed limit would be passed. Those who sped, tended to move in packs.

It offered a kind of coverage with the idea being whoever was in the lead car was more likely to earn the ire of the local or state patrols, while those following could take advantage of the distraction.

While I found it amusing, it wasn't important beyond it would be a distraction for Stone.

"You're not wrong," she said and all at once, she was in analytical mode.

On the one hand, I hated that she had to lose some of the relaxation she'd found with McQuade. On the other, Patch was the best at her job I'd ever seen. There was no one else I wanted covering all the angles for me.

"You told Locke you were worried about a jammer. Were you really or was that just to shut him up?"

I grinned. "Now, luv, don't go stirring up trouble. I can rile the thief on my own."

She laughed. "Fine, but you are getting closer." Her tone went sober. "He's not trying to throw off detection. The route he's taking will get him to I-35 in no time, once he's there, he can head directly north through San Antonio to Austin, and on up to Dallas and Fort Worth."

Translation: we didn't have a way of identifying his destination.

"Agreed," I said. "That's why I think there's a more than fifty percent chance that this is a feint. He wants to pull our attention away. Use the time while I play his game, to dig in deeper there. What does he *not* want us to find?"

"I'd say it's a who, not a what. The who is whoever is working with him," McQuade joined the call. "Stone's got some crazy fucking ideas, but he's not an administrator. Hell, he's not a planner, not the way my father was. Stone is the guy you send in to wreck things. You give him orders. He likes to spout some crazy damn rhetoric, but he will get the job done."

"If someone else gives him a map," Fallon said slowly, her voice thoughtful.

"Yes," McQuade answered and I could practically hear all of them thinking in the silence that followed.

"So," Locke asked. "Who would he listen to?"

"We need to do some research. Keep your comm open for pinging so I can still track and lock in if you need me?" It was a request. One she didn't usually have to make when we were on a job. After her reaction to McQuade cutting her out earlier, I understood why.

"I'll keep it open." I didn't think it was a real problem. "I will cut it if I think they are using the signal to triangulate where you are." Compromise offered, and it was as much as I was willing to concede.

"I can probably mask the transmission. Give me an hour and I'll check in." Compromise accepted.

"Be careful, luv."

"You do the same," she responded, the tart note punctuating the sentence made me smile. I was closing on the red dot. When I had him in visual range, I pegged my speed to his and settled in to follow.

Right on cue, my comm chimed. I tapped it to answer. "I'm here."

"How is it going?"

"He's going straight north. No stops. No pauses, no slowing down or speeding up. You?"

"I did a sweep of his car, and it's definitely him. Apparently, whoever he works for keeps him under surveillance twenty-four seven."

"Hmm. Sounds like someone doesn't trust him." I turned that nugget of information over in my head.

"It does, doesn't it?" There was a hint of a smile in her voice. "Whoever they are, they might be a little smarter than me."

"I find that difficult to believe," I countered.

"Oh? I should warn you, Remy, flattery will not work on me."

I grinned. "Then it doesn't hurt either of us for me to offer it, does it?"

"Hmmph." The little snort made me smile.

"What else did you find?"

Because despite her comment about them being a little smarter than her, she sounded quite pleased about something. To be fair, I would never begrudge her enjoying herself.

"Where he started his day. You see, keeping someone under surveillance with this tight of a leash means the log also keeps track of where it started and stopped each day."

"GPS coordinates."

Oh, that was priceless.

"Exactly. McQuade and Locke are on their way to do an inspection and sweep right now."

I frowned. "One of them should have stayed with you. At least until we cover that this isn't a blatant swap to pull us away."

"Hmm-hmm, he who decides to run off on his own doesn't get to call us on tactical choices." The scold was playful, but I didn't miss the firmer note in it. "I have them on another line. I can link all of you if you want or we can just work with me on the switchboard."

It was how we'd always done it. Yet—how we'd always done it had begun to shift and change. Her being taken had illustrated just how vital she was to me.

To all of us.

"You can handle it," I told her, giving way on the fact that she was very well aware of her own abilities and information. "Read me in on the new plan?"

"Cooperation looks good on you, Remy," she murmured and the ease my cock had gotten from the distance vanished as it hardened all over again.

"Thank you, don't change the subject." It was my turn to point her back to where we needed to be. Flirting would have to wait.

"New plan. You stick with Stone for the moment. I'm working on some code to layer into the one running on his devices, so I can track him like whoever has his leash without alerting the leash holder to my presence. Might take me a couple of hours."

"You can do it." No doubt existed within me. "Soon as you have him tagged, I can come back or bag him for you. Whatever you need."

"I like having options." The playfulness bubbled up for a moment before she sobered. "While we do this, McQuade and Locke are going to find the current 'base' or residence. Whatever it is. We want to know who he is working for and what they have set up out here. I've been keeping an eye on town and it's been—illuminating."

The wariness in that last word gave me significant pause. "How so?"

"It's a virtual ghost town now. Even the diner is closed. No cars. No sign of population. No movement. They were there for a couple of hours *after* you left and now—nothing."

"Reynolds?" The journalist's very real fear had been something visceral.

"No sign of him. I'm sorry, I have been skimming footage from earlier. I don't see anything suspicious, necessarily. Just one by one, folks leaving. The cars pull out and go. No one comes back."

I frowned.

"They were evacuating slowly." That was the only conclusion.

"Agreed. They did it without fanfare or a lot of chaos. Now, Reynolds may still be in his apartment and lying low. But I have no movement discernible through the camera on his windows. His blinds are shut and the curtains closed."

"I should have left a mic."

"I don't disagree," she said, the forgiving note in her voice wrapping around me like an embrace. "But I also didn't disagree with *why* you didn't leave one. We had other issues to deal with."

At the time, McQuade had been missing and Fallon panicked, even as Patch had fought to keep her cool. I understand the divisive nature of the competing desires.

Even more so now, because I had tasted my own fear when she'd vanished. Not an experience I was eager to repeat.

"Keep an eye out for him?" I didn't owe the man anything, but if I read him right, he'd been genuinely trying to warn me off.

"I will. You still good?"

"Haven't been good a day in my life, luv. Not planning to start now."

The surprise snort of laughter followed by her chuckles made me grin. Exactly what I wanted to hear.

"Talk to you soon," she said amidst the amusement.

"You definitely will." It was a promise. The soft beep told me the call muted. We were still online, so she could track me, but we didn't need an open line to do it.

It was entirely possible Stone had done this to lure McQuade out and lull him into a trap. That had occurred to me. I didn't doubt it hadn't occurred to all of them as well.

Patch hadn't mentioned it, but we were all adults here. It would be a solid play to get McQuade off the scent by following Stone. Based on what McQuade had said, Stone wasn't the one likely running the show.

Involved? Yes.

In charge? No.

He sounded like a bit of a prick as it was, and McQuade more than confirmed Stone should be on the kill list. So if this was a trap, I was more than happy to spring it. Stone's involvement was enough for me to agree to scratch him off the board.

TWENTY-SEVEN

PATCH

I nstead of being able to turn Remy around quickly as I would have preferred, we had to let the gambit play out. Whoever wrote the code to keep track of Stone, had used an elegant format. Adding my own lines to it would trigger alarms if I didn't do it exactly right.

By the time night fell fully, Remy was in the Dallas area. He'd followed Stone to a five-star hotel, where the former general had checked in and then gone straight to the bar for a drink. He'd been there for the last—I checked my watch—hour.

McQuade and Locke were running into issues at the location we'd tracked using the GPS in the program. It was a ranch property, large house, bigger barn and a few outbuildings. They were empty.

Worse, there were definite signs of equipment movement with heavy tire treads going in and out. Had they begun the evacuation that fast? Or was it already in progress when Stone confronted McQuade?

I rubbed at my tired eyes. The buzz from the

271

earlier orgasms had long since passed due to my frustration with all of this. We needed a break. Just one—and Stone seemed to be it and yet, here we were running into a salvo of distractions, half-clues, and worst of all, dead ends.

After a brief consult, they'd all decided that McQuade and Locke inspecting the location was vital as was Remy sticking with his target. Grabbing my mostly cold coffee cup, I grimaced. It didn't have much left in it, but I needed more caffeine and I didn't like cold coffee unless I ordered it that way.

One more sweep of my screens and I pushed the chair back. Stiffness invaded my muscles after having sat still for so long. The earlier boneless relief brought on by McQuade's touch and Remy's kisses, not to mention the fact Locke had heard everything—heat rose through me just at the memory—was completely absent now.

More was the pity. Interruptions of all types had demarcated my days for years. Particularly *after* I left my job. Building my life as an operator meant rigid controls, with checks and balances at every stage. That provided safety, but it also meant I didn't have fail safes or coverage when I needed downtime.

Better to not need it, so I learned to adapt. I slept when I could and worked the rest of the time. It kept me alive and my mind stimulated. Maybe it hadn't been the best existence, but it had been one. At least until...

No sooner did I try to think about what happened *before* I woke up after the bullet creased my forehead, than the memories slipped away, Spilling through the cracks like water sluicing away.

Irritated, I stared at the empty coffee pot. I'd made straight brew earlier. With as much work to do as I'd had, it was just easier than making a new espresso every couple of hours.

Now the pot was empty, because I'd filled my mug the last time and then shut it off. I'd meant to start a fresh pot, but then nothing.

Sighing, I stared at the pot, then at my cup. My stomach protested. Had I even eaten? The idea of food wasn't that appealing. Fine, I'd get the coffee started, and make a sandwich. That would be enough to get by on, surely.

The cold unit didn't offer us frozen, but the fridge was more than enough. The water tank was designed more for showering or washing. Probably not the best for drinking. We had bottled water in gallons for coffee.

It didn't take long to get the new pot brewing. I had my headset on, and I'd hear if any of them wanted me. It didn't take me long to build a sandwich and I'd eaten half of it by the time the pot finished brewing.

A part of me wished I'd just gone the espresso route or a flat white, but the fresh brewed coffee tickled my nose delightfully. I made myself finish the sandwich though, because after a full pot of coffee, I was just asking to strip my stomach by adding more without food.

No sooner did I finish the food and claim the coffee cup than my bladder made its protests known. Not for the first time since boarding this lovely moving office, was I grateful for the fact that they'd also installed a bathroom. It was a limited tank and they had to deal with it, but I didn't ask any questions and they offered no details.

That worked for me.

That *really* worked for me. I returned to my desk, swept my gaze over the three monitors and all the camera angles. I was keeping one eye on the town, and the other on the boys. While Remy had taken our SUV, Locke had gone to lift another vehicle. It didn't have the cameras already installed, but we'd rigged something up.

I could see the buildings they were clearing and all the signals were reading strong. No movements grabbed my attention, so I checked their links. All live and connected, just muted.

Good. Pee break time. I snagged my phone which would give me a smaller monitor if I needed it and hurried to the little privacy room they'd curtained. Eyes closed, I tried to think through the code I'd been working on amending. I needed to be more subtle than the original author.

Each call would need to be embedded in a command function they had already created. That would help to avoid setting off any traps that would quarantine the additions and let me use their own tools against them.

The fact that someone had created something quite so elegant annoyed me on a very primitive level. It was also something of a personal challenge. When I finished up, I did a quick wash of my hands using sanitizer then headed back to my desk.

A beep in my ear alerted me to the incoming call.

"Talk to me," I said as I connected us and slid back into my chair.

"I'm starting to think being here is where I needed to be," Remy said by way of greeting. "Connect the boys so I can brief you all at once?"

"Standby." I hit two buttons on the keyboard, sweeping the camera angles by matter of habit as I chimed into both Locke and McQuade's comms.

"Here," Locke said.

"Online, Sugar Bear. Missing us already?"

"Of course, I am," I answered with a grin, then connected the separate lines into one, so that the four of us were on the same call. "Remy is also online and needs to debrief. Are you secure?"

"As secure as can be at a completely abandoned facility." Irritation discolored every single syllable of McQuade's statement.

I sighed. "We'll gather what we can. Maybe we've forced them to move and that's not a bad thing." If their operations were being delayed, it meant we had them on the back foot. Maybe it was petty of me, but I'd spent enough years hiding from them.

"Will do," Locke said. "What do you have for us, Remy?"

I switched my view to the hotel he was at. One nice thing about the location—*lots* of security cameras. *Lots* of them. It took me a minute to find the bar they were in. I zeroed in on Remy first, then did a sweep of the room.

The cameras didn't move, so I had to toggle from camera to camera to find the right angle.

"Stone is in a meeting. He's been in a bar since we got here and he's about six bourbons down. I half-expect him to stumble, stutter, and slur, but he seems to be flushed and that's about it." Mild disgust filled Remy's voice.

There they were. He wasn't wrong, Stone did appear if not ill, at least vaguely off. His face was damp. The cameras were all in black and white and the zoom was a joke. When did they install these? The early aughts?

"Who is he meeting with?"

"Working on that," Remy said. "I want some confirmation. You got them yet, Patch? If you need a better angle, I can move. I'm also sending you a couple of pictures."

"Oh good. The hotel's cameras are *terrible*. They pixelate before I can bring them into focus. Send them over?"

"Already sent." The few second lag felt far longer than it was, but then I wanted to see *now* and in our high-speed world, any delay was too much delay.

The first image loaded via my phone's connection and I switched screens to pull it up. The first one was an angle of the back of the heads of two men greeting Stone. He looked less than pleased to see them.

"Not a friendly meeting."

"Not as far as I can tell," Remy agreed. "I can't tell if these are partners or bosses. But they are *not* happy with him. Guy on the left is Peter Anton. He's a little older and he has a couple of new scars but he's definitely the same guy and when I knew him, he was ASIS."

Australian Secret Intelligence Service. We didn't hear about them as much in the States or even in Western Europe. FBI. DGIS. MI-6. Them we heard about.

ASIS was far more subtle.

"How long since you last saw him?" I asked, already pulling up a screen to try and tunnel ASIS. I wanted more information on Peter Anton.

"Ten years," Remy answered. "Let's just say, we were not friendly then, we're definitely not friendly now. I didn't like his work ethic and he didn't like that I was a better shot."

"Good to know," McQuade said. "We got pictures of him yet?"

"Coming in now," I told him as I tabbed back to the screen then matched the second photo to the ASIS profile. They really did look like the same person.

I forwarded both images to Locke and McQuade. The soft dings over the line told me they'd received the images. McQuade let out a little grunt.

While the third photo downloaded, I rolled back to the ASIS connection. It was going to take a moment to get in. They had some nice encryption. Very nice, in fact. They'd definitely invested in it.

Unfortunately for their programmer, tunneling through these was my bread and butter. I wanted his ASIS file and—there we went.

"He left ASIS seven years ago, while it doesn't say he left in disgrace, he left in the middle of an investigation into abuse of power and position. Reading between the lines here, he was asked to resign and they made the investigation go away."

That happened sometimes. If they didn't want the egg on their face or if they didn't have quite enough to force the issue.

"That's three years longer than I think he should have been there."

"Hmm... I'm seeing a psych hold on his file dating back a decade during recovery time. Remy, it sounds like he had a hard time getting over you."

"If he'd died that would have solved the issue." The bland response made McQuade laugh and I had to admit, I grinned. "So, seven years ago, he takes a walk and now he's in bed with Stone. Who is our third man?"

I flipped back to the screen and stopped cold on the man staring back at me. That was a face I'd never wanted to see again.

"Sugar Bear?" McQuade prompted but I couldn't find the voice to answer them, not yet.

The man staring back at me stirred up a tempest of memories, all better forgotten. I licked my lips and then did a quick search, looking for a photo to match it too. Maybe I was remembering him wrong.

It had been a few years...

No images were prompted by my search and I had to drill down. He'd been scrubbed. That made sense. We had created sniffers, search and destroy protocols, when necessary, to eliminate public data on our operatives.

It protected them from accidental search and

the whole world was connected these days. Those types of programs were exactly how I scrubbed myself, my history, everything about me.

Those programs were how I became nobody. It kept me safe for a long time.

Now that same type of system was protecting him. I didn't think so. I had caches of data on the dark web, set up and accessible via IP address and pass code phrases that only I knew the answers to. They were a combo of pop culture and associated candy flavors.

The system made sense to me, and would likely fuck with anyone else. You only got two shots to get it right and then the info would self-nuke.

I found the file I wanted—

"Fallon," Locke said softly. "You still there?"

"luv?" Even Remy prompted me, the worry in their voices breached the barricade I erected around myself. It was like the water coming over the storm wall.

"One second," I managed and it even came out in an even, and grounded voice. "Just verifying."

The challenge popped up with a Taylor Swift song lyric accompanied by a photo of a woman from the Real Housewives of New Jersey.

The answer was Bruce Springsteen.

The files opened immediately and I paged through them to find the jpegs.

Marty Cartwright stared at me from his identification badge. He'd been my direct report supervisor, and the man who gave me all my instructions. Comparing the photo to the one Remy had sent, I lined them up side by side.

"I know him." No matter how hard I tried, I couldn't keep the tremble out of my voice. "I worked for him. When I left Section Five—when I walked away, he was my boss. His name is Marty Cartwright. Or at least, that's who he went by. That could have been an alias. He certainly doesn't exist anywhere now."

The rather generic name returned a lot of possibilities, too many to parse right now. But even using matching data to filter the search didn't turn up anything with him in it.

"I've got a direct line on him," Remy said, the offer was there. If I wanted him gone, all I had to do was say the word.

"Tempting," I admitted.

"Do it," McQuade said. "If he's in bed with Stone and this Aussie bastard, then we're better off scratching all of them off. Maybe it doesn't kill the body, but I've always found that cutting off the head can do a lot of damage."

"But if they aren't the head," Locke interjected. "We may be open—"

An alarm went off and I jerked. Then flipped the screens back. The alarm was an intrusion on *my* system.

"Patch," Locke said in a tight voice. "Talk to us."

"Right. Now." McQuade's order cut through the chatter and anxiety. "We're on our way to you."

"Standby, we've been on an open-line between us and someone is trying to tag my system. Pretty sure it's coming from where you are." Remy was in a hotel. McQuade and Locke were at that facility.

"What do you need?" Locke was already thinking.

"Kill the power out there." If they had a generator... I couldn't focus on that right now.

"Grenade," McQuade said and I blinked as my fingers froze mid-keystroke.

An explosion echoed over the line as I made myself type. The screen in the corner showed the flash of whatever he'd detonated. The intrusion hiccuped, but it was still going.

"They have a generator," I said.

"Got another grenade?" Locke asked, almost idly.

"Of course, I have another. Got a target?"

Locke's answer washed over me. The banter. The coordinates. Through it all, Remy was quiet, but my screen showed him still connected. I blocked the next intrusion and shut it down.

"Grenade," McQuade called out again. This time the explosion was a lot further away, but the flash was no less intense.

The intrusion ceased.

I blew out a breath. "That did it."

Remy's long exhale echoed my own relief. "Good. Get back to her and move the damn truck."

"Agreed," Locke said and then another alarm sounded, this one was not for my system but for the truck.

"Patch?" McQuade's voice dropped. "Tell me you're armed."

I flipped the screen to see the car parked behind the truck and the two men getting out of it. It was dark out there and they were all in black.

They were also armed.

Yanking open the drawer next to me, I pulled out the gun and slid the full magazine into it to load it. I was not a fan of guns. I never had been. Having one right here was practical.

"I am."

"We're already on the way to you." They didn't give me an ETA.

They didn't have to.

They were too far away to help me in the immediate future. I was on my own.

"I'm here," Remy said into my ear. "Shut off the internal power. Set the spotlights to the access points. It will blind them when they open. You go for center mass, luv. You go for the largest target and you don't hesitate. You just fire."

My heart slammed against my ribs. The gritty taste of fear soured in my throat. This was—brutally familiar. Sweat prickled my skin and icy hot chills cascaded through me.

"You can do this, luv. Trust me."

I'd give anything if they were the ones here. Two keys and the internal lights were off. I left the desk and shifted to where the room divider was. On one side, the door near the cab. On the other, the ramp that slid down when the back opened.

They'd been coming up the sides. I could see my screen still. It was dark, the movement outside hard to detect. But they were going to the side.

"Breathe, Fallon," Locke said. "Deep breaths. You don't want to hold your breath or hyperventilate."

That was excellent advice. Back door or side?

Where were they coming in?

"You have those assholes in your sights, Remy?" McQuade asked.

"Yep. Just one word, and three shots. They'll be done."

"Good."

The silence stretched excruciatingly. The sound of something burning echoed into the rig. They were cutting into the side door. I closed my eyes a split second before the lights targeted the door as it opened.

Then I opened them as I took aim.

And I fired.

TWENTY-EIGHT
PATCH

"Patch?" Remy's voice penetrated the dull roar left behind by firing the gun. It didn't matter how steady my aim had been, I couldn't look away from the two bodies piled on each other. I'd emptied half the magazine into the pair.

Pulling the trigger repeatedly had left me deafened. But I couldn't look away. The lights had gone off. The car was still out there. My screen was still on and the guys were on the line.

"Almost there, Sugar Bear. Are you secure?" McQuade's voice trickled past the ringing. It sounded like he was a thousand miles away.

He wasn't there. Neither was Remy. It was just me and the two dead men.

"Just keep breathing for us, luv. Let out another long breath, you don't have to say anything."

Remy was in Dallas. Locke and McQuade were...

"Sugar Bear, in three minutes, you're going to see our headlights on the monitor. The alarms will probably go off again. It's us."

They were close. That was good. My chest hurt, and my lungs burned. Oh. I was holding my breath. I blew out a long sigh.

"There she is," Remy said. "Don't let go of the line now, luv. We've got you and we're not letting go."

"Two minutes," McQuade counting it down helped. Particularly when it was an eternity between three minutes and two.

"We're on the dirt road," Locke added as McQuade said "one minute," and another shuddering breath left me. Their headlights glowed on my computer monitor.

"Can you see their headlights?" Remy verified.

"Yes." Oh, that word came out so very small.

"Good girl," McQuade said, the rubble in his voice adding more of a growl than normal. "That's my sugar bear. I'm doing a little dance as we walk up... can you see me?"

I had to drag my gaze from the downed bodies to the screen again. It was hard to refocus but there were two men, just like there had been two who came in the door.

The air backed up in my lungs.

"I'm dancing, Sugar Bear. Tell me you can see me." McQuade's order snapped through the haze and I blinked. One of the men was dancing. It was a lot like John Travolta in that movie...what was that movie?

"I remember that one," I said slowly. "Wasn't Uma Thurman in it?"

Why couldn't I remember the name?

"Pulp Fiction," Locke said. "You're right. He's

doing that weird dance. Remind me to get you real lessons, McQuade."

"Fuck. Off." The familiarity in the teasing and grousing helped to crack more of the wall that separated me from the rest of the world. I didn't even know when that wall went up.

My hand trembled.

"They're coming, luv," Remy said, his accent seemed softer somehow, kinder. "Hang on. Are you still pointing the gun at the door?"

"We're here, Sugar Bear," McQuade called from the same direction as the pair of bodies. I heard him on my headset and with my own ears.

I tried to swallow around the lump in my throat. "Is—is Justus with you, still?"

"Yes," Locke answered himself. "We're here and we can see the bodies."

"Hell of a shot, Sugar Bear, hell of a shot." That was McQuade again. They were here.

The shaking in my soul translated to shaking in my arm and my hand. Everything trembled. The pain of keeping my arm pointed hit me and all the numbness holding me in position drained away. It left me pained and cramping.

"You can let them in," Remy said, his words were so soft in my ear. It didn't play in stereo like Locke or McQuade. Because Remy was still there, and the guys were here.

I flicked a look at the screen on my computer. They'd left the headlights on their acquired vehicle on. It illuminated Locke.

"It's us," he said, directly to the camera. Had he been talking to me through it since they got here?

Like someone cut my strings, I sank to the floor abruptly and lowered the gun.

"Come in. I'm lowering the gun." I barely seemed to have finished the words and Locke was there. He'd left the bodies to McQuade, who was checking them. When Locke plucked the gun from my hand, I let it go and then I was wrapped in his arms.

The adrenaline crash was profound. I fought the waves of nausea that hit and let Locke just hold me.

"You did good, Sugar Bear," McQuade said and I managed to force my eyes open to meet his gaze. He was checking the bodies. "I'm gonna deal with this..."

"I can—"

"Stay right here," Locke said, before he slid an arm under my legs and lifted me off the floor. "In fact, you're gonna take a little walk around to the other side. You don't need to see this part."

"Let them take care of you, luv," Remy said, he was so solid. "I've still got eyes on these guys, but tell me right now, do you need me back there?"

I wanted to say yes. I wanted to say yes really bad. "I do want you here..."

"Want is good, luv. But do you need me? Cause if you can let them look after you, I can stay on these guys and see if I can get us more."

It was a choice. Eyes closed, I tucked my head against Locke's shoulder. The steadiness of his heart helped. The fact he was holding me helped.

They came.

I hadn't been alone this time. Or unarmed.

Wait, I'd been armed before. I just hadn't been

able to get to my weapon before they were on me. That reality dawned with crystal clear clarity.

Dammit.

Pain lanced through my head, an icy spike that seemed to stab deep into my brain. The tears burning in my eyes offered no relief, only anger. Gradually, the fact Locke rocked me slowly registered.

We weren't near my computer anymore and my headset was off. Instead, he sat on the bed with me in his lap. The gentle sway accompanied the circular rubbing of his hand against my back. All of it worked to push back the nightmarish reality.

Nothing could make it go away fully. Nothing.

At the moment, I wasn't even sure answers would fix this. In the past few weeks, I'd lost the security of anonymity. I'd been found by three men I trusted, but had never "met" before. At the same time, I'd been compromised and tortured.

The scars decorating my skin served as a road map to some of what had been done to me. I could imagine the rest. I had a very good imagination. If not for them, I would still be in the hands of my tormentors.

The information I'd taken might be the only currency and leverage I had left. Yet, I couldn't help but feel like I was being herded in that direction. The plan they'd drawn out, how "release" might have been manufactured and allies created for me left me wondering how could I ever know if something was *real*?

"Here. I got this." McQuade was back. Tenderness sanded down all the rougher edges in his manner and voice. I forced my swollen eyes open and then winced.

Oh that was a mistake.

"Careful, Fallon," Locke cautioned and then pressed a cool, damp towel to my eyes. It was almost heavenly. I was not a cryer. I'd never been one. Right now, sobbing seemed to be my release for fear, for anger, and even for pleasure.

"My eyes hurt," I told them in a nasally voice that held all the evidence of my weeping.

"No doubt." McQuade settled a hand on my thigh. The contact helped to ground me. "You did good, Sugar Bear. Clean groupings on both men."

Locke sighed. "I don't think *that* is going to help."

"It doesn't matter if it helps right now," McQuade countered easily. "It matters that she knows she took care of herself. She *saved* herself. She did it damn well."

I sniffed a laugh, then reached up to pull the damp cloth down so I could peer at him. Even squinting hurt. "You mean that... Don't you?"

Why I had to verify, I didn't know. But I needed to hear him say it. McQuade didn't sugar coat *anything*. Whether he was calling me Sugar Bear or not, whether he was grousing on the phone or buried inside of me, he was one of the most brutally honest people I'd ever known.

"Fuck yeah, I mean it. You didn't even use the full clip, which..." He mimed a chef's kiss with his fingers before returning his hand to my thigh. "Damn good job."

Somehow, that *helped*.

Still... "We're not done."

"No." Now there was a measure of apology in his voice. "We need to move. I've dealt with the bodies and the blood. We're better off getting back out on the highway and away from here before they send someone to look for them."

I used the damp cloth to press against my eyes as I sat up. Locke helped balance me and then eased me to sitting next to him. It was a lot chillier even with that small distance between us.

Holding the damp cloth to my face, I worked on taking a little self-inventory. The tears had stopped —mostly. The fog of panic wasn't clouding my brain anymore. Right...

I needed to focus.

"Did they have any identification on them?" I took the time to wipe my face. The tear tracks could at least be erased, even if I stayed blotchy.

"Nothing I found useful. A couple of plain white security cards with no numbers, addresses, or names. Likely access to something but who knows. Car appears to be stolen, so nothing in there. They are dressed in suits—look like government issue except..."

I dragged the damp cloth down to meet his measured gaze where he knelt in front of me. "Except?"

"Military issued boots. The suits don't fit them well."

"Wet work operatives made to look like FBI or another alphabet agency." That made a kind of sadistic sense.

"That would be my guess. Their fingerprints

were burned off. I don't have time to do dental impressions but I got some DNA."

"Pictures, too?"

"Yes, but I'd rather you didn't look at those until more of the shock wears off." The guarded suggestion wasn't a bad one.

"I can do that. We need to move right now, more than we need to dig." Bit by bit, I was clawing my way back. "Remy still on Stone and the others?"

"Yes," Locke answered. "We've got him on comms still."

Right... "Okay, I need my headset and some water. Then I'll get on this."

"You can take a beat," McQuade said. "We need to get on the road and Remy is waiting for your word before he acts."

Before he puts a bullet in all three of the targets. "That's tempting," I admitted. "But I'd never know for sure without verification."

The look McQuade and Locke shared said they'd already guessed that. Honestly, that decided me even more.

"Right. We need to drive to Leesburg, Virginia."

"Leesburg?" McQuade verified. At my nod, he continued, "For?"

"We need to identify all the players. We need to know what my former boss, Stone, and the ASIS agent have in common. To do that, we need to get an item from Leesburg and then I can get the data from the dark web."

Locke frowned. "You can't just access the dark web from here?"

I shrugged. "Yes. But without the item, it won't do us any good. You or me."

Their questions seemed to radiate in the air around them.

"Look, it sounds complicated, because it is to someone who isn't me. You need the physical item and the dark web address. But even if you have both, if you don't know how to use them, you still can't get to the data." When Locke would have opened his mouth, I raised a hand. "No, I couldn't tell you how to do it. I won't know until I have both in front of me."

McQuade frowned. "It's a puzzle of some kind."

"I like puzzles. I like to make it a challenge. It's harder to hack something that changes from day to day, season to season—even month to month. Ciphers and keys are great, but you need an X factor to make something as secure as possible."

I killed two people today. I'd never done that before. Not with my own hands. Had I participated in how I helped my contractors in the field? Yes. But that was at a distance. This was much more intimate. Much more personal.

"You okay for me to drive and McQuade to be on watch with me?" It was a fair question, after the assault on the rig, they might know about it. That could create other complications. Ideally, they hadn't confirmed to anyone what they'd found before they began the assault.

"I can even do something to mask the transponder so if they are searching for it, we'll transmit something different to the highway scanners." I wiped my face again. "Give a me a couple of minutes to use the bathroom and wash my face, then we can go."

"Hey," McQuade said, catching my arm as I stood. "You're not okay."

"No," I agreed with him. "But I will be." Then, because I could, I put a hand to his chest and pushed up on my toes to brush his jaw with a kiss. The beard there teased me. Locke had risen to his feet and when I turned to him, he dipped his head for a kiss.

It was light, just a glide of lips to lips. When he steadied me with one hand on my hip, I curled between them and they crushed me in a gentle, all-encompassing hug.

Three deep breaths to scrub the scent of death and blood away, leaving only the hot masculine scent of them.

"Okay." I pushed back and straightened. "Let's get to work."

Ten minutes later, I had my headset back on, my chair locked and a seatbelt in place as the rig began to move. Tapping two buttons, I exhaled a deep breath. "Remy—we have a plan."

CHAPTER
TWENTY-NINE
PATCH

Sleep was a battle. The drive to Leesburg would take a couple of days, particularly if we didn't want to attract attention. Remy stayed on the targets for a few more hours, tagged them before they separated, then met us on the road.

I'd avoided any kind of sleep until we rendezvoused a couple of hours east of Dallas on I-30. It was after three in the morning. The roads were quiet, the rest stops were still. It took no time to find a spot and let Remy pull the SUV on board.

He'd left the vehicle and come straight to me. The grip of his hands on my elbows steadied me as much as it pulled me to him. I didn't quite collapse into his embrace as I had with Locke.

McQuade said something and clapped Remy on the shoulder before he'd pressed a kiss to my head. Then he was gone. A few minutes later, the truck gave a little jerk as we began to move again.

Remy rocked with the motion easily, keeping both of us on our feet. "You need to see sleep, luv."

The words seemed to vibrate in his chest and I soaked up the sound of him and the comfort he offered.

"I don't know if I can." Although the swelling had gone down some, my eyes still hurt—a lot. They were red-rimmed and I wasn't even sure eye-drops would help at this point.

"I'm not McQuade," Remy said. "But I'll stay with you while you sleep."

I blew out a breath.

"Trust me?"

The request cut the legs out from under any objection. "I promise, this isn't about trust. I do trust you." I trusted all of them.

"Then let's see if we can get you some sleep. It'll make me feel better too."

Frowning, I leaned back to search his face. "Did something else happen?"

"Yes, luv. You were caught alone, and had to defend yourself, and I was too damn far away to take the shots for you." The sobriety of that statement and the self-recrimination in his eyes had me reaching to hug him again.

"I don't know if I would have gotten through it if you guys hadn't been on the phone."

"Let's not ever find out, shall we?"

I didn't want to find out. Instead, I let him coax me over to the bed. Shoes off, I slid out of the new sweatshirt, but that still left me in leggings and a tank top. Once I was under the covers, Remy set up a gun on the wall, in a holster he could velcro into place. It put a gun in reach for him.

"Too much?"

After a moment, I shook my head. "Not after today."

A flash of a smile softened his face. I pushed back the blankets when he would have laid on top. One long studying look later, he slid into the bed next to me and wrapped an arm around me—after he rolled me onto my side so I was snug with my back to his chest.

He held up his cell phone and pressed a button. A moment later, McQuade answered. "All good back there?"

"Yep. Getting her to sleep for a while. Try not to throw us around."

"You have faith in my driving," McQuade said in a dry tone and I couldn't help the laugh that escaped.

"Good thing that I'm driving," Locke said, his voice a bit farther away. "Get some sleep. We'll wake you in a few hours for breakfast."

Few hours. I smothered a yawn. Technically, breakfast was a couple of hours away...

"Don't call us," Remy said, almost idly as he began to stroke my hair. "We'll call you." There was just a hint of humor in his voice. "Maybe."

He hung up before they could respond. The slow massage of his fingers over my scalp eased some of the tension knotting my spine. The lance drilling into my skull was still there.

"Go to sleep, goddess," he whispered. "Dream of me." Bit by bit, he smoothed it away. Like water rushing over rock, the slow stroke of his hand through my hair washed the tension out of me.

It was...

~

"TALK TO ME," I said, after hitting the button to answer the call.

"Gorgeous," Boxer said by way of greeting.

"I told you no," was my answer. It was almost four in the morning and I was tired. It had been a long night, I'd juggled both Remington and Locke's operations.

Thankfully, Locke's was more about transport and teasing. Remington's had taken some juggling. The fact they were in completely different parts of the world wasn't lost on me, but I'd made it work and they were both on their way.

"You know," he said, his tone playful. "You always start out with 'no,' before you even hear the question."

I wasn't in the mood for this. "Because the majority of the time, what you want is for me to take on something you agreed to and I'm already busy. You don't want to keep being buried in work, stop accepting jobs. Now, I'm going—"

"Wait," Boxer said before I could cut off the call. "I hear you. I absolutely do. You gave me great advice before. I listened."

"My advice was to trust your gut and if it felt hinky, say 'no,' and then walk away." I reached for my coffee cup. The dregs of the last cup I'd made were in there and I downed the cold remnants in one swallow.

Disgusting, but I'd take whatever jolt it had left. My eyes were so tacky, it was like they had glue as well as sandpaper in them.

"Exactly." Boxer snapped his fingers. Most of the time, I didn't mind Boxer. But the past few months, his excuses for contact had grown more and more out-landish. To be fair, I should probably take my own advice. If it felt off, say no and cut the contact. "It was excellent advice."

"So why am I talking to you?" It better be good.

"Maybe I just wanted to say thank you," he suggested.

"Want to try that again?" I eyed my empty coffee cup and rose. My chair squeaked and my back cracked. Or maybe that was my hips. Fuck, even my ass was numb. I'd been still for too long.

"You know, you have balls that clank." He let out a humorless laugh.

"Thank you," I said.

"I didn't mean it as a compliment."

"Too bad," I retorted. "I'm tired, Boxer. You have three seconds to tell me what you want or I'm cutting the line."

"Goddamn."

"Three," I said, hitting two keys to shut the system down and then turning to open the door. "Two."

"You were right, about trusting the gut. If they were hinky, I should have said no. I didn't say no."

I stopped, but the locks were already disengaging.

"And I'm sorry, I really should have listened to you."

I frowned. Ice slid up my spine. "What did you do?"

"I had no choice. It was do the job or die. So... I did the job."

The door shoved inwards abruptly and there were men swarming toward me.

"I gave them you..." I didn't hear the rest of what he was saying as a fist caught me right in the stomach. I jerked away, yanking the headset cord from the phone and sending the device tumbling.

Another man grabbed me from behind and a bag came over my head. I didn't stop fighting. I just needed another foot. I jabbed my elbow back into the man's crotch and lurched forward.

The killswitch was on the wall. I hit it. And the drives in my main machine fried. It wouldn't kill the backups but they would have to find those.

Then my head was knocked against the wall and the world went gray and fuzzy. The next time I woke up, I was in the buck of a truck, bound, gagged, and a bag over my head.

I groaned.

A mistake, because something icy cold touched me and voltage cascaded through my body.

The next time I woke, it was dark but I wasn't alone. Hands grabbed at me. Pinching. Pushing. Pain.

Then I was out again.

I woke up in the room with Shaggy and Mr. Cold. Mr. Cold did nothing when Shaggy started putting his cigarettes out on me. To be fair, I didn't either.

Pain and I had become fast acquaintances.

The world swayed in and out of focus. I couldn't move and my tongue felt too large for my mouth. But I couldn't even manage to get any spit to form.

"We need her alive for answers," a cool voice said. Not Mr. Cold. This voice wasn't devoid of all emotion. If anything, they sounded annoyed. "Explain to me how your enhanced interrogation is getting us what we need."

"It takes time," Shaggy said. "You didn't tell us she was trained to resist interrogation."

The sound of flesh colliding with flesh echoed around me. I tried to get my eyes to open but they weren't listening. Another blow landed and something damp hit my face.

"Take it easy," Mr. Cold said. "He's an asshole, but he's an effective asshole."

"When I want your opinion, Sergeant. I'll give it to you." The newcomer was furious. "We are on a clock. We need the information recovered or positively identified as destroyed. Then you can clean up the rest of Cartwright's mess."

Cartwright.

Marty...

They wanted the data.

They weren't going to get it.

"Well, we can't exactly drill into her gray matter and pull it out," Shaggy responded in a haggard, breathless voice. He actually sounded like he was in pain. I wished I could see it.

"Make it work. She's one woman, not even a particularly strong one. Use drugs if you have to. But I want that information reacquired. Work like your life depends on it." Then a door slammed as the man left.

"Bastard," Shaggy said, before he spit.

"Don't push him," Mr. Cold stated. "He will put the gun to your head himself and pull the trigger."

"Where are you going?" Shaggy demanded.

"To get the adrenaline. She can't answer anything if she's not awake." The door closed again. Not that I could do anything about it. I sagged against the restraints. They were the only things keeping me upright.

"If he had a better idea, they would have done something with it already." The bag over my head jerked off. *Oh. That was why I couldn't see. Were my eyes open?*

I wasn't entirely sure. Shaggy's grip bit into my face as he yanked my head back.

"This is going to get a lot worse for you," he told me. I tried to focus on him, but nothing worked the way it should. "Do me a favor and don't cooperate. I'll enjoy taking you apart."

The next time I woke up I was in the new cell. *This wasn't right. I didn't go to the new cell then. That was later.* It didn't matter, it was like being ambushed in the dark with a blindfold. The images fell like blows I couldn't avoid.

Across from me, they dropped a woman into the other cell. *Right, the woman they wanted to be my friend.* I tried to study her again without actually looking at her.

She was important, right?

Before I could see her face, I was being jerked backwards and a towel laid over my eyes and nose and mouth. Then water cascaded over me. I couldn't breathe.

Spots danced before my eyes.

Then I was back in the cell. They were talking. "I don't think it's cause we can't break her," a man was saying.

"No?" The woman was talking to him. *I knew I'd been right about her.* But I didn't know who the new guy was.

"No," he said and he sounded almost apologetic. "I think she doesn't know. These assholes are going to torture her to death to get it out of her."

"Stone thinks she has it. Cartwright says she's the one who took it. He confirmed the identification."

"We should pull her out now, offer her protection..."

A door opened and closed somewhere else, but when I forced my eyes open, the man and woman were gone.

Everything hurt.

More images danced through my mind, jerking and twitching as electricity was applied. Memorizing the codes. Getting out of the cell. Making my way up.

Then they were there...

McQuade and Locke.

They were there and they'd come for me.

~

I JERKED UPRIGHT, a scream half-formed in my throat. Light pooled in the dark, but it reflected off a familiar bald head and a pair of familiar hazel eyes.

"Remy?" I was shaking all over. My body still hurt with all the phantom pain. The scars and the marks made sense now. It was both right there and a thousand miles away. My earlier headache was definitely present.

"I'm here, luv," he promised and I surged up to meet him. I wrapped a hand around the back of his nape and dragged him downward. Our mouths crashed together and I drank him in like the air I so desperately needed.

CHAPTER
THIRTY
PATCH

"Fallon," Remy said, in between terrifically sharp and biting kisses. "You're safe."

They'd been telling me that a lot. Locke had promised me. McQuade promised me. Now Remy—only he promised me before too. Falling back against the bed, I stared up at him.

It was mostly dark and the hum of wheels rolling over highway filled the space. It was kind of soothing in its way. The low lights at the top were on, a yellow-gold cast. Bright enough to see, but not so bright as to blind me.

Remy was a man of complicated shadows. I stroked my hand from his nape to his head. The faint prickles at the base of his skull and around to just over his ears belied the smoothness of his skin.

"Yes," he said in that perfectly delightful accent. "I shave part of my head."

"I don't care," I whispered. "I mean—I do, but I don't. I just love that I can touch you."

"Well, then," he said, a slow smile curving his lips. "Touch away."

Licking my lips, I studied. He really was a contradiction. So there, and present, on the surface, you didn't see the shadows. You saw the simple man who didn't bother with pretense. Yet, he wore a mask.

We all did.

"Honeysuckle," I said, exploring all the dips and divots of his skull. The head was such an odd shape and hair hid so many of its features.

"My favorite." He touched his nose ever so lightly to mine. "And yours?"

I grinned. "I don't think I ever really had a favorite...or maybe I did. But that Fallon isn't me anymore." The Fallon who believed the lies, who drank the Kool-Aid, who took the job. That Fallon had stars in her eyes and a streak to do good.

I had no idea how much bad I'd actually done and someday, I would make myself learn. I would find a way to make up for the work I did in the service of liars.

"That Fallon—she used to like sunflowers, because they were beautiful, and did you know that a sunflower will turn to look at another sunflower if the sun isn't out? They need the light so much, they will look to each other to find it."

I was rambling.

"They're quite beautiful," he agreed.

"They are—that Fallon loved the poetry of them. I thought I was like them. I looked to my fellow workers for the sunlight because I worked in the shadows." I shifted beneath him but when he would have moved, I hooked a leg over his hip. "Stay."

"You're sure?"

"That I want you? Yes. That I want you to stay right here, where I can wrap around you? Also, yes." No hesitation in me at all. We'd been on a course for this for a long time. The flirting and the playfulness had been there.

He settled himself into the cradle of my legs and let his weight rest on me more fully. Oh, I liked the way he felt. All long and lean. Where McQuade was big and brawn, Remy was lean and sharp. Locke was somewhere in between, but they were all perfectly them.

"I pretended to not notice the flirting." It wasn't so hard to admit. "I'm very good at pretend. When I walked away from Section Five or MadOg or whatever they want to call themselves... that Fallon died in a way. She had to die. She had to leave the life she'd been building, the friends, the few family relationships I still had, and just—vanish. One day I was there and the next not."

Framing his face with both of my hands, I indulged myself in exploring his features. Remy also lived in the shadows and at a distance. Contact had to be as alien to him at times as it had become for me.

"It was really easy," I admitted. "Maybe too easy. I'd already been isolating myself so much because of the work. I had few relationships that didn't include time at the office. I think I had maybe four friends who weren't online gamers too."

Grimacing, I shook my head.

"I know how I sound."

"Do you?" He raised his eyebrows.

"Kind of pathetic."

"Not the word I would use, luv."

"No?" Then I shook my head. "I'm not fishing for compliments, I'm trying to be real with you..."

"I believe you," he said, then pressed a soft kiss to the tip of my nose. "You're beautiful, dedicated, and devoted. You're also incredibly loyal. The people at fault are the ones who abused your loyalty, Fallon. The ones who put you in a corner and forced you to make the decision to excise yourself so formidably."

My mouth opened then closed again. When he put it like that...

"Choices were made. You did the best you could with what you knew at the time. You made that choice to serve when you started working there. You made it again when you pulled yourself out. You did one more time when you set up to become an operator..."

He feathered a hand down my face.

"What I see is a fighter, who took them with everything she had and has been kicking their ass from the beginning. You're going to destroy them and I get to help. I know everything I need to know."

That playful smile of his returned.

"Well, everything except one thing." He gave me such a serious look, I didn't know what to do with it.

"What?"

"Your favorite flower."

"I—" I frowned at him and then laughed. It dislodged all this rubble that had been weighing me down. The memories were there. Everything that happened. Every moment of "meeting" them and then discovering that they'd come to find me.

"You?" He added another kiss to the prompt and I forgot about the question, savoring the contact as he massaged my lips with his.

"I don't know what my favorite is going to be now..." I slid my hand back down to his nape. "I barely know who I am going to be now. But I want to find out. I want to make them go away, then I want to find out."

"What do you need?" He stroked my cheek with his thumb, then pressed another kiss to my forehead.

"You," I said, tugging him back down. His mouth crashed into mine, drowning out the broken voices in my head. He blanketed me, answering every demand I made with equal fervor.

His clothes were in the way and pushing at his shirt, I had to break the kiss to get him to pull it up and over. I stopped at the criss-crossing scars over his chest. There were marks that looked like knife wounds. Puckered ones that had to be bullets.

Of course they had scars. McQuade had them too, I'd felt them but I hadn't really had a chance to explore them. There was a small cluster of bullet scars near his left shoulder. Over his heart...

"Someday—will you tell me?" I didn't want to pry but I wanted to know everything.

He caught my hand and pressed a kiss to my palm. "That was another life, but if you need to know, then yes, I'll tell you."

When he nudged up my tank top, I wiggled to

pull it up and off. As though mirroring me, he explored the scars littering my chest and my arms. "I can tell you—"

That snapped his gaze up to mind. The featherlight caress of his fingers sent goosebumps over my skin. "You remembered?"

I nodded slowly. "Yes."

"Are you all right?" Concern bled through the passion in his voice.

"I think by definition of the phrase? No? But... yes?" It didn't make sense to me and at the same time... "It's weird. I remember it and it all happened to me. I remember being afraid. I remember fighting. I remember the conversations I heard and the pain. But I wasn't giving in and I wasn't going to. I know everyone breaks eventually, but the more pain they put me in the less I could help them."

I let out a little laugh and his brow furrowed. "That's not funny, Patch. Your pain is never something to laugh at."

"Maybe not, but I won." Petty? Probably. But I didn't give a damn. "Right now? I'm still winning. I got away. They can't take back from me what I took with me and I'm not alone anymore."

"No," he said in a voice that seemed to swear an oath. "You are *not* alone."

This time it was his hand around my throat and his mouth devouring mine that ended the conversation. He alternated between exquisitely gentle and demandingly sensuous.

All at once, he pulled away and shoved the blankets back. A bump in the road shuddered through us and he caught himself with one hand on the wall. Laughter swelled up through me.

We were in the back of a rig, on a highway, on our way to wage war and we were making out like teenagers. When the ride smoothed again, he reached for my leggings and peeled them down.

"Thank you for not cutting those off," I murmured and that earned me a definite eyebrow.

"You sounded like you enjoyed his knife play," he teased as he undid the snaps on his slacks.

"I did. I enjoyed everything with McQuade and with Locke." I grinned. "You seemed to enjoy me with McQuade too."

"Oh, without a doubt, luv. You are absolutely perfect when you're glowing with an orgasm, all flushed and sweaty, then you scream against my mouth."

I shuddered at the description.

He paused at another bump and glanced toward the side like he could see them through the truck.

"Think they're doing it on purpose?" I rather doubted it but it was kind of funny.

"No, if they knew what we were doing, McQuade would have already pulled over and come back to watch."

What a decadent idea, I shivered.

"Give me a moment." Remy rolled off the bed and tugged his pants down, boxer briefs and all. The angle kept his cock in shadow, but when he rolled back onto the bed, there was no mistaking the erection pressed against me and the...

"Michael Remington," I said. "Are you pierced?"

"Could be," he said, giving me a little nudge back against the pillows. "Want to find out?"

Not bothering to answer him with words, I wrapped my arms around his neck and dragged him down again. His mouth feasted on mine and every time there was a bit of rough road or the faintest bump, we were both laughing.

It was ridiculous and magnetic. He took turns massaging and kissing my breasts. Then he rolled over so I could explore his chest. The heat would flare to life and threaten to consume us and then we'd lock eyes and laughter wrapped us up in its embrace.

In so many ways, I was drunk on Remy. When I finally got to play with his cock though, I took my time and I wished for more light. For now, I let my fingers do the work. There were two barbells, placed right along the ridges around the head of his cock.

The combination of warm metal and silky skin, even with the springier hair at the base— "You're not bald everywhere."

He chuckled. "No, I'm not. Finish your playing or fuck me and put me out of my misery, woman." For all his protest, he laid there, hands beneath his head and watched me as I knelt over him.

There was something deeply erotic in the way he studied me as if he didn't want to miss a single thing.

"I don't know anything about piercings," I told him and gave into the impulse I'd had since I'd first seen them. I dipped my head to wrap my lips around the tip of his cock. I explored the ridge with my tongue and teased over each piercing.

His low groan was even more enticing. Oh, I wanted to play here for hours. Each time I felt him stiffen more or when he let out a low groan, I'd repeat the strokes with my tongue. I wasn't quite giving him a blowjob but I had a very good idea of the geography of those piercings when I lifted my head.

"Done, luv?" The low-voiced question demanded an answer.

"Remy... I'm never going to be done with you." I wasn't going to be done with any of them. Maybe I hadn't been certain of much in the beginning. But they'd literally stopped their lives and come to find me.

The idea they'd found each other at my home and then come looking for me...

"Good, then I can be fine with letting you play later." He hauled me upward, flipped us over so I was below him and he had both of my thighs up and my legs over his shoulders.

"Deal," I said, but the word came out in a rush as he teased his cock over my entrance. I was already so damn wet. I never looked away from him as he cupped my breast, nor when he teased the nipple.

He threatened to drive me mad with the gliding friction that offered no real pressure. Maybe it was to get even with me for the tiny little flicks of my tongue. At the same time, I was utterly desperate for him. Dragging a hand between us, I wrapped it around his cock. He hissed out a breath before he swooped down to steal my mouth again in another toe-curling kiss.

Maybe he hadn't been determined to make me insane before, but stroking his tip and those glorious piercings up and down and teasing my own clit with them was better than a vibrator. Particularly when he alternated between laughter and gasping.

A wide variety of pleasure for both of us. But when I tilted my hips higher and angled him just right, it was both of us groaning as he filled me with one thrust. So aware of his piercings, I savored the way they teased me with each thrust.

He pulled out and another hard bump sent him thrusting deep again. Another bout of laughter filled the air between us. He cupped my face in both hands and the deep drugging kiss he gave me held me there as we set a brutal pace for each other.

Between us and the rig's motion on the road, it was a torrid little dance of ecstasy. I writhed with every strike and the scrape of his teeth against my throat or the way his tongue darted in to tease mine at each kiss just eddied me higher and higher.

The tension was a delicious spiral. The laughter only fed the languid heat, the tension so tight it threatened to snap. Then I came, sudden and abrupt. The orgasm startled me as my vision whited out. I hadn't realized how close I was. Clinging to him, I wanted to draw out more for both of us but he let out a shout as my inner muscles spasmed around him.

He fused his mouth to mine as he filled me, much like he'd kissed the gasps from my lips when

McQuade had done the same. We collapsed together. Gradually, the little bumps in the road, the hum of the wheels, and the creak of the metal penetrated the haze around us.

I stroked my fingers over his scalp, as much massaging the skin there as savoring the right to touch him. We were both panting and his heart seemed to be beating as fast as mine. Even as we closed the distance toward the fight ahead.

It was more than okay. We had this interlude to be drunk on each other. There would be more.

Dammit, I wanted more. I wanted them and we were going to win for real. Then... then we could have this.

CHAPTER
THIRTY-ONE
REMY

Forty-eight hours later, I followed the GPS toward the sprawling estate in a North Virginia suburb of Washington D.C. Power brokers came in all shapes and sizes. This one was retired military intelligence who amassed wealth considerably more than his pension would support.

Patch identified five separate revenue streams, all funneled through projects he was either in charge of or on the "board" of. His wife brought generational wealth into the marriage, but not enough to account for the literal hundreds of millions safely stored away in off-shore accounts.

Once we'd retrieved the safe deposit box from the tiny little local bank in Leesburg Patch used, she was able to open the dark web IP address she'd locked the data mine away in. Fortunately, she hadn't had to go to the bank herself. Hot on the heels of someone having gotten so close to her again, we were all running at full caution.

Locke was more than happy to fetch the box,

using her keywords, codes, and memorizing a thirty-six-digit number for the account itself.

I didn't mind admitting I was impressed. Once she had the *snow globe* of all things, everything went into motion.

"I'm still not a fan of leaving you there by yourself," Locke complained. While I didn't disagree, her reasoning and logic were sound.

"So you've said," she answered in a patient voice. "However, these concerns are why we picked this extremely *well lit* rest area to park the rig. All three of you vetted it, and I'm plugged into all the local security and cameras…"

The huff Locke released said he *knew* but he wasn't satisfied with it. None of us would be until at least one of us was back with her. Unfortunately, the plan in play required coordination, three separate targets, and Patch in the chair playing conductor every bit as much as operator.

Unperturbed, Patch continued, "Which are currently showing me all clear. I also have two guns. The one under my desk and the other next to the coffeemaker."

"Left a third one for you in the loo," I chimed in. Luck had been on our side, along with a little forethought, to make sure she was armed. We were going to keep playing that card. "Velcro'd to the wall next to the chain."

"Still don't like it," Locke muttered.

"Stop your bitching," McQuade ordered. "We agreed to the plan. Sugar Bear agreed to the plan. Do your damn job."

The grousing was so McQuade. Unrefined,

blunt to the point of painful, and very much a what you saw was what you got type of man, he also possessed incredible loyalty, determination, and a fierce kind of devotion to the woman who held all of our hearts.

"Be nice boys, we're all on the same side." Her scold had one corner of my mouth turning up. A lot of our conversations as a group went this way. If McQuade wasn't trying to take the piss out of me, he was doing it to Locke.

"That is nice," Locke commented, a grin in his voice. "For McQuade that's downright genial."

Shaking my head, I reserved my own opinion. Roughly a mile from my target's property, I parked behind a hotel and took out my backpack before setting off overland.

There were any number of approaches I could take to St. James' place, the retired colonel had decent security on his property, including a gatehouse, and electronic gate that didn't allow you in without being buzzed by the house.

The guard in the gatehouse was only there during the day. Otherwise, it was all camera surveillance and monitoring from another location. I studied the angles, the lack of blindspots required Patch and I to work in tandem. The system, however, had protocols to deter hacking. We would be on a clock from the moment she started redirecting the cameras.

Looping them would set off an alarm. So would a reset. While knocking out the power might seem a good idea, the house had generators and it would also trigger another set of protocols.

Complicated, however, only took you so far. Patch had come up with a far easier idea. Once I was in position with the fence in sight, I tapped my comm. "Ready for my kiss."

Her throaty laugh titillated, particularly after savoring her orgasms *while* she laughed. Sex and humor had become my favorite companions. Particularly when it came to her.

"Kiss incoming, three seconds, then start your clock."

After tugging the mask down firmly to cover my face and head, I did the mental count to three. On cue, I hit the stopwatch function on my watch as she said, "Go."

Seven seconds to clear the wall. I took it at a run, jumping to catch the top of it and pulling myself up and then rolling over and dropping to the ground.

"And go."

On my feet, I ran following a straight trajectory and hit the ground amidst shadows at the seven-second mark. I'd covered roughly fifty meters.

Three more sprints would bring me in range to the house.

"Go," Patch said and we repeated the process for the next three sprints. She was monitoring the cameras' rotation and had been gradually adding seconds to them over the past several hours to delay their range and it gave me mobile blindspots to run through.

Fortunately, I was a solid sprinter. In range of the house itself, I moved with the shadows beneath the trees that lined the edge of their garden. The retired officer didn't care for personal monitoring, so the cameras were sparser on his private spaces, such as the garden.

He likely trusted the system he had in place to alert him before anyone got this close. It was a very nice system. But *nothing* was fool proof against a determined man.

I was quite determined.

"You've got a thirty second window coming up," Patch said as I took a beat to get my air back. "In five, four, three..."

On one, I was up and went directly through the garden to the trellis that attached to the side of the house. I didn't bother with the doors or windows downstairs. Every single one was wired.

Instead, I climbed the trellis to the second story, then up to the third. The house boasted a very nice attic that Patch found featured in a Town and Country article from four years prior. The windows were narrow, but I could get through them.

They were also not wired.

Sloppy.

It took a little effort to get the window opened and slid up. Then I wiggled through the opening. Careful not to make too much noise once inside. On light feet, I crossed the interior of the attic to the door. They had a proper door at the top of the stairs.

In the Town and Country article, the attic had been converted into a cheery little reading space. The four different windows allowed for a cross breeze and the furniture had a lot of floral, and pink accents.

At the door, I used a small can of oil to lubricate the hinges and gave it a beat. A lot of older houses did the creak and groan. I didn't want to alert my target. The door opened silently after that. The lights were on low, the occupants were likely asleep.

A cat sat on the staircase below and stared up at me with feline indifference before sauntering away. Once down the steps, I began a sweep of the house. The occupants, well occupant since his wife was on a cruise with her sister in the Caribbean, was here somewhere.

It was why we'd chosen to hit all our targets in the middle of the night. It was just after one in the morning here. A soft murmur from downstairs drew me to the living room.

The flickering of a television offered alternating light to the room and cast wild shadows. The movie playing was a classic Bond film.

No comment.

My target, however, was sprawled in a recliner, an empty heavy crystal glass on the side table. The scent of bourbon reached me as the retired colonel snored heavily through his film.

Lips pursed, I studied him for a moment, then scanned the room before returning my attention to him. The curtains were closed, the windows blocked and no obvious signs of camera surveillance.

Still, I wasn't going to take any chances. I pulled out the device that Patch had made for me. It had two small antennae on it and basically looked like a wifi signal booster. Once I had it plugged into the wall, my comm played three dashes, a dash-dot, then two dots, and a dash.

She was in the system.

Withdrawing, I kept my gaze focused on the target until she sent another signal in Morse code for all clear. Pushing away from the wall, I did another sweep and removed any possible weapons from St. James' reach, along with his cell phone. Dropping it into a sealed pouch for Patch to do what she wanted with it, I finished my search.

Once satisfied, I pulled out the pressure injector and crossed the room to where my target continued to sleep blissfully.

I could just drug him while he was out. That would be efficient. Except...

They terrorized Fallon. Tortured her. Took her life from her. Threatened to do it again.

He didn't deserve an easy path. I kicked his chair once and his eyes jerked open. The pupils dilated as he focused on me and his mouth opened.

"Good evening, Colonel St. James—we need to have a word." Then I planted the pressure injector to his neck and fired it. The paralysis of just waking kept him from responding immediately and by the time he thought to fight, he was already going slack from the paralytic.

"You're going to be uncomfortable for a while, but I assure you, it's nowhere near as unfortunate as the treatment you have approved for others." I withdrew a step and pulled off the backpack before tapping the comm. "You there, luv?"

"Talk to me," she invited. Three magical words I craved more than my next breath. Because those three words meant she was still safe and still watching my back. It also meant *she* answered. "Well, talk to us."

"I'm on property. I've located the owner." I hadn't bothered to remove my mask. Being loomed over by a masked man with an accent couldn't be comfortable for the retired officer. "You need a retinal scan and his left thumb print, correct?"

His pupils tried to swell as the television lights flickered then retreated again. The paralytic was doing its job.

"Yes." The unguarded answer held just a single hint of a question. She knew what I was implying. However, to be clear for both of us, I asked the question more directly.

"Any message you want me to leave with him?" No judgment existed within the question. Patch's ethics and morals had been what drove her to leave their operation in the first place.

It had been what compelled her to take critical information. She'd excised herself from her own life, then rebuilt a new one. As much as I regretted her suffering, it was hard to not be grateful she was in my life.

If not for this bastard and the others like him, I might never have known her. That would be a bloody shame.

Section Five, the MadOg project was the brain-child of powerful and influential men. They left the day to day execution in the hands of actual mad dogs and sadists. Everyone answered to someone, in this case, St. James was at the top of the pecking order.

His information network had made him billions more than most people realized. It had also cost many people their lives.

It had cost my Fallon.

It had cost her dearly.

So I waited for her decision.

"Never again," she said quietly. "They don't get to do this again. Scorched earth."

"Yes," McQuade exhaled the word like a triumph. It had been his argument all along that we were better off killing them. Dead men couldn't hunt us down.

Hunt *her* down.

"Gloves off, Sugar Bear?"

"Make sure we have what we need first," she cautioned. "I know you may want in and out, but we need to make sure we have it locked and loaded."

"Done," McQuade said. "Also, I'm here. Going silent running for fifteen, twenty max. Standby for transmission. Even if you had the lead, I bet I get mine before you get yours, *mate*." Then he beeped off.

McQuade was a prick, but he was growing on me. "I'll take care of it. Talk soon." Then I went back to silent running. What came next, she didn't need to hear. "Colonel St. James... the next hour or two are going to be very uncomfortable for you. I'd ask you if you were ready to talk, but you can't. You also have absolutely nothing to say that I want to hear."

I collected his thumb print by removing the thumb and storing it in a safe box. The pain helped to flush fresh motion into his eyes and I took full retinal scans of both. The flexing of the pupil was vital to accuracy.

When Patch let me know she had it, I nodded to myself. Business secured, I pulled out a knife and studied the colonel.

"You owe a friend of mine at least a pound of flesh, but I plan on charging interest..."

Even with the paralytic in his system, he did manage to scream after I carved out the first pound.

It was good practice, I had a call to pay on the man formerly known as Marty Cartwright when I was done here.

CHAPTER

THIRTY-TWO

MCQUADE

"Gloves off, Sugar Bear?"

"Make sure we have what we need first," she cautioned. "I know you may want in and out, but we need to make sure we have it locked and loaded."

"Done," I said. "Also, I'm here. Going silent running for fifteen, twenty max. Standby for transmission. Even if you had the lead, I bet I get mine before you get yours, *mate*." I couldn't resist the chance to taunt Remy.

The arrogant Brit turned out to not be so bad. The fact he'd spent several hours in bed with our lady while we did the driving and the watching didn't irritate me at all. Well, it hadn't after I'd seen her relaxed expression, and this while she admitted to remembering.

She remembered being taken.

How she was taken.

She remembered the people who had taken her.

Then she'd given me a gift once we retrieved her *snow globe*. I was still wrapping my head around the

324

fact her key to the data had been hidden in a snow globe, or at least the triggers for it were.

It didn't matter, she knew how it worked and she was able to unlock the files. Once they were open, she went on a search for the names of specific people. My three targets were all directly related to her interrogations.

The site in Louisiana might have been scrubbed but the operatives there were one of the senior black bag teams working for Colonel St. James. My father's name had also been in the files, but his information had been listed under a sealed warrant.

Patch cracked that like an egg. She really did make it look easy. The warrant was a no touch order. Dad was out, he'd cut ties with the organization, but he respected top secret and eyes only authorizations.

They were stalemated.

He wouldn't shut them down. They wouldn't touch him.

I got it. I didn't like it, but I understood it. Once upon a time, I wouldn't have cared much either. Not my circus and not my monkeys. But all of this involved Patch. They *hurt* her. They targeted her. They were going to keep coming for her and she didn't have a rank or career to shield her.

But she had us.

Fisting my temper and putting it away, I climbed out of the car. The interrogation facility might have been in Louisiana, but Robert "Bobby" McCoy and Karl Seward were based out of a nondescript little office building a five minute's drive from Dulles Airport.

Patch had tracked them arriving back in state three days earlier and they hadn't left as far as she could tell. The shitty little office building was down a side street, with a lot of other industrial offices and what looked like a tractor repair shop and a detailing place.

At this time of night, it was dead quiet. Nothing moved. There was a vague hum of traffic from the state highway to the north of me, but nothing back here.

The fact there was a subdivision of townhouses at the end of this road was strange. The road dead-ended into trees. A hiking and biking trail were located on the other side. The former site of railroad tracks had been replaced with a paved path that paralleled a more natural one that was kept clear for those wanting to walk dogs or ride horses. A touch of country right there in the burgeoning tech corridor.

The location was just odd. The homes and trails could account for traffic at all hours while the industrial park provided decent daytime coverage for their activities. Most people were just too damn busy doing their own things.

I pulled out the black duffel from the trunk and then checked my weapons. Pausing a beat, I tapped my comm, "Sugar Bear?"

"I'm here, Sugar Lips." The throaty tease made me grin. She could call me whatever she wanted.

"Tell me you're still safe."

I just needed to hear it.

"I'm still safe. All clear here. How about you let me worry about my ass while I watch yours?"

"No can do, Sugar Bear. That sweet ass is all I can think about."

"Focus, McQuade."

"I am focused." On getting some justice for her. "Talk soon."

"I have eyes on you." The promise sent a frisson through me and electricity skated over my skin. No one else I'd rather have at my back. Swinging the duffel back over my shoulder, I freed the Smith & Wesson M&P M2.0 from its holster as I strode across the cracked pavement lot.

With Patch keeping an eye on security, I didn't have to worry about cameras. She also hadn't indicated there were civilians anywhere. It meant I got to have some fun with my prey.

Circling the building, I approached the side door that was hidden from direct sight of the parking lot. Shifting to put the duffel strap over my head so it hung crosswise from my shoulder, I studied the heavy door.

I had charges that would work.

Four small devices, each planted at key points for lock and hinges, and I backed up and around the corner. The blasts were localized, but they would do the job.

I hit the trigger and there were four small pops, followed by a distinctive thud of a heavy door falling. I loved a dramatic entrance.

Striding forward, I walked through the debris and smoke straight inside. A guard fumbled to his feet, but I didn't wait for him. He didn't match the photo I had for my targets, so he got the express pass to getting the fuck out of my way.

Two bullets to the head.

Continuing forward, I slowed at the curve in the hall. Pulling out a flash bang, I flicked out the key pin and then tossed it around the corner. Eyes closed, I gave it the three second count to stun and disorient. Then I started forward.

Two more guys were staggering, one had dropped his weapon. The other was waving his around. Close contact gun to the chest of the gun wielder. I fired twice. Then another clean grouping into the staggering one.

No joy on the targets. But they did have security keycards.

Helpful.

I'd memorized the layout of the place. The offices were down one flight. Everything up here was just for show. The guys did their work in their hellish little pits.

At the end of this hall was an elevator and I used the security pass to open it, then reached inside and inserted a key to lock the elevator to this floor.

Then I went to the stairs.

No easy exits for them. If they had soundproofing down there I might still have time to surprise them. My evening was looking up. I unlocked the door at the bottom of the stairs and opened it, threw out a couple of flash bangs then closed the door to wait.

Violent cursing carried through the door.

Bingo.

Yanking it open, I stalked through to make my way down the hall. The body armor I was in was light, it would take a shotgun shell, but I'd prefer to not give them that opportunity.

The first guy rushing toward me went down with a swift gun to the face. I had more magazines, but I didn't want to waste the ammo. I zip-tied his hands and feet, then continued on.

I found Robert "Bobby" McCoy first. He rushed me, swinging a knife. I avoided the first two wild slashes easily. Then caught the arm he was using, twisted it back and then broke it with a solid blow to the elbow.

His scream was pure agony as he dropped the knife and to his knees at the same time. Gripping his hair, I jerked his head back. Shaggy brown hair, a scar distorting his upper lip on the right side and dirty stained clothes. The man had no pride in himself.

"Hello, Bobby." I smiled and then slammed him headfirst into the wall before securing him back in his office. A good choice because bullets struck the dry wall next to the door as I started back out.

Oh, someone was actually giving a real fight. Adrenaline surged in my system. I lived for this shit. Especially when it involved dealing with scum who deserved zero mercy.

I returned fire, four shots in rapid succession. Then I released the magazine and reloaded as I headed out. I went low, but I'd already made it halfway down the hall when Karl Seward twisted into the hall again, firing.

His first two shots went over my head, but the third slammed into the tile in front of me. I'd admire his aim later, I returned fire and chased him around the corner. Just as I reached the edge, he pivoted to face me again.

I had a headshot and center mass. He was already a dead man. But I wanted him to suffer first. So no fast passes for him.

Instead of the easier shots, I went for the shoulder of his gun arm. The first shot knocked him back, the second spun him around. He lost the gun, but grabbed for it with his good hand and pointed it.

Clever.

Another two shots in rapid succession. This took his second shoulder and he slammed back against the wall in a spray of crimson. Smears of blood followed him as he sank down to the ground.

"Asshole," the man said through gritted teeth. He wasn't spitting or swearing. His face didn't contort. If anything, you wouldn't even know he was in pain if not for all the damage.

"Pleased to meet you," I told him. He was perfectly manicured, though that wasn't going to do his useless hands any good. His face was smooth, there was no stubble. His expression devoid of even the normal human reactions of shock, pain, fear, or fury. "Karl Seward."

"You know my name," the man said in an empty voice. "Should I be impressed?"

"I don't care if you are or not," I told him then stomped on his right hand as he twitched his fingers toward another weapon at his side.

Now he let out a low-pitched scream. With little regard for his pain or blood loss, I did a quick search of him and removed his weapons before dragging him back toward McCoy's office.

The downstairs offered limited spaces for discussion. Once I set him on the floor and zip-tied him to McCoy, I headed back out to do a full sweep and clear.

Finding no one else, I tapped my comms.

"You're late," she told me tartly and I grinned.

"Couldn't be helped. Shopping was a bitch."

"Did you find what you were looking for?"

"Yep, so it was worth it." I made my way back to McCoy's office. "You have any words for these guys?"

A camera on the wall shifted and began to turn slowly. The red light blinked at me once, almost like she was winking and I stepped to the side so she could see into the office.

"That's Shaggy and Mr. Cold." Her confirmation was good. I'd already identified them, but it was helpful to be sure.

I gave her a moment to consider her answer. She'd already taken the gloves off and I had plans for these two. That said, ladies first, and she was the one these assholes hurt.

"No," she said slowly. "They really aren't worth any last words. They were merely the sadistic tools of their masters. I'd be happy to never think of them again."

"Anything you want, Sugar Bear."

"Anything?" Intrigue punched up that word and it wrapped around my dick like she was stroking it. Not the time, I told myself.

"Anything," I promised.

"Dealer's choice then," she said, giving me blanket permission. "But I expect you back here promptly."

"Copy that." The soft beep of going silent had me studying the pair who stared up at me. The confusion on McCoy's face was almost funny. Seward, however, wasn't similarly open in his reactions.

He clearly knew what was coming.

Good, it saved me time and explanations.

"You don't know who we are," McCoy yelled suddenly, trying to lurch forward. Course, the broken arm made such motions excruciating, but couldn't happen to a nicer guy.

"Don't care," I told him.

"You care," Seward informed me. "You don't just break into a secure facility and mow your way through people for fun."

"You misunderstand," I told Seward as I secured my gun and then dropped the duffle onto the top of the desk. I had lots of fun tools inside of it.

I'd start with the pliers. I checked the pair as I took them out.

"I don't care who you are. Or were. Because as of five minutes ago, you're a footnote in someone else's story, if you even rate that much."

"What are you talking about?" McCoy demanded.

"He's not really bright," I said to Seward. "Is he?"

Seward grimaced.

"That makes you the brains and him just the actual mad dog let off his leash."

McCoy shrieked something incoherent, spittle

flying from his lips. Yeah, he didn't like being dismissed.

I studied McCoy's hands, and then looked at his legs. Oh... yes, that would work. I put the pliers back and then pulled out a glass bottle from the interior of the bag.

The sudden stuttering silence amused me.

"Who wants to go first?"

Neither volunteered, but I hadn't really expected them too. I did glove up though before I stripped their pants and planted the first bottle up McCoy's ass. He passed out screaming. Seward actually sweated the whole time and he even threw up when I did it to him.

Not the easiest job and it definitely stank, but the whimpers of pain were worth it. That was one piece of flesh she was owed.

Now I'd take the rest.

CHAPTER
THIRTY-THREE
LOCKE

There was a party in full swing when I arrived at the Sommerland, in Washington D.C. The exclusive club required more than just a membership to enter. It required a key card, a passcode, and a pat down. They even used airport level x-ray to make sure you weren't carrying weapons or recording equipment.

My comms were off, and I wasn't armed. This was considered one of the most secure clubs for the elite in the district. You could buy anything and anyone. Every vice was catered too and you had to be someone if you were here.

If no one recognized you, that just added to your cachet. It wasn't hard to affect a bored look as I went through the expected procedure. Once complete, they handed me back my card.

"Welcome Mr. Green," the concierge said. "Is there anything you are looking for specifically this evening?"

"I haven't decided," I told him. "I think I'm

going to get a drink and check out the entertainment."

"Of course." The concierge smiled. "If I can get you anything, please don't hesitate to ask."

"I won't." Then I wiped my hands on a handkerchief before I returned it to my pocket. I was already walking away from him and across the foyer into the main atrium of the club. A bar in the center offered up drinks. Women in skimpy outfits sauntered through, serving a little bit of everything vice.

While I'd half-expected to take a while to find my target, he was visible on the far side of the room in a tall-backed round booth, glaring out at the cheerful crowd as some girl worked his needle dick under the table.

Poor thing seemed to be going very fast, head bobbing, but the man's expression didn't change. Maybe it was just a limp dick. With that in mind, I strolled to the bar.

I recognized quite a few of the men in this room. I'd imagine the gossip columns and political reporters would pay a fortune for these tips. As it was, I went to the bar and waited for one of the beautiful women to drift over in my direction.

"What can I do for you, sir?" Not what could she get me. But what could she do for me? There really wasn't any fun with people just offering you everything. I'd rather get it myself. She was definitely *not* Fallon.

"Do you know how to make a Copper Drop cocktail?" I raised my brows, inviting her to challenge herself.

"I've made one or two..." She tilted her hair. "Do you like creamy or just straight?"

"Creamy sounds like the right thing." I used the bare minimum for emphasis.

"Coming right up." She winked. The suggestiveness was all there, but I just nodded. She was definitely *not* what I wanted.

Leaning back against the bar, I let the atmosphere wash over me. The poor girl under the table looked to be struggling briefly and the guy had his hands down there on her head.

His grimace was followed by her jerking her head away and a long trail of spittle with cum stretched from her mouth to the shadows hiding the man's penis. Small mercies.

I glanced to the bartender as she slid the cocktail across the bar to me along with a napkin and her phone number. "The drink is all I need," I assured her as I pushed the napkin back.

Sampling a mouthful, I nodded. It tasted correct. Drink in hand, I left the bar and made my way across the room. Letting my gaze drift from person to person as though I wanted to find something to entertain myself.

I nodded once or twice, always when I wasn't locking eyes with someone. Act like you belonged and they would treat you that way. An older gentleman reached out a hand to stop me. His crown of snow white hair added to his very flushed appearance.

"Carter?" The man squinted at me. He smelled like he'd taken a bath in his Scotch.

"I'm afraid not, sir."

Rather than being put off, he patted me on the shoulder. "Well, you look like him," my new drunk friend said. "Let me buy you a round and you can tell me who you are."

"I have a drink," I said easily enough and raised it to show him.

"So you do." He peered blearily. "Well, if you're not Carter you have to be someone and I need someone to talk to or I have to go home. I'm not sober enough to go home. The wife will definitely know where I've been."

Honestly, unless he planned on bathing and changing his clothes, it wasn't his inebriated state that would give him away. "Why don't we find you a seat and then I'll buy you a round—maybe an espresso martini to start the sobering up part."

With a boisterous laugh, the man slapped me on the back. Drunk or not, the man had some force to his excitement. "Oh, I like you."

The timing really couldn't have been more perfect. While I didn't believe in luck, not really, my target was charging across the room to leave. He sort of strode like he expected people to just get out of his way.

It took almost no effort to step into his path and collide with him. The glass broke in the force of him trying to shoulder me away and splashed us both. He stumbled and I slid a couple of steps, but I patted his jacket as I kept us both on our feet.

Oh, there it was. I swapped my pen for his and then smoothed his suit as though trying to undo the damage from the drink. I would regret the damage done to my suit, but it was a worthy sacrifice to the cause.

The retired general snapped his head to look at me and snarled. "Watch where the fuck you're going."

"Well, that was unnecessarily hostile," my new best friend said as he leaned into the fray between and exhaled his fumes. "We have rules here, my good man. Don't make me ask for someone to deal with you."

Abdias Stone just *looked* like a dick. He scowled at me and then my friend.

"Tell you what, just let me know what it costs to clean the suit and I'll cover it." I patted Stone on the chest once more and then nudged my companion back. "Let's let the man go on his way."

We were almost to the bar when a gasp went up around the room and the music cut off abruptly. Across the room, Stone had gone down and his face was rapidly swelling. Two of the servers went to help him.

It was such a spectacle as he fought for air against a rapidly closing windpipe. His epi-pen came out of his pocket and he tried to stab himself with it but failed.

One of the wait staff took it and jabbed it against his thigh, but nothing happened. "It's not working..."

"I'm a doctor," another man called as he pushed through the crowd. I kept an eye on the whole thing, gawking like the rest of the influential crowd. "Let me get in there..."

The doctor tried the epipen again. Then they were calling for someone to find another epipen.

"It's all very dramatic," the man next to me said.

"It is."

Then he peered up at me. "Do I know you?"

"No, sir," I said. "I think you were on your way to find a room for the night."

"Oh, that's right. Right." He wandered off a few steps but then paused when the unfolding medical crisis captured his attention all over again.

I checked my watch as the doctor fought to get Stone's airway opened but he didn't have the equipment and no one else had an epipen. A medical kit was being rushed into the room, but it was too late.

Stone died in just under ninety seconds from our collision. Peanut rum creme was just as deadly as the peanuts themselves. It didn't take long before the concierge and the staff were trying to clear the room. They were going to need to deal with a death on the property.

Most likely by removing him from the property. The members of this club did not pay such exorbitant fees to be caught up in the scandal. I followed a couple of senators and a man of old school wealth on their way out the main doors.

Limos were pulling up to collect their people and still others flowed to where their cars waited in the secure lot. Once I was back in my car, I followed the train of other vehicles until I could head out of the district proper.

Once on the highway, I slid my comm back in and tapped it.

"Talk to me," she said, welcome in every syllable.

"Did you miss me, beautiful?"

"Of course, I did. How did it go?"

"Scratch Stone off the list. Easy peasy. Though next time, I'd rather just grab you some jewels or maybe some art for your new place." I loosened my tie as I drove. "In fact, once we've cleared everything up, I want to take you somewhere."

"Are we all invited?" McQuade asked. "Or is this just you?"

The sun was coming up behind me as I headed south and west. It was a lot later than I realized. Still, a new dawn, and clearing the decks was a good thing.

"Sure, you can come and bring your favorite mate too…"

"Don't you start," Remy said with more than a little snap and I grinned.

"But it's done. I'm an hour away, want me to grab you some breakfast?"

"No," she said and that surprised me. "Come on back, we need to get on the road again. There's one more thing I want to do before we release the file."

"Read us in?" McQuade asked and the concern in his voice echoed the tension in my gut. Her earlier playfulness was absent and I wasn't sure what I thought about the grim certainty that had replaced it.

The plans had worked. We'd eliminated the major threats.

Right?

"I will as soon as you're all here." It was a promise. "Trust me."

"On my way," I promised. A sentiment the others echoed. I didn't doubt that we were all accelerating to get back to her.

To go to *her*. I liked that thought. I didn't even mind the others. They fit, just like she did. Maybe she just wanted to get out of here and back to her life. When we were done and released the files, there would be nothing stopping her. The people who knew about *her* were gone.

She could go home.

My stomach sank.

Then I shook it off. We still had time to persuade her and if she really wanted out, then I'd find a way to retire, or at least just take smaller jobs so I could stick closer.

Flexing my hands on the steering wheel, I grimaced at the smell of the alcohol on my clothes and adjusted my speed.

Whatever she wanted, we'd make it work.

Look what we'd done so far. Anything was possible.

The positive thinking did nothing for the worry eating away at my stomach. Twice I went to call her and twice I made myself stop. She asked us to come to her.

Whatever it was, we'd *take care* of it just like we had everything else. I almost had myself convinced by the time I reached the rest area where we'd left her parked.

CHAPTER
THIRTY-FOUR
PATCH

One week after Abdias Stone died, the news was full of stories about his body being discovered in a hotel room. The peanut allergy, well known to his close associates, was detailed as the cause of death. A faulty epi-pen had been found with him, and it seemed law enforcement was comfortable in labeling the death as accidental.

The club had done the heavy lifting on covering up the death. The death of retired Colonel St. James in a house fire earned a paragraph on page thirty of the post, and a slightly more detailed obituary released by the family.

No one reported on the deaths of Robert McCoy or Karl Seward. They simply vanished. They were ghosts *before* McQuade made their occupation a reality. I didn't know the names of the others who'd worked there. I made my peace with not knowing who they were too.

Section Five had been gutted as well as having its head chopped off. I'd identified five politicians in key positions and four journalists, including Mark Reynolds, I would trust with the information. He turned out to be an excellent resource once we cracked it all open and I felt like we owed him since we'd chased his leads off. I would also make sure that both sides knew that someone on the other side had it.

The carcass would be ripped apart soon enough. But before that could happen, I had one last task. This item I'd saved for myself. The guys hadn't been thrilled when I detailed my plan, and there had been a few arguments.

Ultimately, however, they dropped their objections. The fact they'd dropped them at all told me I had one or more of them following me.

Oddly, I was okay with that result. They needed to watch my back the way I needed to watch theirs. I'd probably have okayed them following me anyway. The trip had brought me almost full circle, I suppose. Only instead of Colorado, I was in Washington state.

I'd arranged to pick up a rental car, setting up a false id and taking care of the payment all electronically. All I had to do was use my phone to access the car and the keys were in it. I pulled out of the airport rental place and followed the flow of traffic.

Seatac was a busy damn airport. It had been so weird sitting on a plane. Weirder still to read a book rather than open my laptop. I'd been tempted, but I was almost positive Locke was four seats behind me. I could afford to relax. So I took advantage of the time and the space to read.

Being outside in the open air, even with my

hair pulled into two long braids, green-lensed sunglasses, tie-dye shirt tucked into an ankle length Bohemian skirt and looking as far away from my old self as possible, was still almost violently weird.

I was used to walls being around me, shielding me from prying eyes. Having someone, even a flight attendant, make small talk was alien. Now behind the wheel of a car, driving south on I-5, I was wrestling with so much green in the trees, and even more people around me as I moved with the flow of traffic.

My phone worked as GPS and I followed the directions. The shakiness that I'd fought on the flight came back, and I struggled to keep it suppressed. This was what *freedom* was like. Freedom I'd lost a long time ago.

The same freedom I'd nearly had ripped away from me all over again. While I didn't have any long-term plans *set*, I did have them. Those terrified me almost as much as all this openness.

Maybe I should have had one of the guys come with me. No sooner did that thought take purchase than I dismissed it. No, I had to do this on my own. I didn't mind them watching over me, but from a distance.

If I merely traded the cage I'd built for myself to one constructed by them for safety, then it wasn't freedom. As I crossed the Tacoma Narrows Bridge, the rain gave way to watery sunshine and I grinned.

This was all insane. The last five years had been insane. The years before it had been crazy. Somewhere, the idealistic kid I'd been in college and my early twenties had become this jaded woman in her thirties.

I was okay with that. Because this jaded woman had survived. It didn't take long before I pulled up a long and winding road and passed several other homes built into the hill and all the way down to the water. The house I was heading for was all by itself at the top.

There were gates over the drive. I had a device to mirror the signal that opened them and it took it all of thirty-eight seconds to find the right frequency. The gates opened and I drove right up to the front and parked.

No doubt he had cameras. He would know I was here. Maybe he'd answer.

Maybe he wouldn't.

But I was getting out of the car and I was knocking on his door. Shoving the door open, I climbed out. The breeze carried the promise of water in it—whether it was the rain I'd just driven away from or the water below, I had no idea.

Standing in front of the door, I debated whether to ring or knock, then I turned to the camera pointed right at me. Tugging my glasses off, I stared up at it.

"Hello, Boxer. I think you owe me a conversation. Don't you?"

There was no immediate response. I waited, leaning back against the wall next to his door.

"I've got time," I said. "But you might not want to make me wait too long."

Another arduous five minutes passed achingly slow, but I just leaned there, staring at the camera.

The air around me was fresh. I was outside, getting to enjoy it. I wasn't locked away in my house in one of the prettiest parts of the world and never leaving it.

I wasn't dying in some cell, wishing the pain would go away. I wasn't hiding from life in the back of an eighteen-wheeler as the three men who'd never let me go fought to give me back my peace and my freedom.

A lock finally tumbled, then another. The door opened slowly, just a crack and a guy peered out at me. Yeah, that wasn't working for me. I shoved the door hard. It caught him off guard and he stumbled back, then the door hit him in the face.

Boxer was maybe five foot nine? Five foot eight? It was hard to tell. He wasn't much taller than me. A little overweight, his cheeks were ruddy, his hair was dark and his eyes terrified.

Yeah, I got that.

The stained shirt and the hint of Cheetos dust on his fingers was also painfully familiar. Boxer had locked himself away in this house and lived through the screen on his computer.

"Do you know who I am?"

"I—" Boxer stuttered, then raked a hand through his hair not seeming to realize he spread the Cheetos dust to it. "You're—Patch."

His gulp was almost comical. I stared at him for a long time, saying nothing. I wasn't even sure what I expected to feel when I got here. Anger? Resentment? Betrayal?

Sure, they were all there, but Boxer was younger

than me. Maybe five or six years younger. Not that it excused him.

"Yes," I said. "I am."

"You're—okay?" The uncertainty in the question almost made me laugh. He really didn't have any answers. He'd sold me out to save himself. Compromised me because fear was such a vicious animal.

Having run from that beast for a long time, I got it.

I really did.

The only thing I felt staring at Boxer was pity. Sliding my sunglasses back on, I said, "You're out of the business. Find something else to do. Forget my name and my number. But you're done. No more operational work for you. Shut it down, and go get another life."

"Or what?"

"There is no 'or what,' because you're going to do what I told you. You're done, Boxer. Boxer is dead. You're Ned Johnson from Madison, Indiana. Maybe get yourself a dog and go for walks outside. The fresh air will be good for you."

He jerked his gaze past me and paled. I didn't look. I knew exactly who was there.

"You can't just tell me to quit everything in my life and go somewhere else," Ned tried to argue and I tilted my head.

"You sure about that? Because while I'm telling you to do this, the guys behind me won't ask. They won't even care why you did what you did. You and I both know and that's enough for me—if you get out and you get a life."

I backed away from him, hands spread out to the sides. "But you know what," I pitched my voice louder. "It's your choice. Do it. Don't do it. Just remember, I can find you. If you don't get out, the next time, it won't be me knocking. Consider this the courtesy you didn't give me."

I shrugged and pivoted to find Remy, McQuade, and Locke standing there. Locke met my gaze, but Remy and McQuade were staring past me at Boxer.

"Gentlemen," I said by way of greeting. "Do you guys like seafood?"

"I could eat," Locke said. "Know somewhere good?"

"Not off the top of my head, but I think we can find something... you guys up for it?"

"We just leaving this guy here?" McQuade asked finally.

"For now," I said. "I gave him a choice. If he doesn't listen, he's all yours."

Satisfaction crossed McQuade's face and Remy nodded once. A ridiculous bubble of laughter fluttered through me.

"Who wants to ride with me?" Cause it was time to go. Time to find food. To talk to them about what our future could look like. I was the woman in the chair. But only for them.

Only ever for them.

Aware of Boxer staring at us, I didn't hide my smile as I slid back into the car. Locke made it to the passenger seat and McQuade circled the car to give Boxer a hard stare. Whatever Boxer saw in his face made him go pale before hurriedly retreating.

"McQuade really does have a way with people," I said as Remy climbed in behind me.

Locke chuckled. "That he does."

Once McQuade was in, I handed my phone to Locke. "Find us somewhere to eat?"

"On it." Then I started the car and headed back down the hill. The gates opened automatically.

"Do you guys care about your rental?"

"No," Remy and McQuade answered in one voice. I grinned.

"There's a place about fifteen minutes away on the water. It's supposed to have an amazing menu." Locke pulled up the GPS and hit the directions to go.

"Did you find out what you needed?" Remy asked me.

"I did," I answered. "But we have a lot of other questions to answer now."

"Such as?" McQuade challenged.

"Well, where our home base is going to be for a start. I like the rig, but we need a bigger bed..."

Locke covered my hand with his and leaned back with a smile.

"I know what I want," I continued. "So talk to me...let's figure out how to make this work."

Because we could.

It wouldn't be a fairytale and it wouldn't be magic. It was going to take work and probably some arguments. I flicked a look at the rearview mirror at McQuade's stubborn face and then grinned.

A lot of arguments.

I really couldn't wait.

END

AFTERWORD

Whew.

When I write, I sometimes become utterly absorbed by the story and it plays out like a movie in my head. More often than not, my brain will begin to go much faster than my fingers. In those moments, I'm in the zone and I can feel the pulse of the story.

That happened so many times while writing this duet. I dreamt about it, I couldn't stop thinking about them. Even when they were being tight-lipped, they were vivid and alive.

If you're wondering will there be another book this characters? I don't know. I don't plan on it right now. Their story is done. It's not all wrapped up in a bow, but it's a new start for them. I may write a couple of bonus scenes going forward for the omnibus when it's time. But anything I post in a special edition will also be available on the website.

I have so much more coming up! Including another dark romance duet, so be sure to visit my website and sign up for news and updates . Then don't be shy, jump into my reader group on Facebook, I love to hear from my readers!

xoxo

Heather

Website:
heatherlong.net
Reader group:
facebook.com/groups/heatherspack
Spoiler group:
facebook.com/groups/teammadatheather

About Heather Long

I *love* books. Not just a little bit, but a lot. Books were my best friends when I was growing up. Books didn't care if I was new to a town or to a class. They were always there, my trustiest of companions. Until they turned on me and said I had to write them.

I can tell you that my own personal happily ever after included writing books. I've always said that an HEA is a work in progress. It's true in my marriage, my friendships, and in my career. I am constantly nurturing my muse as we dive into new tales, new tropes, new characters and more.

After seventeen years in Texas, we relocated to the Pacific Northwest in search of seasons, new experiences, and new geography. I can't wait to discover what life (and my muse) have in store for me.

Maybe writing was always my destiny and romance my fate. After all, my grandmother wasn't a fan of picture books and used to read me her Harlequin Romance novels.

Follow Heather & Sign up for her newsletter:
www.heatherlong.net
TikTok

ALSO BY HEATHER LONG

82nd Street Vandals

Savage Vandal

Vicious Rebel

Ruthless Traitor

Dirty Devil

Shamelessly Loyal (Novella)

Brutal Fighter

Dangerous Renegade

Merciless Spy

Reckless Thief

Fierce Dancer

Dirty Dancer

Bay Ridge Royals

Shamelessly Loyal (Novella)

Battle Lines

Deceptive Truce

Wicked Surrender

Violent Chaos

Desperate Victory

Blue Ivy Prep

The Quick & The Fevered
A Man Called Wyatt

Heart of the Nebula
Queenmaker
Deal Breaker
Throne Taker

Lone Star Leathernecks
Semper Fi Cowboy
As You Were, Cowboy

Shackled Souls
Succubus Chained
Succubus Unchained
Succubus Blessed
Shackled Souls (Omnibus)

STANDALONES
Kiss of Fate (w/Blake Blessing)
Taste of Karma (w/Blake Blessing)
I'll Be Home... (w/Tate James)

Untouchable
Rules and Roses
Changes and Chocolates
Keys and Kisses
Whispers and Wishes

His Moonstruck Wolf

Thunder Wolf

Ghost Wolf

Outlaw Wolves

Wolf Unleashed